PENGUIN BOOKS

THE CEASELESS CHATTER OF DEMONS

Ashok Ferrey is the author of five books, four of them nominated for the Gratiaen Prize and the fifth for the State Literary Award. By day he is a personal trainer.

ALSO BY ASHOK FERREY

Colpetty People
The Good Little Ceylonese Girl
Serendipity
Love in the Tsunami
The Professional

The Ceaseless Chatter of Demons

ASHOK FERREY

PENGUIN BOOKS

PENGUIN BOOKS

USA | Canada | UK | Ireland | Australia
New Zealand | India | South Africa | China

Penguin Books is part of the Penguin Random House group of companies
whose addresses can be found at global.penguinrandomhouse.com

Published by Penguin Random House India Pvt. Ltd
7th Floor, Infinity Tower C, DLF Cyber City,
Gurgaon 122 002, Haryana, India

Penguin
Random House
India

First published in Penguin Books by Penguin Random House India 2016

ISBN 9780143428657

For sale in the Indian Subcontinent only

Typeset in Minion Pro by Manipal Digital Systems, Manipal
Printed at Thomson Press India Ltd, New Delhi

www.penguinbooksindia.com

For Francesca and Rehan

Acknowledgements

I am hugely indebted to Professor Nimal de Silva, whose vast and encyclopaedic knowledge of the Kandyan Kingdom I have freely drawn upon, and to K.K.S. Priyantha, descendant of a long line of sorcerers, who furnished me with details and procedures of the *thovil* ceremony, as traditionally performed by his family.

PART I

1

I was born ugly. That's what my mother always said.

'Sonny,' she said, 'when are we ever going to find a girl good enough to marry you?' A cunning choice of phrase, because by *good enough* she didn't mean would the girl match up to my exacting standards, but rather, would she be good-natured and *kind* enough to take me on. It made me sound like a charity case or something. I had visions of a girl in pinafore and plaits. (All good Sri Lankan girls those days wore plaits, also heavy glasses.) My mother had a smile in her voice when she said this, as if she were joking, but I could see the glimmer of shrewd assessment in her eyes—the look a butcher might give a lame horse, possessed of some vital secret known to all but the horse. As with all secrets, the import of it had seeped into me long before her meaning became plain and I grew up—this was back then, in the eighties—with this great burden of ugliness upon my shoulders.

I had thick curly black hair and flat features. But I had lustrous, velvety skin, even if it too was rather black for my mother's refined Sanskritized tastes. My one great feature was my smile—it truly lit up the darkness I seemed to carry around with me—and it was surprisingly popular with the girls. Naturally, I smiled an awful lot. As expected, the only woman who was immune to this smile was my mother.

Because of this ugliness—or, perhaps, in spite of it—I was attracted to beauty in all its forms. The special incandescence that seemed to emanate from anything beautiful: I could feel this glow burning up my fingers till they began to vibrate, the resonance of like calling to like. (Or in this case, of like calling to unlike.) This resonance fed and nourished me: it was enough for me to stand in front of something beautiful—even if it was only a beautifully appointed room—for me to be subsumed by it. It did something to my brain, it filled the cavity of my stomach with a fluid that was equal parts joy, equal parts sadness. Joy because this beauty was so alive, all fresh and tingling like a shiny, round fruit in a market stall. Sadness because the fruit said, look at me—look, but don't touch.

At the age of six I contracted a particularly bad throat infection. Nothing that a course of antibiotics would not have cured, but my mother decided that it was plain to anyone but a moron that a demon had entered my body which, quite obviously, needed to be exorcized. Her case was strengthened by the fact that my voice had dropped an octave and I could only speak in a growl. Add my looks to this, and could you blame her? Those days, there were many demons said to be flying about the hillsides of the walauwa and I had a big mouth, so it was quite possible that one had just slipped in while it was open.

The exorcism ceremony was quite a complicated one. A bamboo-and-thatch structure was set up on the terrace in front of the house. The people on the mountainside worked for days. Costumes were brought out of storage and mended, drummers and dancers hired, the whole thing being as much a theatrical performance as a medicinal remedy. People came from far and wide to watch.

The exorcist was a man by the name of Kodivina Peiris, a distant relation of my mother's. Kodi, as he was called, worked himself into a trance to the beat of frenzied drums and, at its height, took a long, rusty sword and slashed in half three limes on a single stalk: the reasoning being that the demon had been tricked into leaving the comparative four-star safety of my throat to enter the limes, and was then disposed of.

But I was curious to see that other people too felt free to gibber and squeak, shiver and shake, finding themselves 'possessed' during what should have been my command performance. Once they had taken a turn or two around the dance floor they fell back exhausted, writhing and moaning occasionally to show what good sports they were. This ceremony lasted the entire night and I was truly shattered by morning. ('Naturally he's worn out,' snapped my mother irritably, 'the devil's hardly going to leave without a fight, is he!') But here's the strange thing: we learnt next day that just about the time Kodi was preparing his lime juice cocktail, our family GP, Dr Dep—he who would have prescribed the antibiotics had we only consulted him, as my aunts had suggested—fell down the stairs of his home and broke a leg.

'Serves him right,' said my mother, 'for trying to inflict his Western mumbo jumbo on us, the charlatan!'

In the light of all this, was I perhaps something of a weirdo? Oh I was, you see, I was.

∽

Every Sunday morning Luisa and I took the bus into central London all the way from Putney, past the many green commons of south London, past the Indian restaurant with the big sign that said *Bring the one you love, it's too good for the wife*. We smiled and held hands tightly. If it was too good for the wife, it was certainly too good for us. In all our time in Putney, I don't think we stepped in once.

Sunday was the day reserved for Bond Street. Back then shops closed on Sundays, so the whole street was ours. Nowhere was it more obvious that London had, till only recently, been the imperial capital. Each window held a treasure more precious than the last, culled from some hazy outpost of the empire. Here, for example, was the satinwood bed of a maharajah, very wide but only five feet long.

'It's so small!' Luisa said. 'How did he sleep in it?'

I looked at her small frame. 'Maybe he was your size. Maybe the bed wasn't for sleeping in. Who knows?'

Two shops down, in the dead centre of the window was a single jewel, a small, panther-shaped brooch of sapphires and diamonds. 'Property of the late Duchess of Windsor,' said the card. The sapphires were cunningly set, like paving stones, so you couldn't see the grout in between. My fingers began to tingle.

'You like?' I asked, putting my arm around her.

'Hmm, it'll do, I suppose. You brought money?'

'Certainly, dear girl.'

'Cash or card?'

She scrutinized for a moment the card I held up. 'That'll do nicely,' she said. It was my London Transport travel card.

We giggled and moved on.

'Now this I really like. Really, *really* like.' In a corner of the next window was an armband, twisting and rearing out of its case, a serpent studded with rock crystals and sapphires, crudely cut, opulently mismatched. The emerald eyes of the serpent glittered poisonously against the black velvet. You couldn't call it beautiful, but it had a magnificently barbaric splendour that held you in its thrall. 'Part of the State Regalia of the last King of Kandy, Sri Wickreme Rajasinghe, 1775–1822,' said the card. We looked at it in silence.

'Now this I can get you,' I said after a while.

'Really? What were you planning to sell? Your soul?'

'I know where the matching one is,' I said quietly. 'At home.'

She looked at me in pitying disbelief.

'I mean not at home, actually. Underneath it.'

'Fairy tales,' she said, taking my arm. I had somehow ruined the mood of the morning, though I didn't exactly know how.

'Let's go,' she said.

Luisa and I lived on Upper Richmond Road, all the way to one end, in a former council flat her parents owned. They were American and rich; I don't know what circus tricks the estate agent must have performed to persuade them that an ex-council flat in Putney was the very zenith of London living. Glamorous it was not. The week before we moved in, they discovered a dead body in the dumpster of the basement car park. Taking the rubbish bags down on a Thursday night was often a rich and rewarding experience.

When I say Luisa's parents were American, I mean that they were the children of Italian immigrants. They were both doctors, though only the father practised. Her mother played the share market, Luisa said. I got the impression she played it greedily and guiltily, the way you might polish off that last piece of chocolate cake in the fridge, pressing every last crumb to your finger, and that she was immensely successful at it. 'My mother made a hundred thousand dollars on the stock exchange today,' Luisa would occasionally remark. A hundred thousand is a lot now. You can imagine what it was then, particularly to the country boy from the Third World. Her parents also owned a diner in New York—in SoHo—the Blue Plate Grill, on Thompson and Prince next to a Chinese laundry. This was the true love of their life and they were fonder of it than they were of medicine or the stock exchange or even Luisa. 'If the President of the USA ever came to visit,' Luisa would say darkly, 'they'd probably take him to the Blue Plate Grill for dinner.'

Our flat was the last one in a long, open corridor on the third floor. We called it Cell Block D, on account of the lavish use of purple brick and the grim-faced residents peering out at us through small windows that barely opened. The only thing missing was the exercise yard, of which many were in sore need. We walked up three flights with heavy shopping when the lift was broken. (It frequently was.)

Inside the flat was a passage with a kitchen and sitting room to one side, a box room and bathroom to the other, and at the end, a bedroom large enough to fit a double bed and not much else. The sitting room was furnished with a single leather sofa against one wall, paying homage to the TV opposite. This self-imposed minimalism—of course, we had no alternative—meant we only had each other: for distraction, for entertainment, for love, for sex. There was no easier way to get to know each other, no easier way to fall out. When I look back, it seems a strange and wondrous thing that we didn't.

I was always quite good with my hands, spending many of my waking hours, when I should have been writing, at DIY. So the bathroom got itself hand-painted Italian tiles whose blue undulations, glaucous and blurred, made you feel you were swimming at the bottom of the Mediterranean. And I installed wooden cupboards in the kitchen underneath a work surface of matte black tiles, and felt proud that, in some small way, I had added value to Luisa's existence, though it was her money that funded these operations. I was a kept man, you see, struggling with his first book.

'What's for lunch?' she asked when we got back.

'Omelette.'

'For a change.'

'There's a bit of Gorgonzola in the fridge for afterwards.'

'Oh, now you've really made my day!'

'There's no need to be cynical,' I said. 'It's only four more days to pay day.' I hugged her because I knew she didn't really mean it.

You may wonder why Luisa's parents, with all their millions, didn't do more to help us out. They had given us the use of the flat; as far as they were concerned, it was enough. It was my first lesson in the rules that obtain in this great white world I found myself in: where it is every man for himself and God for none; where parents did not see any great necessity to pass on their achievements to the next generation. What they made was theirs to enjoy during their lifetime, even if it meant drinking up every last drop of it.

Was there more to it than this? Perhaps. Luisa's parents were not racist. They simply felt their daughter could have done better than an impoverished writer. It offended their go-getting entrepreneurial immigrant sensibilities that she hadn't. I might have had more acceptance, for instance, had I been a second-hand car salesman. But I was a writer—who happened to be black, *and ugly,* as I thought.

'Do you find me ugly?' I asked Luisa when we got married. 'What, you?' she replied.

I was left to decide what exactly she meant by that. But I loved her all the more for giving me that choice.

My mother was the daughter of a famous astrologer who, at the height of his career, had been consulted by just about everyone from the President downwards. For, in Sri Lanka, no one moves without the help or sanction of divine providence. There are certain hours of the day when the streets of Colombo are eerily empty of traffic, simply because it is a *bad* time. Couples have been known to plan the precise time of birth of their children, by Caesarean section, in order to give them the best possible start in life. It has always been a source of wonder to me then, that in spite of all these precautions, we Sri Lankans seem to do so badly in life.

My mother's father met his downfall when he advised a former President to hold snap elections two years before they were due. The President was riding on an unprecedented wave of popularity at the time, and it seemed there was no way he could lose. But lose he did. My grandfather had to go into hiding because there were threats to his life when the government fell. After years of dodging irate party supporters and enthusiastic, machete-wielding goons he emerged a broken man, spending the last years of his life calculating auspicious times for toddlers' birthday parties and telling unmarried men of sixty that yes, their best years were still to come.

But long before all this, he had been astrologer to the Mahadewala Walauwa, the big house on the mountain that belonged to my father's side of the family—in Kandy, the ancient capital of Sri Lanka. The astrologer would sit for hours on the verandah steps, working out his calculations and shuffling his palm leaves, answering the many questions my father's rather haughty mother, the Kumarihamy, put to him.

The story goes that one fine day, he climbed up the verandah steps, flung his cloth bag with insouciance on to a side table and, sitting in a chair next to her—a startling breach of caste and etiquette—said, roguishly, 'It seems, my lady, that we are about to be related. It is foretold in the stars.'

To which my Kandyan grandmother replied, 'Stars? What stars? Shut up and get out, and don't ever come back here again!'

The astrologer lived in a small timber shack on the other side of the hill, down near the bottom. My father, walking into town one day, had caught the eye of the pretty girl who was the astrologer's daughter. In spite of all entreaties and threats, the romance persisted and the subsequent marriage went ahead; my parents were banished from the big house by my father's family. It was only years later that they were allowed back into the walauwa, when a reconciliation of sorts was effected by my Kandyan aunts, who accepted their new sister-in-law into the fold with a gracious, if slightly supercilious, air. They were far too well-bred to be rude to my mother's face, but behind her back they called her the *akuru deke gani*, the woman of two letters.

How did I know all this? I hung around at every family gathering discreetly, in the background, my very ugliness giving me a cloak of invisibility. I learnt early on that no two people take away from any event the same understanding of it, that the truth always lies somewhere in between. I learnt that this truth is frequently and mistakenly associated with goodness and beauty, and untruth with ugliness and the bad. My own truths, however beautifully I phrased them, were always treated with the greatest suspicion.

'Sonny says the sky is blue,' my mother would say. 'Sonny says the grass is green.' She would smile her butcher's smile and the very prefix 'Sonny says' would warn her audience of the improbabilities to come. It was ironic that the astrologer who had always been believed had been granted a grandson whose fate it was never to be believed.

No wonder then, that I escaped from all this at the age of nineteen, in the late summer of that year, 2002.

2

Like thick, grassy slabs of cake covered with luminous green icing, the swards were arranged geometrically around the circular pond at whose centre was Giambologna's Mercury, poised for flight. Tom Quad was the largest quadrangle in Oxford and quite possibly its most beautiful, but all I could think of was the cold. Oxford is built on a river and, as day ends, the cold comes creeping out of the water like some noxious effluent, dressed in rags, enveloping the town in the toxic embrace of its bony fingers. Once you have walked those streets at three in the morning and allowed the cold to enter your bones, you realize it is something that will never leave you. Years later, in the tropics, I could summon it at will from within my system in seconds by merely thinking of it.

I got to the interview with two minutes to spare, dressed in my best school prefects' suit. I had to hold myself down to stop shaking from the cold. My left shoe had split open, the upper coming away from the sole like a half-peeled banana, revealing my toes at unguarded moments. I gingerly placed my right shoe on my left to prevent it opening up any further, praying they would not notice.

There were three of them facing me: the Senior Censor all in black, and two dons.

'You're from Sri Lanka?'

I nodded.

'So you must play cricket?'

I had half a second to decide. Do I lie and brazen it out, or do I tell the truth? I told my own, ugly truth.

'Sorry,' I said. 'I'm hopeless. Hardly ever held a cricket bat in my life.'

You should have seen them hang their heads in disappointment. They must have been expecting so much of me. At this point I nearly said, shall I go now? But I desisted and hung on. There was, after all, the possibility that my truth might be disbelieved.

The man in black was the first to pull himself together. 'You took English A Level? What plays?'

'*Macbeth*,' I said.

'Can you tell us why Shakespeare put witches into the play?'

I could have leapt out of the chair and kissed them at this point. 'James I was an expert on demonology,' I said. 'Shakespeare was socially ambitious and had hopes of currying favour with the king by bringing witches into his play.'

They looked happy with this answer.

'My grandfather was an expert on demonology too,' I added. 'He was always being called in to exorcize evil spirits from people's bodies and things.' I could see I had their attention now.

'Is this very common in Sri Lanka?'

'Oh, yes. We're all supposed to be Buddhist or Christian or Hindu or Moslem, but this belief in good and evil spirits goes back much further. It predates conventional religion by thousands of years. Much of our life in Sri Lanka is spent driving out evil spirits and propitiating good ones. For instance,' I said, 'for a long time my mother used to think there was a demon living inside me, and that was why I looked like this.'

Suddenly, they were looking everywhere else but at me, their faces painfully contorted. I took pity on them.

'Actually,' I added, 'I think she got that all wrong. She's the one with the demon inside. I'm actually quite good most of the time.'

They accepted me in spite of that outburst, to read politics, philosophy and economics at Christ Church—one of the richest, certainly the grandest, of all Oxford colleges. Pure bloody fluke. Oh, they'll rue the day, I thought gleefully, shaking my curly black locks.

∾

My flight from Sri Lanka arrived two days before Freshers' Week at the start of Michaelmas Term. I found I was sharing four splendid high-ceilinged Georgian rooms with Tamas—or Thomas—Vaclav, the top maths scholar of the year. The Canterbury Drag Rooms, as they were called, were assigned on the express condition that they could be booked for parties any day of the week by any member of college. Many a time I would come back to find some rather stuffy drinks party going on in our rooms.

'And who might you be?' the host would ask rather grandly.

'Don't mind me,' I would reply, 'I only live here.'

There was an enormous drawing room overlooking Canterbury Quad, an even bigger dining room overlooking the Picture Gallery Gardens at the back, and two separate bedrooms. The bathrooms were two floors down in the basement. ('Bathrooms?' one don had said when they were first installed. 'Why do they need bathrooms? They're only here for eight weeks at a time, aren't they?')

The drawing room contained a George III sofa with square tapering legs on block feet; the dining room a mahogany table for eight which cranked out to fit three extra leaves so you could seat fourteen; and a bow-fronted satinwood sideboard.

Tom looked me up and down, and then impatiently at his watch. 'It's a good thing you're early,' he said. 'It's now three in the afternoon, the perfect time for a dawn raid.'

We went from room to room around Peckwater Quad. By the end of the raid we had acquired a fall-fronted bureau veneered in burr walnut and two enormous Turkey carpets. 'Let us start as we mean to go on,' said Tom.

Possibly the cleverest person I ever met, he was a figure straight out of the middle Europe of the early twentieth century, an image he reinforced with his pencil moustache, his cavalry twill trousers, his brown tweed jacket. Effortlessly good at whatever he did, his ramrod-straight, rather superior pose hid an essential shyness: girls who were attracted to this esoteric Secessionist image found soon enough that the steel walls he erected around himself were impenetrable.

But not to worry. I was there, lolloping along happily in his wake, picking up the pieces. For the first time in my life, I found my looks not a hindrance. Even more enchanting, people actually believed what I uttered. They say there is an essential colour blindness between races: that the colour of your face camouflages your features from people not used to its hue, disguising what you really think, hiding who you really are. If so, I was the beneficiary of this dictum.

Every Sunday afternoon, people from all over Oxford came to tea in our rooms. These were not necessarily people we knew. Friends brought their friends, who next week brought theirs. Tom had a quartet going in the dining room: violin, viola, cello and bassoon, no prizes for guessing which *his* instrument was.

It must have been a Sunday in the middle of term when I came back from the library to find Tom up a ladder outside our door. He had a plastic bottle of water in his hand which he was attempting to balance over the door.

I looked at him. 'What on earth are you doing?'

'Go inside and don't come out,' he ordered. I could hear the musicians tuning up within, creaking and sawing like a group of DIY enthusiasts.

'Our first guest gets this,' Tom said gleefully. 'Penalty for the unforgivable rudeness of turning up on time.'

'Tom, you can't!'

'Oh, shut up. And stop being so wet. Wet, get it?'

I went inside. Don't ask me how Tom himself crept in without upsetting the water, but he did. Five minutes later there was an almighty shriek. An extremely good-looking girl stood on the Turkey carpet, dripping, like a very elegant rat that had just swum across the Cherwell. Tom was innocently blowing away on the bassoon in the next room.

'What the bloody hell do you mean?' she asked angrily.

'I'm so sorry,' I said, trying hard not to laugh.

'You don't sound sorry at all! Do you realize this is a vintage silk dress?'

'I'll pay for it to be cleaned.'

'This is what happens when you go to strange people's rooms,' she said bitterly.

'You have to believe me when I say I wasn't responsible.' I gave an involuntary guffaw.

'Oh really?'

I held out my hand. 'People call me Sonny.'

'I'm sure they do,' she said. 'But I would call you a bloody idiot.' She stormed out.

Another one gets away, I thought. Thank you, Tom, thank you.

It was something of a wonder to me that Oxford did not seem to house any demons. It was almost that by discounting any question of the presence of evil, you obliterated it. Here people were neither good nor bad: they just got on with life in a pragmatic sort of way. Any misfortune had an explanation. There was neither gratuitous good nor gratuitous bad, except in a theoretical sort of way. Things you might read about in newspapers that you never came across in real life. There was Rosemary West, of course, and the Yorkshire Ripper. But evil was rather vulgar—it never happened to *nice* people, and for every case you read about in the papers, for every murderer that came to trial, there seemed to be three or four psychiatrists queuing breathlessly to testify that it wasn't really his fault: it was the fault of a deprived childhood, a chemical imbalance in the brain, a momentary lapse of judgement.

How different from my part of the world, where people wore their evil (or goodness) on their sleeve. Back in Sri Lanka, we were all part of a medieval passion play, our roles—hero or villain—assigned to us at birth. It took just about everything you possessed to break out of character, if indeed you ever wanted to. There were many who never did, who at the end of their lives were supremely satisfied that they had fulfilled their role in life, taking the trouble to explore the extreme aspects of their character to the full, investing it with the flourishes and grace notes so essential to a winning performance. And when they died, it was this character that lived on in the memories of other people, not the man himself.

One of the great delights of our set of rooms was that it commanded a grandstand view of Canterbury Quad below. At any time of day or night there were random tourists, drunken revellers or disconsolate dons, appearing and disappearing off this stage set, as if propelled this way and that by some unseen divine hand, wilful and capricious. Every evening at precisely 5.45 p.m. a flood of very attractive girls entered, fanning through the courtyard like a flock of brightly coloured birds of paradise.

'Ah,' said Tom, 'the fishing fleet has arrived.'

'Fishing fleet?'

'The girls from the local secretarial colleges and language schools. They're here to find a husband. Of course, we have our own Christ Church girls, but who wants those? These are so much prettier, having no brain to speak of.'

'You bloody chauvinist pig!'

'No, seriously. This year in Christ Church we have the heir to a dukedom—a practice duke, if you like—the Premier Earl and a couple of barons. Oh, and a minor cousin of the Queen, to say nothing of two very wasted German princes. A girl could do very well for herself if she was of such a mind.'

But I wasn't listening. I raced downstairs and caught up with them just as they were going into Peckwater.

'Excuse me,' I said breathlessly. She didn't seem to hear, so I touched her arm.

She turned. 'Oh, it's you,' she said resignedly. 'I try not to look up at your room each time I pass this way.'

'Again, I'm so sorry for what happened. You know it wasn't me.'

'Oh, sure.'

'Can I make it up to you? Take you out for a coffee or something?'

She thought for a moment. 'Actually, coffee won't do. I'm starving. Any better ideas?'

I took her to the burger joint on the Cornmarket. Brave choice for a first date.

We sat in the window, looking out at the sodium-yellow lights of the Cornmarket through the thickening night air: shops closing and people going home from work, weighed down and listless after nine hours of drudgery. The icy neon lights inside the restaurant bleached her face of all complexity of feature, making her look younger than she probably was.

'My name is Sonny, I'm first year. What do you do?'

'I'm with the Banbury Language School,' she replied, sucking up her milkshake noisily through the straw.

'Funny, I could have sworn your English was perfect.'

'Ha, very funny. I *teach* them English.'

'You don't look old enough to be a teacher.'

'You don't look clever enough to be an undergraduate.'

'Now we've got that settled, can we meet again?' I asked, setting the banter aside.

'Only if you promise not to put water bottles over the door.'

I grinned. 'Can't promise,' I said.

Luisa and I started seeing a lot of each other. I can't exactly pinpoint the moment we became boyfriend and girlfriend; other people saw us together and gradually began to assume we were an item, till one day we began to assume it ourselves. There was no sex. Her Catholic scruples prevented her, she said, but I wasn't so sure. She was heart-stoppingly, finger-quiveringly beautiful: a profile straight off an ancient Roman coin, corkscrew curls falling on either side of a perfect oval face. How on earth could she find me attractive? So I didn't push the sex part. I must have still been in character. I hadn't taken the greasepaint off yet.

We went everywhere together, the Beauty and the Beast: a striking, much-talked-about Oxford couple, even if for all the wrong reasons. And I finally began to believe that the pall of darkness I had been surrounded by all these years was starting to lift. And no, I did not notice then the little pucker at each corner of her mouth that should have spoken to me of the wilfulness of this poor little rich girl.

3

The Catholic Church of St Frideswide dated back to the eighth century, when it had been part of a nunnery. Absorbed into Wolsey's new Oxford College and subsequently confiscated by King Henry VIII in 1532, it had been renamed Christ Church. The church still functioned as the college chapel, even if it was also the Anglican Cathedral of Oxford.

It was cold and damp among those old stones. The Devil shivered in his discreet pew, tucked away behind a fat Romanesque column. Seated in the purple shadows in his long black cloak he looked like a grand old Canon of Christ Church. But the silken ruff around his somewhat scrawny neck and the crimson lining to the cloak revealed a certain uncanonical Restoration flamboyance, accentuated by a black felt hat pulled low over the horns, giving prominence to his pointed, goateed chin. All in all, a good look to sport around a college that had housed the Cavalier King Charles I during his wars against the Roundheads.

The Devil was safe from recognition (where safer than a church?) and he knew it: after all, the ancient laws of good and evil decreed he could only be seen by anyone who was truly good or truly evil, and there were very few of those to the pound nowadays. Contrary to popular belief, things were bad down in Hell. Numbers were dropping: people were just not interested in being wicked any more, though they were even less interested in being good. It was all to do with those mumbo jumbo Eastern philosophies which told you that to understand all was to forgive all. How could there be evil in the world if as soon as it popped up it was forgiven? A shameful state of affairs. Hellfire and brimstone were unknown quantities among the youth of today. The very concepts were deeply dated and unfashionable: as dated as spam or sandwich spread, or purple flared jeans with patches sewn on them. In his more maudlin moments, the Devil longed for a good old-fashioned hot cocktail of brimstone on the rocks.

In the light of these depressing statistics he had been sent Upstairs on a recruitment drive, to drum up interest among young people in the dark arts. Oh, it wasn't easy. The youth of today hadn't even heard of Black Sabbath let alone the Black Mass. All they worshipped was capitalism, the girls in their pussy bows like mini Margaret Thatchers, the boys all young fogeys in their shapeless cords and dull brogues. All they wanted in their spare time was to go beagling. *Beagling!* Chase me, muttered the Devil, I'll give you a good run for your money.

The next hymn, 'From Greenland's Icy Mountain', was announced and the congregation stood up.

What though the spicy breezes blow soft o'er Ceylon's isle
Though every prospect pleases, and only man is vile.

In vain with lavish kindness the gifts of God are strewn;
The heathen in his blindness bows down to wood and stone,

sang the Devil in his fine countertenor voice. The old lady next to him was almost beside herself with the lustiness of this aged Canon's voice.

Ceylon, thought the Devil, the old name for Sri Lanka. He had heard a lot about the wickedness there. It had always had a reputation for the Dark Arts, from the time of its demon King Ravana. Maybe that's where I should go, he ruminated. Used to the über-tropical temperatures of his natural habitat, he couldn't quite cope with the rheumatic damp of an Oxford autumn.

Just then a frigid blast of wind swept through the cathedral door and around the Romanesque column, and the Devil's teeth chattered.

The service finished. The congregation stood up to leave. Enough talk of Greenland's icy mountains, he said to himself. Ceylon, that's the answer. There was a young couple ahead of him, as they all filed out into Tom Quad. A rather dark Asian man with a white girl, who was small but with startlingly good looks.

'In Kandy, where I come from, the temperature is a constant 80 degrees all year round,' he was saying.

'Hmm,' said the Devil as he followed them out into the icy headwinds of Kilcannon Passage. 'Hmm.'

Tom was at the open window listening to Janacek, very loud. He seemed to be trying to initiate the whole of Canterbury Quad into the delights of Czech music.

Luisa went straight past him into the bedroom, and shut the door.

He stopped me as I attempted to follow her in. 'Watch out for her.' He gestured at the closed door. 'She's a tart. She's after you.'

'Tom!' I said.

Things were not good between Luisa and him. They hadn't been since that first day: she had never forgiven him that ruined silk dress. For that matter, things were not that good between Tom and me either. I had somehow failed to live up to his expectations and I didn't quite know why. Our rooms were becoming famous throughout Oxford, people coming from far and wide for those Sunday afternoon salons: to mill about and listen to music, to eat crumpets toasted on the single bar electric heater with hot butter and Marmite. All this was part of the plan. I was not aware of the sort of Bridesheadian student life Tom must have envisaged—his aristocratic Sebastian to my rather middle-class Charles— because I must have been the only student up at Christ Church who had not read the book. 'At least try to be a little polite to her,' I said.

He didn't reply, just turned up the music. I went into the bedroom and shut the door behind me, though the Janacek seeped through, loud and unconvincing, rather like Tom himself. Luisa was already in bed, and I took my clothes off and joined her. Bed was our favourite place. The no-sex rule meant it was neutral territory. We could each be ourselves without having to put on a show for the other. Holding my hand firmly to stop it wandering, she spoke on.

'He's a little in love with you, you know that?'

'You just have a dirty mind,' I said, though secretly I was flattered with all this attention I had never received before in my life.

'And so, he resents me.'

I turned to face her. 'Tell me about you,' I said. She talked then about the rather swish Manhattan apartment her parents lived in at the Essex House, which was actually a proper hotel. There were a few—very few—privately held apartments nestling among the hotel rooms, though from the outside corridors you couldn't tell. Their neighbour was David Bowie. She talked casually and rather disparagingly of all this, though I could see within her a quiet air of contentment: the satisfaction of the rich man who can afford the luxury of criticizing a splendid dinner once he has had his fill.

'But what I really want,' she said, 'is to go to Italy. To learn Italian properly, to see where my family came from; to get a sense of where our story began.'

Funny, I thought. I had a very clear idea of where *my* story began: all I wanted was to obliterate it and jump, hands outstretched, both eyes closed, into the present. Here she was, if not forgetting her present, at least putting it aside like money in a bank deposit, to venture down into the unexplored vaults of her past. Part of the game plan of teaching English to Italians at the school was to learn Italian from them.

'But I loathe my boss. He's always patting my backside or putting his hand on my shoulder. When I push him off, he gives me an amused look, as if I'm being prissy or over-reacting, as if somehow I'm the one at fault.'

'I'll kill him,' I said.

She laughed. 'Please don't. I need him alive. I need the money.'

And there we were, back at that sordid question of money again.

'Maybe you can ask David Bowie for some,' I said, softly.

What I meant was, ask your parents, surely they can spare some? But I didn't know her well enough. I knew every inch of her body: but the topography of her finances was a mystery unknowable, particularly to someone from a society whose grasp of money was rudimentary at best. At home, in the small-time countrified Sri Lanka of my childhood, money hardly existed. Favours were granted, their repayment always in kind. Money was so essentially *not* a part of our lives: our currency was property or crops or jewellery. The real irony here was that 200 years ago, my famous ancestor had been the last king's treasurer, a fact my mother kept banging on about. He must have been an aberration, I decided. A complete freak of nature.

The term ground on. Luisa became a part of my life in a way I had not thought possible. I had never had a girlfriend before, let alone any friend who was a girl. Discreetly and silently she had built up around me the four secure walls of my new life, locking out the demons of my past. Oxford had eight-week terms, and the last week was upon us before I knew it. I had barely been to lectures.

Luisa had Tuesdays off every week, and more often than not we had gone up to London, sometimes staying the night at a cheap B&B. Luisa's parents had sent her, by post, an aqua-green American Express card, a rare and wondrous thing as far as I was concerned. We would take the early morning Wednesday train back and I would squeak into my tutorial with minutes to spare, producing as my week's work an essay so thin and meagre, I was ashamed. It would not have fooled my don, though he never made it an issue. There was an unspoken assumption that, because the entrance requirements were so high, if you were good enough to get into Oxford, you were good enough to last the course. There was the end-of-year exam anyway, Mods, which would weed out the ones truly beyond redemption. So they pretty much left you alone the rest of the time.

On one of the last days of the term, Tom had gone out for a raucous end-of-term party and I was alone in the rooms, listening to Strauss's *Four Last Songs*, sung by Elizabeth Schwarzkopf, or Betty Blackhead as Tom called her. Her voice was cold—the thin, mystical notes creeping around the room, a trace in sound of the fingers of mist trailing through the air outside. There is nothing so lonely as an Oxford winter's night at the end of Michaelmas term.

I heard someone at the door. I looked up to see Luisa standing in the half light, hesitant. There was something about her posture which was completely different from the self-assured, self-possessed figure I was used to.

'I'm leaving,' she said quietly.

'You told me. You're off to Italy to look up your old aunts.'

'No, I'm done here. Finito. I'm gone for good.'

'*What?*' I felt the floor of my heart give way. 'No,' I said. 'You can't!'

How could she do this to me? I felt abandoned, bereft: a child who has had his rattle taken away.

'I can't take it any more. Today he forced himself on me in the office. Oh God, his rancid breath!'

'I'm taking you to the police.'

'No.' She put her hands out as if to ward off something unpleasant. 'It's not going to get me anywhere. This is not New York. It'll be his word against mine. The only thing that'll happen is that I'll never be able to work in this town again.'

'But he'll only do it again to the next girl that comes in.'

'Do I care?' She was shouting. 'I'm not here to fight other people's battles. It's difficult enough fighting my own.' She began to sob and I took her in my arms. The strength in her which I'd gotten so used to had melted, as breath into the wind, and I was shocked. I wanted to say, don't go, we'll fight this thing together, we'll find you another job. But I realized I would be doing this for all the wrong reasons. I wanted her to remain for my sake, not hers. The knowledge of this dishonesty, coupled with my inadequacy, made me somehow reticent.

'Stay with me tonight,' she whispered. It suddenly became clear to me what she had in mind. Leaving the Strauss to play on, I led her to the bedroom, praying that Tom would not be back early.

We were famished and greedy for each other. For much of that term she had been my chaste bedfellow, so the sensuousness of her hunger was both deeply satisfying and mildly disturbing. I had thought till then that sensuousness was the province of ugly people, requisitioned by us for our coarse needs. Its expert and extravagant practice by someone so spare and refined in everyday life was both shocking and pleasurable: as if she had been found, suddenly and unexpectedly, to be an accomplished sorcerer, having passed the exam secretly at night school.

It was our first time, perhaps our last. I do not remember much about the early morning stumble to the railway station, only the picture of her face framed in the train window, getting smaller and smaller as it receded into the distance. And my body awash in its private grief; private because I was too proud to let it show.

Looking back I wonder to myself, why didn't I fight back? Why did I let her go so easily? I could have said: What about me, where do I fit into this picture? I could even have chucked up Oxford and gone out to Italy with her. The only defence I have is that I was young then, with the fatalism of all young people: aware of change all around them, never for a moment imagining they could be agents of that change. For me, at that precise moment, there really was no concept of the future: only the present, the undying and undiluted present, pulsating, ugly and alive.

4

Clarice, Mahadewala Kumarihamy, sat on the verandah of the big house on the mountainside, sipping her coffee. By her side stood her walker, a rigid four-legged aluminium contraption, as much in use as a weapon as for a means of support. Below her lay spread—like a millionaire's picnic—the Palace, the lake they called the Sea of Milk, the Cloud Wall and the Temple of the Tooth. It was a view of which she did not tire at any time of day, though mornings were best, when the sun gilded the ripples on the water and dazzled the golden tiles of the temple roof. Already from below she could hear the muted roar, as of some vast beast, of the town coming awake.

The Kumarihamy mused, as she often did, on her early life. It had been a hard climb from where she had been to where she was now: both physically and metaphorically. She remembered the one-room clapboard house of her astrologer father, the comforting feel of the rough mangowood planks lashed to the uprights with hairy coir rope, and the corrugated tin roof —deafening in the rain, stifling in the sun—on which crows joyously bounced as they landed, as if it were some sort of avian trampoline. Her father had had the ear of just about everyone who was anyone in the country and offers of better habitation had come frequently from this politician or that, but the old man was adamant that they not move. This was a lucky house and he was not about to tempt fate by abandoning it. He knew only too well that the higher up you went, the further you had to fall, and when his own fall came, he took a certain perverse satisfaction in the fact that he was where he had always been: at rock bottom, with nowhere further to go. True, he had had to abandon his home for a short while after that fateful election when there were threats to his life. But he knew too well that in Sri Lanka, today's white van victims are tomorrow's heroes. You only have to bide your time: it is a country with the longest of histories, the shortest of memories.

Notwithstanding this humility, the astrologer had been the first to encourage the match when his pretty daughter caught the eye of the heir to the big house further up the mountainside. His horoscopes told him that they were a perfect match; here again it was a question of patiently waiting, till the ranting and raving, the threats and tears, against this 'hideously unnatural' inter-caste marriage had fallen silent. The boy was, after all, sole male heir, the carrier of the Mahadewala name. Without him, nothing.

The astrologer's young daughter had not been so sanguine. It was she who had had to listen to the insults and innuendoes, the snide comments and honey-smooth patronization. She had borne it all with dignity because she truly loved her husband; but she never forgave, she never forgot. And now, after his death, when she was in sole charge, she wielded her absolute power quite absolutely. They say that in any religion, it is the convert that is most pious. The Kumarihamy was a far more rigid practitioner of the medieval way of life that she had married into than her sisters-in-law, who were to the manor born and could therefore afford to be more relaxed about it.

Clarice Mahadewala was a fine-looking woman, with aquiline features and fair skin—the result, if truth be told, of her mixed Portuguese ancestry. It was a source of unfailing satisfaction to her that she looked more Sanskritized and Kandyan than her sisters-in-law, who were much darker, retaining in their features some slight suggestion of the atavistic fuzziness of the hinterland. To put it rather vulgarly— and the Kumarihamy allowed vulgarity to flourish like some glossy weed in that most secret place within her heart—she had the money, she had the power, she had the looks. Oh, and the title too. Only one thing marred this idyllic existence: her son, Sonal, known to one and all as Sonny.

Her reverie was interrupted by the insistent ringing of a bell. The postman had wheeled his bike through the walauwa gates and right up to the verandah. Again. He stood below the Kumarihamy, waving a blue airmail letter at her, grinning importunately.

The Kumarihamy ignored him. Instead she rang her own little hand bell, which she kept by the chair. An old man came from inside the house in a dirty mud-streaked sarong and torn vest. There was mud on his face too.

'Ah, Girigoris.'

'My lady?'

'Will you tell the postman that there's a letter box at the gate for his letters. He can ring the bell on the gatepost if he wishes to inform us he has delivered.'

The postman grinned. 'That bell doesn't work. Anyway, the gates were open, so I came in.' He shot an expert stream of crimson betel juice at a double-petalled blue hibiscus, to the extreme annoyance of the Kumarihamy.

'The gates are always open,' she said, still addressing her words to Girigoris, but speaking very slowly as if to a moron. 'This does not mean that we are at home to everyone.' She smiled sweetly, a smile of cold steel dipped in saccharine. 'Please see that this doesn't happen again. Otherwise the postman might find himself delivering letters in the Wanni jungles.' She gave a little silvery laugh, which matched in colour the steel.

This suggestion of the Wanni jungles, where a war was currently being fought, was outrageously improbable—but the seeds of the threat were very real, you were never sure how far the Kumarihamy's influence might extend. The postman knew when he was beaten. He turned the bicycle around, giving the bell another vigorous ring before preparing for descent. He paused a moment. 'Oh, I nearly forgot this,' he said, throwing the flimsy airmail letter on to the verandah. It fluttered through the air and landed on the hibiscus, an extra blue flower harvested swiftly by Girigoris before it too was stained with betel juice.

The letter could only be from one person. With trembling hands, the Kumarihamy placed it by her side, forcing herself, with supreme self-control, not to look at it till she had calmed down. Her problem was a simple one. From the time of her childhood—and her astrologer father had only reinforced this idea—she had been good. Too damned good for everyone else. Indeed she had been able to counteract the malign influences flying about the mountainside only because of her goodness. Her kindness. Her charitablenesss. How then to come to terms with the hideously unpalatable fact that your son, your only child, was in some way tainted by evil? That, in fact, he might actually be the work of the devil? It hadn't been easy, oh no. If she had been American she might have had to undergo an extremely long (and expensive) course of Park Avenue counselling treatments. Here, alas, she had to manage with the servants—to whom she spoke incessantly about this problem. Like psychiatrists, they were trained not to talk back.

In her heart of hearts the Kumarihamy wondered whether she was perhaps being punished. In spite of her father's astrological assurances, had she in some way transgressed the ancient natural laws by marrying into this family? Don't be silly, Clarice, she said to herself. They are bloody lucky to have you.

Dearest Ma,

I'm sorry I haven't written for such a long time. Life here has been hectic. Oxford works you very hard, and I'm happy to say that my essays so far have been getting top marks. Anyway the real reason I'm writing is to tell you that I've met someone who I think is very special. She's American but of Italian ancestry, and very, very pretty. Daddy would have loved her had he still been alive. (Ha, I bet he would have! thought the Kumarihamy.) I would like to bring her home. I know you're a bit tight for money, and that the arrangement was that I would work here during the holidays, but Luisa (that's her name) says she'll treat me to the ticket. So you may see us sooner than you think!

I hope you're keeping well and that the eyes are not troubling you too much. Please give a fond hug to Sita and all the others.
Your ever-loving son,
Sonny

The Kumarihamy rang the bell again, with trembling fingers. 'Sita!' she called out. 'Sita!'

'You rang, my lady?'

'Sit here.'

Sita sat on the verandah steps at the Kumarihamy's feet.

'He's trying to come back.'

'But he only just left.'

'Exactly. He's found himself some rich white bitch.' (The Kumarihamy was very fond of the B-word—it was a B-word in Sinhala too, *bally*, and guests at the walauwa were often startled by her lavish use of it, the casual savagery of her conversation.)

'She must be a demoness,' said Sita.

'Don't be silly. She's just white, she can't help it.'

'He'll be wanting his old room back.'

'Well, he can't have it, can he!'

'What are you going to do?'

'If I knew that, you stupid girl, would I be asking you?' The Kumarihamy gave Sita a sharp knock on the head with her knuckles.

'Ow!' said Sita.

'Let me see your fingernails,' commanded the Kumarihamy.

Sita held out her fingers for inspection. 'They're clean!' said Clarice, disapprovingly. 'What are you doing with clean hands? Wicked girl, you're supposed to be helping Girigoris with the soil!' She gave Sita another sharp rap on the head. Sita yelped good-naturedly.

∽

My mother had made it very plain that she could not afford to support me during the holidays, that I had to get a job. Someone had told me about this place in London, in Earls Court, where you went at 5.30 any evening. Your would-be employers turned up at six and if they liked the looks of you, if they thought you were willing and able—or, more important, stupid enough—they'd bus you out to wherever the job happened to be.

There were three lucky lads that first day, me, an Aussie and a New Zealander. I soon found out that the Aussies were absolute masters at this game. They could tell you where to go for a free meal, a free bed for the night, a free anything. They could work the system beautifully, they knew it backwards. Our place of work was about the size of a football stadium with ceilings fifty feet high, the entire place kept at sub-Arctic temperatures. Coming from Sri Lanka, I expected several hundred people to be working in there. Wrong. There can't have been more than ten of us in all: the maintenance guys, the drivers, and one lone, bearded Sikh. Inside were boxes and boxes of frozen chicken. In fact, the place was one dirty great Palace of Chicken. All lit by this unearthly blue neon light, so you almost felt you were in heaven. Which in a way was true for the chickens.

The Sikh drove the forklift which brought the pallets laden with boxes out front. He was the lucky one, he had the donkey jacket. He drove recklessly up and down the aisles all night with this frozen rictus of a grin on his face. I swear by dawn I could see icicles forming in his beard. Our job was to load the boxes on to the lorries. We worked through the night so the lorries could leave by four in the morning. The Aussie and the New Zealander were used to their Antipodean winters, they kept each other warm, so to speak. The only thing I was used to was my sleep.

I'm ashamed to admit I lasted barely a week. I couldn't take the late nights, I couldn't take the atmosphere in there. They were all cold towards me, especially the chickens. I longed for somebody to say something, I prayed in vain for a squawk from one of the boxes. The only satisfaction I got was knowing that during that particular week, in eating-houses all over London, people were sitting down to their chicken, fried, grilled and curried, all packed by my own fair (well, metaphorically fair) hand.

I had found myself a room in a huge house off Gloucester Road, Ambrose House, full of immigrants, all as soft and stealthy as I was. We passed each other in the corridors on silently slippered feet—on our way to and from the shared bathroom at the end of the corridor. If you were in the bath (and I was, a lot, it was virtually the only way to keep warm) and someone tried the door handle, you gave a loud cough; immediately you heard a scuttling noise, as of rats running away. When you passed other people's doors you could hear BBC World Service from within, and the sizzle of roasted chillies and of dried fish being fried. Some days, I could swear I heard the pop and fizz of Elephant House ginger beer.

And all the while I could not get Luisa out of my head. I played and replayed endlessly the late-night conversations we had had, the things we had done together. We had talked about visiting Sri Lanka. So much so, that I had felt betrayed when she came to me that last night to say she was leaving for good. Why had she decided to let me have sex that day? Was it a mercy fuck because she knew she would never have to see me again? Did she have to shut her eyes and think of Italy? I had her address in Monte San Savino, the little village in Tuscany where her relatives lived, and the first thing I did from Ambrose House was to write to her. There was no reply. A week later when I could bear it no more, I wrote again. By the third week I had given up all hope. Perhaps this was the civilized white way of doing things: when they were with you they were all over you, when they were gone they were gone, and might as well not have existed at all. The knowledge of this was like a chip of ice stuck in the heart.

After the chickens, I went on to something far more respectable, cleaning the lavatories at Wembley Stadium. I got to see inside the press box (while vacuuming it) and the view from the grandstand (while picking up cigarette butts and sweet wrappers from under the seats). I thought of Tom, who had no idea of what I was up to, and who would have been horrified and deeply ashamed of my unBridesheadian behaviour.

In no time at all, it was the start of the second term.

5

The train up to Oxford was packed with students returning for Hilary Term. The sky hung low, its luminous silver skin shining through the grey like the vast underbelly of some airborne fish. The first thing I did was to check my pigeonhole at the porter's lodge in Tom Tower. And there it was, a yellow envelope addressed in turquoise ink, in Luisa's curly-wurly handwriting. My heart bursting, I took it back to my rooms to read. Inside, a single piece of paper with three lines.

'There's something I have to tell you. Not sure exactly when I can come. See you when I see you.'

At the bottom was a large heart with the word *baci*, kisses, written inside. If there was a faintly ominous tone to the words, I did not care. She had written! That was all that mattered. She did not want to end our relationship, and I was willing to continue on whatever terms she dictated. Just for it to exist was enough for me.

The door opened and Tom burst in with his friends: Matthew Stonehouse, whose father owned an island in the Caribbean; Paul Higgitt, who was possessed of the finest dinner jacket in all Oxford (far more precious than a mere island); and Jane Shilling, all Gothicked up in black lace. They were brandishing a jeroboam of champagne and I got swept up in the revelry. Even as I sank gratefully into the din and clatter of their good life, the knowledge of that yellow letter remained, a small, comforting stone lodged deep within my gullet, anchoring me with its weight.

There was no one to spend my evenings with, no more distracting visits to London. I found to my consternation what a mess my studies were in. It had been easy so far to wing it at tutorials, when I knew absolutely nothing. Now that I had genuinely started reading the prescribed books I realized with horror how little I knew, how far I had to go to catch up.

Tom was no help at all. Why should he be? Those days there were far fewer women up at Oxford than now. To be in a relationship with one (however sketchy) gave me infinite cachet. With Luisa coming in and out of my room at all hours it was easy for us to lord it over him: we genuinely believed ours was the 'true' life and Tom's the fake. All his champagne breakfasts and punting picnics did not fool us—they were mere attempts at recreating an Oxford past which indeed might never have existed at all. We pitied and patronized him with our superior attitude. Now with Luisa gone, I was back to being single and it was all too easy for him to put the boot in. And he did, viciously. I had to sit there in the corner and take it like a man, all the snide comments about cheap girls in language schools and the fools who fell for them. In a perverse masochistic way I lapped it up: I craved attention at any price, anything at all to dispel my loneliness.

My Kandyan father's family was Catholic and, until his early death, my upbringing was very much in that tradition. But it was the Catholicism of tropical Asia: of flickering red lamps and silver gilt monstrances; of bodies packed tight into whitewashed baroque churches, the women smelling of camphorwood and coconut oil and the freshly plucked jasmine in their hair. I remember the annual pilgrimage to St Anne's on the north-west coast in the last week of July. We went in caravanserai, with pots and pans and servants, camping out in the little thatched huts surrounding the great church ('It must make Clarice feel *quite* at home,' said my Kandyan aunts cattily). I remember the rows of stalls selling miraculous medals and prayer cards and fluorescent plastic statuettes, all the detritus of holy commerce; and everywhere the plaintive chant of *yarkña*—the onomatopoeic word for prayer—issuing from loudspeakers strung high on coconut palms. Above all, I remember the long, late lunches of crab and prawn, fresh from the ocean, simmered in turmeric and coconut and lime, and eaten al fresco on the sand.

When my father died, my mother took over the reins of the walauwa and all this came to an end. Perhaps my aunts still continued to go, but we at the big house stopped; then began the slow, almost imperceptible slide into the demonry and necromancy that informed much of my later childhood. This was the way in Sri Lanka, where conventional religions were happy bedfellows of prehistoric rites, the symbiosis between the two considered entirely natural by all. My mother had a tame priest—should I call him a familiar?—at the Ampitiya Seminary. Father Rosario was always ready to speed up the hill to our house on his little blue Vespa when the need arose. His speciality was the finding of amulets buried in your garden by those who wished you evil. He would begin with a few lengthy incantations and imprecations to get you in the mood, so to speak; having worked himself up into a thoroughly trance-like state, he would fly around the property like a water-diviner with the tools of his trade. He was followed closely by Girigoris, bare-bodied, with a pick over his shoulder, a tropical grim reaper in a hitched-up sarong.

'Dig here,' Father Rosario would say, and Girigoris would wield the pick. Almost always they would find, less than a foot down, a fragment of bone or hair or nail clippings wrapped up in cloth, which would be taken off ceremoniously and burnt in full view of the participants. My mother would let out a sigh then, as if a great rock had been lifted off her back. How did this happen? Did Father Rosario come the night before and bury the charm? All I know is that I have witnessed this ceremony many times, and every time there has been a result. Everyone on the mountainside was at it, you see, casting charms on everyone else. A charming neighbourhood.

As for this question of evil, I had been taught by the Church that you could never achieve a good result through evil means. This worried me deeply: was it not worth shooting one man to save the lives of a hundred others? If not, then how could you justify war? Particularly wars the Church itself has condoned over its long history? And how about the reverse: could you, with the best of intentions, end up accidentally committing evil? If so, did the evil of the deed rub off on you, or did your Teflon-coated goodness leave you pure even if the deed itself were dire? Worst of all, how could you explain natural disasters like Pompeii or Krakatoa? Was that the work of the Devil? Or was it God polishing off so many thousand truly evil men who deserved to die? If so, was God Teflon-coated too?

I was unclear where I stood on all this. As far as my mother was concerned I was born bad. Was this the reason then for my blindness, my inability to judge? Was I morally dead in the water? Was I lost before I had even begun?

In that second term, after Luisa left, I took to going to the Catholic Chaplaincy for Sunday morning mass, across the road from Christ Church and a little further down St Aldates. Many people attended, not all for the correct reasons, I fear. At the après-mass you stood around drinking plastic coffee out of plastic cups, one of those esoteric Oxford events all the more snobbish for the banality of the surroundings. The university was packed to the gills with sons and daughters of ancient English Catholic families, many of whom looked down upon the Whig ascendancy of later centuries with the nicest possible disdain. The Chaplaincy was their headquarters: I got the impression that Sunday mass was their exclusive weekly get-together, and God should have considered himself lucky to be invited along.

There was this French girl, Bettina, whom I was vaguely keen on, from St Hilda's College, who encouraged me to attend. I liked being with her, she had charm coupled with eminent practicality, a condition the French seem to specialize in. I think she found me exotic, my very ugliness a sort of Gallic fashion statement. Sadly for her, I could not get Luisa out of my head. We were drinking our undrinkable coffee when there was a commotion at the door. A somewhat overtanned Arabic man in headdress and robes swept into the hall. He was wearing dark glasses. The whole room fell silent at this wondrous spectacle of an Arab in church. He seemed to be heading straight for me. I froze.

'Ah, Sonny!' he said in guttural accents, throwing his arms around me. He kissed me fulsomely on both cheeks to my huge embarrassment. Then I recognized Tom.

'Meet my wife, the Sheikha Fatima,' he continued. 'I call her Fat for short.' He paused, looking at the figure behind him. 'Though really, I should call her Fat *and* Short.'

From the shadow of his voluminous robes stepped a slim girl in a bright yellow skirt. 'I'm sorry about all this,' Luisa said with a smile. 'I went to your rooms looking for you, I was going to wait. This was all his idea.'

'Luisa!' I yelled, sweeping her off her feet and whirling her round. I was trembling with happiness.

'Can we go back to the rooms?' she asked in a low tone. 'There's something we need to talk about.'

'Can't it wait?'

She gave me a strange look. 'I don't think so,' she said quietly.

6

'Are you sure?' I repeated for what must have been the tenth time.

Luisa shrugged. We were in bed and I was holding her tight. I could feel the tepid unhappiness of her body, its lifeless languor, like water draining through my fingers under the tap. My world had just come crashing down but I plunged on recklessly, almost daring her to say what I least wanted to hear. It would be the end of my degree, the end of Oxford.

'Do you want to keep it?' I asked aggressively. As if my sternness somehow managed to put me in the clear and her in the wrong.

'That's not what *you* want, is it?'

'You don't have to give a fuck what I want. It's your body, your decision.'

'It's your baby too.'

'Is it? How do you know? We only did it the one time, remember? How is it possible?'

She looked shocked. 'You bastard,' she said quietly. 'What are you trying to get at?'

'Whatever you want me to get at,' I replied viciously, turning my back on her in the narrow bed.

A little later I felt her fingers, slightly cold, touching the back of my neck. I ignored them.

I realize how this must show me up: in what bad light. But it is the sad truth—though I am praying you will not believe it. There is nothing I can do about it. No rewinding of the tape, no words of apology could ever cover the grossness, the sheer evil of my behaviour. If my mother had been around, she would have said, Didn't I tell you so? Didn't I tell you my son was evil? She would promptly have identified which particular demon was in possession of my system, and the requisite remedy for its eviction. As it was I was alone and demonless, in a country cold and far from home.

All I can say in my defence is that I was twenty and Luisa twenty-five; and that five-year age gap is far, far bigger in your twenties than in your forties. I had barely begun life after my daring escape from a medieval Kandyan hillside. All I knew and understood at that moment was the glittering present, winking like the sequined scales of a fish, not the matt black permanence of wives or babies or houses.

Next morning I woke up and Luisa was gone. Not far, because the small case she had brought from Italy was still there, open and spilling its contents out over the wooden floor. I went to lectures feeling rotten, all the while making excuses for myself. It is easy being a man: we can afford the fakery of our high-minded justifications, we do not have to deal with the realities of the monthly blood, the ticking clock, the sheer physical weight of birth and being that underpins every woman's reality. I went around inventing manly reasons to be angry with her, showing what an unmanly child I actually was.

Two days later I came back to find her seated on the bed, her face wan, the colour bleached from it, dead and wintry as the sky outside. When she saw me, she began to weep; silently, inconsolably. I sat on the bed and held her, and all I could feel was her body shuddering wordlessly, a silent reproach that will live with me as long as I live.

'I am so, so sorry,' I whispered, caressing her hair. It was too little, too late.

An hour later, she was packed and gone. I had lost her, yet again.

The Devil took the direct flight to Colombo on Sri Lankan Airlines, UL 504—better known as *Usually Late* 504. As it happened it was bang on time, so it might have been better to call it UP 504—*Unusually Punctual* 504. Because the Devil was invisible to all but the very good or very bad, he felt safe, up in the air amidst all these morally mediocre travellers. He slipped into a large business class seat; kicking off his satin Restoration shoes with their gilt buckles, he tucked his hooves comfortably under him.

An unusually well-nourished Sri Lankan woman accompanying a small girl went past.

'Mummy, mummy, look, that Auntie has hairy legs.'

'Oh, shush. You have to learn, Hiranthi, to keep your comments to yourself,' said her mother. 'One day you too will be old, and no doubt you will have hairy legs too.'

The Devil took umbrage. He sat up in his seat and poked his face at them. 'Your mother's fat. Do I go around telling people she's fat? Do? *Do I?*' he thumped his thin chest aggressively. 'On the contrary, I would take great pains to say, "My, Sakuntala, *how* you have pulled down. Have you tried Sustagen?"'

Before he had finished, the mother and child had bustled away, and the Devil sank back into his seat fuming. Really, these Sri Lankans! He was proud, though, that he had been able to insinuate *My, how you have pulled down* into the conversation, a phrase gleaned from the *Handbook of Sri Lankan Idioms* that he had been poring over night after night prior to this momentous journey. Surreptitiously slurping down a Bloody Mary off the circulating drinks tray—there had been Virgin Marys too, but that wouldn't have done now, would it?—the Devil gave a delicate belch and prepared himself for sleep.

'Only man is vile,' he crooned to himself as he drifted off. 'Only man is vile. . .'

A little while later, when the shades were down and the lights off, he felt a tap on his shoulder. It was the Captain, lecherous and elderly, his face creased and lined and shiny like mahogany shoe leather. 'You fancy a good time when we get to Colombo, lady?' He was swaying a little and his eyes were bloodshot.

'Lady? *Lady?* Do I look like a lady to you?'

'I know what I like,' said the Captain. 'I like what I see.'

'Then put your glasses back on,' snapped the Devil irritably.

'Temper, temper!' The Captain wagged his finger. He turned and sashayed back uncertainly to the cockpit. 'That ain't no lady,' he said, shaking his head sorrowfully.

The big house, or Mahadewala Walauwa, as it was officially known, was a smallish Palladian villa with a sixty-foot frontage. It stood on Bhairava Kanda or the Mountain of Bhairava, overlooking the town of Kandy. Bhairava was the four-headed Demon King who had lost his fifth head when the god Brahma had cut it off with his fingernail. During the time of the kings, human sacrifices had taken place on this mountain—young virgins, usually—to propitiate Bhairava. The sacrifices had stopped some 200 years back.

'Where can you find a young virgin in Kandy these days?' Clarice Mahadewala was fond of asking. 'It's difficult enough finding an old one.'

The Mahadewalas, hereditary treasurers to the kings of Kandy, had been granted ownership of the mountain because it commanded one of the only routes into the then almost impregnable city of Kandy. They weren't allowed to build on it, because royal protocol decreed you could not build above the level of the palace. Indeed the king had preferred to herd all his court officials into the narrow criss-cross of streets facing the palace—Malabar Street and Trincomalee Street and so on—where they lived cheek by jowl with the rest of the king's Nayake relations, squabbling and plotting, in as much pomp and circumstance as those crowded conditions would permit. This was where the king liked to keep them, on the sound principle of *keep your friends close and your enemies closer*. On the mountain was stationed a small garrison of the king's soldiers, a watch-post guarding the entrance to Kandy.

Perhaps as a result of all this ceaseless plotting and double-dealing at court, the king himself was becoming increasingly paranoic, prone to bouts of manic depression and vicious cruelty. With this behaviour he played straight into British hands—they had only been waiting for an excuse to move in—and with the connivance of certain treasonous and treacherous nobles, the British took Kandy in 1815, ending what was then the world's longest-surviving continuous monarchy. It was time now for the treasurer to reclaim his land, and he wasted no time building the walauwa—with its precisely cut and fluted Grecian pillars. The dharma chakras on its battlements were a nod to the official religion of the country though this was one which neither he nor the king practised in private. In addition, the house boasted many other accoutrements hitherto forbidden to ordinary citizens of the land: clay tiles and bronze finials, and windows with little squares of pink- and green-coloured glass.

The Devil's crimson silk shoes with their gilt buckles were not the ideal footwear for climbing mountains. They were already ripped a little and caked with mud. A quarter of the way up he noticed a boarded shack with a line of laundry outside, flapping in the breeze. Leaving the shoes carefully on the doorstep—the Devil abhorred waste of any sort—he continued up on sensibly cloven hooves. Back in hell they had told him about a wicked Kandyan princess living on a mountainside in Sri Lanka. It sounded like something out of a fairy tale, and the Devil was inclined to be cynical. Nobody is that bad, he thought, as he walked further up. Trust me, I should know.

The Devil had a fine eye for architecture, and the first thing he noticed about the villa was the bulging bow window to one side, which entirely destroyed the symmetry of the façade. Then there was the matter of the front door, a few feet off centre. Disgraceful, he thought. I could have done a better job myself. He knew why they had done it, of course; according to the ancient laws of vastu, enfilade openings were a strict no-no as they allowed forces of good fortune to enter through the first opening and exit through the last. By having doors out of alignment, you hopefully managed to trap your good luck forever inside. It occurred to the Devil that these benevolent spirits must really be rather foolish if that was all it took. Sadly, the asymmetry ruined the Devil's own flight path too. It was most inconvenient to come flying in at great speed and go smack against a brick wall where you expected an opening.

He saw seated in the purple shadows of the deep verandah a shrunken old woman, not at all princess-like. She was looking with difficulty at pictures in *Hi!!* magazine through a magnifying glass.

'Good afternoon, Madam,' said the Devil touching his hat.

'*Madam?* You're on private property,' said Clarice. 'Now get out.'

Who was this stranger in her midst? Through her macularly degenerate eyes she could see the vague outlines of a figure of indeterminate sex. Was that a cape? Was it a dress? Was this one of those transgender people she had been hearing so much about of late?

'So sorry,' said the Devil. 'I'll come back another time if I may. I've just moved into the neighbourhood. You'll be seeing a lot more of me in the future, I assure you.'

Just then, as if on cue, the solitary phone in the walauwa began to ring deep in the bowels of the house, and the Devil vanished. 'Now where did he go?' thought the Kumarihamy with some asperity. It was one thing to order your neighbours off the property. It was another for them to vanish without so much as a by-your-leave.

'Hi, Ma, it's me!' said the voice on the other end of the line, when she went to the phone.

'*Who?*' asked Clarice suspiciously. 'Who is this?'

'Your son, Sonny. Remember?'

'Oh.' She paused a moment in order to let the smile sink into her voice. 'I suppose you're calling to say you've booked your ticket. Well, I'm sorry. You can't . . .'

'I'm not coming, Ma.'

'But your friend? The white, the white . . .' Clarice cast about for a word that didn't begin with B.

'She's gone, Ma. Left England.'

'Oh, *what* a pity,' said Clarice changing tack smoothly and instantly like a politician. 'And I'd just got your room up looking so nice.' She paused. 'So. Why are you calling?'

'I was missing you guys.'

'Really. What's that noise? Are you having a party?' Clarice's sympathies vanished in an instant.

'That's the TV in the JCR. I'm ringing from the call-box outside.'

'Oh.' The Kumarihamy remained unconvinced. 'Well, don't call again. Complete waste of money. An airmail letter will do.'

She put the phone down. Using her walker, she made her painful way down the corridor to Sonny's former bedroom. There were piles of dank earth everywhere, stacked against the walls. Girigoris was in the pit, digging by the light of a kerosene lantern.

'Anything so far?' Girigoris shook his head. The Kumarihamy looked at the piles of earth. 'Where's Sita?'

'Just left, my lady. She's taking her father to the doctor.'

'Doctor? He looked perfectly well to me.'

'It's the diabetes.'

'Diabetes, cholesterol, piles. Ha! Tell me, how do *I* survive without any of this nonsense? And these bastards : . .' She brandished her walker like a weapon. Down in the pit, Girigoris ducked instinctively.

Sita was, in fact, still in the house, gathering up her bits and pieces in the kitchen. She had made good her escape from the dig when she heard the click-click of the walker down the passage. If she had been caught, the Kumarihamy would have detained her for another hour at least.

Pandu the garden boy was seated at the kitchen table, drinking tea. He grinned. 'Shall I tell her you're still here?'

'You do that,' said Sita sweetly, 'and you'll be getting salt in your tea for the rest of the year.'

Pandu was not allowed in the house at all, not even in the kitchens. His tea was made by Sita or Karuppayah the cook and drunk on a bench outside. He had taken matters into his own hands today, because Sita was busy with the amateur excavation inside, and the cook was in his room snoring after a heavy, late lunch of yellow rice and black pork curry.

'I'll miss the doctor if I don't hurry.' She turned back to look at Pandu. 'Make sure you're out of here in five minutes. Otherwise you're in trouble, you hear me?'

'Yeah, yeah, yeah,' said Pandu. He watched her strong legs under the thin dress, her saucy calves. I wouldn't mind, he thought. I wouldn't mind.

Taking off her rubber slippers, Sita ran down the hill breathlessly. She lived with her father on the other side near the bottom, in the very same shack the Kumarihamy had been born in. It was a source of perennial puzzlement to her—and to everyone else—as to why she had been singled out for such preferential treatment. All the other servants of the walauwa lived in the quarters at the back of the big house where they could be summoned day or night, and they were. Sita, by contrast, came in at six thirty every morning and was out by six thirty in the evening.

The Kumarihamy's character was more complex than one might at first imagine. Mean and tight-fisted in so many ways, she had been incredibly generous to Sita, offering the shack as a home for her and her father. Most puzzling of all was this: Why had she preserved such a structure, which only served to remind all and sundry of her lowly beginnings? Might it not have been more natural to demolish it and pretend it never existed? Though the Kumarihamy hardly left the walauwa these days, when she did—Pandu driving her at two miles an hour in the ancient bottle-green Toyota Crown—she always asked to be taken past it, and seemed to take a certain perverse pleasure in its existence, with its neat bed of zinnias in front and the laundry flapping jauntily in the breeze.

When she got home that day, Sita saw that someone had left a pair of silken shoes on the doorstep, a little ripped and mud-spattered, but nothing a needle and thread could not cure. They fit her perfectly.

'Hurry up!' she called out to her father. 'We'll be late for the doctor.'

7

Next holiday I found myself a room in Wardour Street and a job at an insurance company in the City. I was one of an island of four desks—together with three rather good-looking girls—and, of course, we spent much of our time gossiping. The work was easy, logging client data on to the computer, and I did most of it, being the youngest of the four, a sort of bureaucratic gallantry, watched with bemusement by the other three. I wondered what they would have done had I not been there? Pressed the delete button probably.

While I filed their entries the girls filed their nails and discussed their roots—trichological, not genealogical. These were beautifully varied and balanced, one a flaming redhead, another a brunette, the third a platinum blonde: as if God had decided to be fair on his way through the insurance company, or rather, Boots. If one of them had decided to upset the delicate ecological balance of this island by changing her hair colour, the others would not have spoken to her for weeks. In addition they discussed the problem of my uncontrollably frizzy hair and What to Do with It. It was variously suggested that I straighten it, bleach it, thin it. It was a source of great amusement and much forgiveness.

Then, they discussed their plans for the evening with boyfriends. They all had 'steadies', so they pitied me; poor little single, curly-haired me. They were aghast that I had to live in central London—'Isn't it noisy? Isn't it unsafe?'—and that I was forced by poverty to eat dinner at dodgy Chinese restaurants in Soho. They all lived in the decent and respectable outer suburbs of London. Soho was where their boyfriends went occasionally on stag nights to commit unspeakably degenerate acts. What happened in Soho stayed in Soho. But I stayed in Soho. Yet I came every morning to work with them, which I'm sure gave them a delicious tingle of horror.

It was interesting to learn how many things I was to different people. To the Outer Londoners I was a small, furry animal, to be cuddled and petted and pitied; to Oxford I was atavistic and unreadable, and ultimately worth pursuing for the sheer shock of the new. As for Luisa, for all her Italian ancestry she was unquestionably American in her attitudes. She brought to the table no preconceptions or prejudices. She really did like me for myself, I liked to think.

And to my mother? To my mother I was, quite simply, the work of the Devil.

That summer—or Trinity Term as it was called—there was an air of throbbing urgency and golden expectation: the feeling that anything could happen. I plunged recklessly into study because my exams were coming up. I couldn't really call it revision because most of it I was coming across for the first time. The practice Duke invited me to his rooms to teach me backgammon, as part no doubt of his ducal CSR; one of the Barons invited me to the Cathedral Gardens for Pimms. All I could think of was Luisa, whether she would write. Every day, I went to the pigeonhole praying for a yellow letter with turquoise ink. I found instead a pasteboard invitation: 'Bettina de Rohan, At Home, St Hilda's Gardens, dress Angels and Devils.'

I cut out two horns from a polystyrene egg box, painted them red and stuck them on my head. In my second-hand Oxfam tails, I did indeed look diabolical.

Bettina took my hand and walked me down to the river. There was a slow mist rising; the slightly purplish evening undulated like the notes of an oversentimental song. 'You and me,' Bettina said. 'What are we going to do about it?'

'Not much,' I wanted to say. Of course I didn't. I just took her hand and stared vacantly into the middle distance.

Sita and her father sat in the covered walkway leading to the doctor's room together with literally hundreds of other patients. By the time their number was called, she was almost fainting with hunger.

'It is extremely important that your father inject himself with 30 units of insulin twice a day, once before breakfast and once before dinner, understand?' the doctor said. 'He could fall into a coma and die otherwise. Is there anyone at home to monitor him?'

Sita looked up helplessly. She was at the walauwa all day, there was no one else at home. 'We'll manage,' she said defiantly.

'You will need to buy the insulin and a set of needles at the pharmacy. These are things we are not able to provide free of charge.'

She did not tell the doctor that she had sold the last of her small collection of jewellery. It was getting difficult even to find money for his food. Basic healthcare was free in Sri Lanka, but the extras were not. She was the sole breadwinner, and there were no old age or disability benefits she could claim on account of her father being too old and feeble to work. At least she had a job and a place to live thanks to the Kumarihamy's generosity.

The next morning she got up before dawn as usual and cooked the old man his lunch—a bit of curried dry fish, a ground chilli sambal—and was at the walauwa by six thirty sharp, in time for the Kumarihamy's levée.

Clarice was sitting up in bed with her breakfast bowl of coffee. 'You're late,' she said.

'I'm sorry, my lady, I was seeing to my father. And on that subject there's something I have to ask you.' She knew it was the wrong time—early mornings were possibly Clarice's worst time—but she plunged on recklessly, like a walker over a cliff. 'Could I possibly ask for a two-month advance on my salary?'

Clarice smiled thinly. She patted the edge of the bed. 'Come and sit here. You know you are more than a daughter to me?' Sita nodded. 'Have I not given you a roof over your head?' She paused. 'Are you not fed and clothed by me? So what more can I do for you?' Clarice shook her head sadly, as if she had been let down badly by an old and trusted friend.

'You know how I have had to cut back on my own needs to send Sonny to England? Look at these walls.' Clarice pointed with an attenuated dramatic hand. 'Don't you think they need a coat of paint? Do you think I *like* to live like this? Do you think I enjoy being the laughing stock of everyone on this mountain?'

Yes, but this is a life! Sita wanted to shout. Not some wretched wall that needs painting! She got wearily to her feet. 'I'm sorry to have troubled you, my lady.' Her own breakfast was waiting for her in the kitchen.

She had just got to the door when the Kumarihamy sang out, almost joyfully: 'Of course, it'll all be different when we find *the treasure!*'

When the British finally broke into the king's palace, they found crates of empty wine bottles and not much else. The doors to the treasury were wide open—and empty. Later, they tracked the king and queen to their hiding place in a small house a few miles out of the city. The men who led the search party tore the queen's earlobe in their haste to get at her earring. They ripped her blouse open. The British commanding officer put a stop to this, shocked at the savagery of their behaviour. The queen asked for a glass of claret, which she was served, and the king and queen were escorted, under arrest but with all due dignity, to Colombo. There was no sign anywhere of the treasure, either then or later.

So where had it gone?

It was the astrologer, Clarice's father, who had first alerted her. 'I see incalculable wealth,' he said, 'such as you and I can only dream of.'

'Where?' Clarice asked breathlessly. '*Where?*'

'Underneath the house,' the old man said.

The more Clarice thought about it, the more it made sense. Where would the king's treasure be but with the treasurer? If the king was fleeing Kandy, and could not take it all with him, to whom would he have entrusted his valuables? The traditional method of building houses in Sri Lanka anyway was to bury handfuls of jewels in the foundation. Was it so far beyond the bounds of possibility that the king's treasure lay beneath the walauwa?

Clarice had broached the subject with her husband, who had been alive at the time.

'You mad woman!' he had yelled. 'Are you trying to break up the house as well?' (The marriage had been on its last legs by then.) And that had been the end of that. Till a month ago, that is, when an article in the newspaper had caught her eye, about some of the king's jewels turning up at auction in London. Thoughts of treasure burned inside her like fever. The fact that she could have even read the article with her half-blind eyes was a sign. The fates were conspiring to lead her in its search—and now that that diabolical son of hers was finally gone, it was time.

First of all, she called in a reputed contractor, silver-haired and dressed respectfully in a white sarong. She showed him the floor of her son's bedroom. (Where else would the treasure be? The Devil protects his own, doesn't he?)

'I need this excavated,' she said.

The contractor looked doubtful. 'How far down?'

'Oh, ten feet?' The Kumarihamy was suitably vague. 'Twenty? You see there's an evil charm buried deep down. I need to have it cleared before my son comes back.'

'You need a sorcerer, not a contractor,' the man nearly said. But he knew of the Kumarihamy's influence in town—he might never find work again—and held his tongue. He began work the following week, bringing in a team of enthusiastic young labourers in bright T-shirts and geometric hairstyles. The Kumarihamy sacked them a day later. 'They're wearing shoes,' she explained.

'They have to wear shoes,' the contractor snapped. 'Building regulations. They might injure their feet otherwise.'

'Not in my house they don't. Not while I am still alive.'

So the contractor brought in the next lot, selected with care for their non-confrontational dowdiness. They came in humbly and barefoot, leaving their assorted footwear on the verandah steps.

After a day, the Kumarihamy accosted the contractor. 'Tell your men,' she said, 'that this is a house. People still live here. It is not, I repeat, not, a building site. So I want silence. While they work I want silence.'

Telling a Sri Lankan worker to keep silent is like telling a pregnant woman to hold back till the doctor comes.

'You can have all the silence you want,' the contractor said. 'Because we're leaving.'

The Kumarihamy was non-plussed. For all of a second. She turned to Girigoris, who was standing open-mouthed on the sidelines. 'In that case,' she said, 'you will dig. And you,' she added, pointing at Sita, 'will take the soil out. In this bucket here.'

It was the only way out, this treasure, the only hope. Like many very rich old people, Clarice was panic-stricken she would have to spend the last years of her life in straitened circumstances. So the older she got, the more she deprived herself and the more pleased she became when she did so. Occasionally, a chicken would be brought to the house, to impress the very rare luncheon guest; as for the rest of the time, it was vegetables all the way. 'Veggies are good for you,' she said to the servants. The fact that the servants had to follow suit in this deprivation added a spice to the vegetables that no curry powder could ever hope to achieve.

Clarice was down to one egg a week now—which meant that the servants were down to none a week. The rubber slippers she wore at home were on their last legs, even if the legs they shod were not ready to go yet. What pleased her most about this deprivation was that she had become so very good as a result of it. She felt sure that the day she died, the angels would carry her straight off to heaven in a sort of celestial Ruhunu Kumari. There would be no need for requiems or novenas or those endless sleep-inducing prayers by Father Rosario for the repose of some damned soul or other. Indeed, she realized with some satisfaction, she was currently roller-blading at dizzy speeds on the Plains of Higher Goodness, where visions were commonplace. Every morning she surreptitiously checked her palms for signs of stigmata.

And so, thoughts of angels and other celestial beings were uppermost in Clarice's mind when the Devil happened to visit again.

'You're not . . . surely you're not . . . Oh, my Lord you *are*, aren't you?' she said, in wonderment.

The Devil waved a modest hand. 'Enough of that. We don't believe in titles where I come from.'

'And where is that?' asked Clarice archly, knowing full well.

The Devil laughed. 'Well, shall we say Down Under?'

Clarice was a little disappointed. 'I didn't know they had angels in Australia?'

'Australia? Who said anything about Australia?'

Clarice's suspicions were now fully aroused. This was not an angel at all. Just that nosy transgender neighbour from Australia. 'Oh, go to hell!' she snapped.

'I will,' said the Devil. 'I just need a little more time.'

8

To my surprise, I passed the exams. That entire week I had not bothered to check the pigeonhole and when I did there were not one but two yellow letters. One just said: 'In case you've lost the address, it is: *Borgo Forte 9, Monte San Savino.*' The other was a proper letter. She was happy and settled and had quite a list of students wanting to learn English. The tone of the letter was chatty and friendly, in a way that worried me more than not getting a letter at all: Had I stopped meaning anything to her? Had she moved on to another love?

'I know you won't be going home for the summer vacation,' she wrote, 'so come and spend it here. Tuscany is dazzling in summer. I can introduce you to plenty of girls!'

Girls? I didn't want any girls. I wanted her.

Sri Lankans did not need visas those days, and I took the train down to Italy on my student rail card. In Paris, outside the Gare du Nord, I watched a man selling oysters from a cart early in the morning. People ate them from the shells, on their way to work, crowding around him. There were signs all

over the train—*Defense de Cracher* (Spitting Is Forbidden)—
and I got told off by the guard for putting my feet up on the
seat opposite. In Switzerland, they woke me up in the middle
of the night to check my meagre possessions, letting me go
reluctantly, with the deepest suspicion; finally, in the early
hours of the next morning, we rolled into Milan.

The man at the ticket office gave me the wrong change for
my ticket to Monte. When I queried the amount, he pushed
the rest of it under the glass to me with a philosophical and
elegant shrug of the shoulders, and a charming smile, as if the
fine art of short-changing were the most natural in the world.
It was like being back in Sri Lanka again and I immediately
felt at home. At Arezzo I changed to the Locale, which wound
its way over the mountains at a leisurely pace. My mother
could probably have made it more quickly on her walker.

The Italians, I found, were an extremely fine-looking
race, men and women both, with glorious skin and flashing
eyes and teeth—they should have had a reputation for
unblemished goodness with looks like that, really. The men
had the disconcerting habit of massaging their crown jewels
at regular intervals, as if reassuring themselves their manhood
was alive and well, and still in working order.

At Monte I lugged my suitcase off the train with a sharp
thud, and the whole station stopped and stared, motionless in
disbelief. I don't think they had seen a black man before. I felt
like God on the seventh day. I had picked up a word or two of
Italian from Luisa, and this, coupled with sign language, set
me on the steep slope up to the walled medieval town that was
Monte San Savino, at the top of the hill. It was like climbing
up to the walauwa from the town of Kandy.

Luisa lived in a flat above her great-aunt, the Signora Sirra, who let me in through the front door. A stern woman in black bombazine, with iron-grey hair and a slight grey tinge to her sallow skin, she spoke in a harsh, guttural voice, like a man. Luisa was out. The signora asked me, in a gabble of Italian, to come and sit inside her flat but I declined. Instead I heaved the suitcase up the flight of stairs to Luisa's front door, sat on the top step, rested my head on my knees and promptly fell asleep.

In my sleep I was conscious of something moving on the back of my neck. I thought that the Signora Sirra, tired of waiting, had flitted up the stairs with a feather duster for a bout of tickling. I heard suppressed giggles and choking noises. I opened my eyes to find Luisa peering at me, laughing, a leaf in her hand. With her was a young man.

'We thought you'd never wake up!'

I got to my feet wearily and dragged the suitcase into her flat.

'And this is Ugo.'

The young guy stuck his hand out. He had a full-on smile. '*Ciao ragazzo,*' he said.

Luisa's front door opened out into a large hall, off which were two bedrooms with a kitchen at the far end. Beyond the kitchen was the bathroom, down a couple of steps. There were green terrazzo floors everywhere, with large white marble chips embedded in them, and green louvred shutters on the windows. The place was sparsely furnished but huge, like a mausoleum. It echoed.

Luisa showed me into the bedroom that wasn't hers. I looked at her questioningly but didn't say anything because there was a stranger present. His back was turned to us. I pointed at him with eyebrows raised but all she did was open her eyes a fraction more. I knew that look: it said, don't mess with me.

Luisa sat on my bed with Ugo while I unpacked. They laughed at the clothes I had brought.

'You really think you're going to wear that black tie here?'

'Of course,' I said huffily. At Oxford there was a current belief that you never travelled anywhere without your dinner jacket. It was more essential than your toothbrush. (You could clean your teeth with a twig in the desert; you could not turn up to dinner at the oasis underdressed.)

They laughed at my frayed shirts with their loud, stockbroker stripes ('Mattress cloth,' said Luisa to Ugo), they laughed at my scrappy underwear. Ugo gave me a conspiratorial wink as he left, though whether in solidarity with me against Luisa or the other way around I could not tell. I had yet to master the art of reading the Italian face. After he had gone ('He's only one of my students, Sonny'), I crept into her bed.

She looked at me sadly. 'We're not going to start that all over again, Sonny.'

It was only then that it really hit me. How the thought of that dead baby still hung between us, unspoken and breathless, as suffocating as the hour before the monsoon breaks. Now it struck me: how much she had had to go through, the decisions she'd had to make—alone. It seemed to me that Luisa had come to terms with her actions a long while back. So she was sad not so much for herself as for me, for the distance I had yet to go. It occurred to me that perhaps I would never be forgiven. I fully deserved not to be.

ℰ

It was early summer and everywhere the landscape shimmered in the mountain stillness—a Chinese painting on silk—the palette of blues and greens reminding me of the mountains around Kandy. We spent the weeks ranging far and wide over that Tuscan countryside in Luisa's cream Fiat Cinquecento, to little fortified towns and villages where she taught English: to the children of the gold merchant in Arezzo, to the family Maianni in Palazzuolo, to the servants at the Castello di Gargonza. While she tutored, I tramped around the villages, mostly seething in indignation at the unusually high number of good-looking men she seemed to be giving lessons to.

'Oh, Sonny,' she said laughing. 'Don't be so old-fashioned and Sri Lankan! If I was really having it off with all these men, don't you think I'd take a little bit more trouble to hide them from you?'

On one such evening in Anghiari I pushed open the doors to the church and sat in a pew at the back, in the pitch dark. I thought of Leonardo da Vinci's lost painting. I had recently seen the sketches at the Ashmolean. Had Leonardo ever been to Anghiari? Perhaps he had sat in this church too, in this very same pew.

How foolish I was to assume I had any claim over Luisa! She was a free agent as was I; she had always been the strong one, not me. That brief vulnerability she had shown during pregnancy—for which I had only despised her, a fact of which

I was now deeply ashamed—was a thing of the past. Whatever minute proprietorial stakeholding I might have had I had relinquished with the abortion. It just showed how deeply Sri Lankan I was in my thinking, imagining that a shared past automatically conferred rights. Or, perhaps, a man-woman thing?

My Kandyan father would talk about how his mother had stood behind his father's chair at the dinner table, serving him while he ate. It was only after he finished that she sat down to eat with the children. But what was interesting was the note of pride in his voice when he recounted these primitive Kandyan customs. Perhaps there was regret too, because it was the first thing *his* wife—my mother—put a stop to after she married him.

Sitting in the dark in that ancient church I realized how the medievalism I had sought to flee was still with me, an iron ball on a very long chain, pulling me up short just when I thought I had got away.

What annoyed me most—and made me most jealous— was how fully and easily Luisa had made a life for herself out here, how popular she was. Her Italian-ness seemed to vanish in the camouflage of Italy. What remained instead were her American highlights, carrying with them all the old-style glamour of Hollywood and Manhattan, of Mission-style houses and Art Deco skyscrapers. They would not have understood, these enthusiastic Italian youths of the village, the realities of the Blue Plate Diner; this was a malicious thought, and I suppressed it as being unworthy. As for Luisa, she played up to her American-ness for all it was worth, giving me secret looks in between, sly and bemused. *See how I can ham it up? Aren't I the star? Aren't I just?*

Ugo was her most adoring fan. As is the case with many Italian men, he lived at home with his mother and teenage sister. There was a father too, a long-haul trucker whom we hardly saw. It was unclear what Ugo did for a job, but every free evening he was with us at the flat, or we at his. His mother never let us go without long and copious wine-enriched dinners—rabbit fried with olives or home-made sausages with polenta. Under her watchful eye—and mine—this potential romance flourished like a weed, putting out noxious new leaves every day.

I suppose as far as his mother was concerned—another unworthy thought, this, though yet again I could not help myself—Luisa was a damned good catch, this rich American, Ugo's passport out of the village.

That evening, back at home after another boozy dinner, Luisa said, 'I think we need to have a talk.'

'Yes,' I said nodding sagely, with the wisdom only half a litre of red wine in the stomach can give.

'I need to make it clear that you are here as my friend, nothing more, nothing less. You don't own me, I don't own you. Understand?'

I nodded glumly, her meaning barely sinking in.

'There are lots of lovely girls out here dying to get friendly with you, so stop brushing them off. Make the most of your life. You never know when it might be taken away.'

I sat there, playing with her door keys, not looking at her.

'Remember how lucky you are. There are those whose fate it is to die before they are even born.'

Her voice cracked a little as she said this. I looked up to see tears streaming silently down her face. There it was then, out in the open: the foetus on the operating table. It was the first time she had ever referred to it, and I realized what courage it must have taken for her to say it.

She stood up and gave me the smallest of kisses on the top of my head. She went into her own room, closing the door behind her.

9

Tuesdays are the worst days. Ask any Sri Lankan: they will tell you of the CEO who does not go into office on Tuesday, playing golf instead; whose swing may swerve and hit the caddy on Tuesday; who will consider himself fortunate because a caddy is always replaceable, whereas a bad business decision is frequently not. They will tell you of the mother who keeps her child back from school on Tuesday, because God only knows what they will learn on Tuesday, and don't you know how dangerous education can be? And then there are the roads: it is a ghost town at rush hour on Tuesday morning.

This astrological fatwa covers all but Sri Lankan Catholics, who in their contrariness (or cunning) have declared Tuesday the holy day of St Anthony. This means, of course, that the churches of St Anthony—there are many island wide—are full on Tuesday not only of Catholics, but Buddhists and Hindus as well, who come to light a candle and spend five minutes in prayer, because in Sri Lanka it is wise to have all your bases covered.

On Tuesdays the Kumarihamy did not bother to go to church. The church came to her. Tuesday was the day Father Rosario arrived for his weekly drink (two shots, no more, of milk wine measured out into thimble-sized glasses).

On Tuesday, Clarice sat in the gloom of the verandah under the faded light of the long-life bulb, deep in thought. It was still only five thirty, but the sun had long since crept to the back of the house, leaving her shrouded in the thickening dusk. She had embraced with enthusiasm the invention of the CFL bulb when it first arrived on her shores, buying one—just one—for the verandah.

'Five-year guarantee,' said the salesman. Two years were up and the bulb was no more now than a flickering firefly; but the Kumarihamy hung on, determined to get three more years out of it. In this ghastly gloaming she sat, musing on the strangely dichotomous relationship she had with Sonny, her son. It is galling for any mother to admit she does not love her son and, in all fairness, she did her best not to face up to this unassailable fact. Under normal circumstances, she far preferred the conscious hammer blow of words, her quick-fire language guided by a sureness of instinct—like the marksman who, having found his mark, closes his eyes to shoot, sure of his kill. So she was not one, usually, for such wordless introspection as this.

She knew in her gut that Sonny had been a bad lot from a young age. As a child he had caught a bad case of demons the way other children catch measles or mumps. The Kumarihamy had vainly tried to build up his resistance to evil with tonics and *cassayas*. He had been administered with frequent *thovils* the way other children are given worming syrup. The

Kumarihamy had even dared to hope that his proximity to the plain unvarnished goodness that was her might immunize him from infection. All to no avail. In a final act of desperation she had dug deep—selling fifty acres of coconut—to send him to Oxford. Whoever would have thought he had the brains to pass that infamously tricky Oxbridge interview? But the Devil protects his own, and Sonny had got in.

It was essential that he go abroad, crossing the sea, because as every good Sri Lankan knows, demons cannot cross water. To go abroad was essentially an act of purification. It was equally essential that he not come back: the devils were ready and waiting, and a relapse of evil is often life-threatening. The Kumarihamy knew full well that all she possessed—and there was plenty—would go upon her death to this only child, but she was prepared to do anything, even dispossess him of his birthright, to ensure his safety.

Her musings were interrupted by the familiar *put-put* of the Vespa coughing and spluttering up the hill. The good father was in long khaki shorts—somewhat incongruous tropical attire for a priest in mufti. With a pair of Ray Bans on a strangely unlined face, he looked like a Sixties Italian actor who had accidentally strayed off a Cinecittà film set.

'Sita!' shouted the Kumarihamy. 'Sita!'

Sita appeared from the back of the house with a heavy silver tray, on which were placed two long-stemmed, wide-based liqueur glasses and a bottle of milk wine. This arrangement had been kept ready since morning. Father Rosario leapt lightly up the steps and sank gracefully into the planter's chair opposite the Kumarihamy. 'How's the dig?' he asked.

Clarice threw up her hands. 'I've had to sack two lots of workers so far. But Girigoris is carrying on.' She discreetly inspected Sita's fingernails as she put the tray down. 'With Sita's help, of course.'

'And Sonny?'

The Kumarihamy was silent. 'You know how he had found himself a white friend? Well, he says she's off the scene now. I'm not sure I want to believe him.' She looked out into the darkness. The town lay far below, a black flying carpet encrusted with jewels now. 'Are there devils in other countries, Father?'

'Why not, Clarice? There is no colour bar to evil.' He stood up and walked to the edge of the verandah. And suddenly, as if he had ordered it, there drifted through the chill mountain air the familiar smell, potent and ancient, from deep within the bowels of the molten sulphurous earth. 'I sense something,' he said softly.

'But how, Father? Sonny's long gone.'

'I told you not to dig up the earth.'

'It's only treasure, Father.'

Father Rosario said nothing. Who knew how much misery had been caused, how much bloodshed, in the long history of those jewels? Some things were better left dead and buried.

'It's time for me to go,' said Father Rosario. 'They'll be waiting for me.'

'But you haven't had your second glass of milk wine.'

'Next Tuesday,' he said. 'Call me if you need me before that.'

As he rode the Vespa downhill he felt the faintest breeze ruffle the hairs on the back of his neck, and he smelled it again, the familiar, almost comforting smell of the enemy.

Father Rosario loved Kandy because it reminded him of his hometown, a medieval village in Sicily. He wasn't the only Italian father in Sri Lanka. There were many, including his almost namesake, Father Rosarti of St Anthony's, and the legendary Father Perniola of the Jesuit House. He had been sent at a young age by the order and every time there was talk of a transfer he had begged to be allowed to stay.

Sri Lanka, like Italy, was an ancient country, with many of those beliefs and superstitions clinging on stubbornly in the modern age. There were demons and sorcerers here: they were a very real part of the everyday life of most people. He was in a tricky position as far as the Church was concerned. You could not be an official exorcist till you were appointed by the bishop, and most bishops were reluctant to take a stand on the matter. It was a grey area: while the Church tacitly acknowledged the existence of demons, it did not like to make too much of a song and dance about them. Demons were démodé, an old-fashioned disease like TB that you thought had been eradicated years ago. But like TB, they seemed to be making a comeback.

Father Rosario had realized early on that he possessed certain gifts, though he was far too modest to put it like that. It was like having a rare and esoteric condition, an ear attuned to the vibrations of evil, a sort of moral perfect pitch. Of one thing he was sure. There was a positive plague of evil spirits on the island: and here he was, a doctor with a cure, albeit one without a licence to practise. When asked to help, how could he refuse? He knew, too, that there were bigger forces at work here, and that his own role was a small one. He was a tuning fork vibrating in the wind, but the wind was about to turn into a howling gale.

Father Rosario braked sharply at the bottom of the hill by the police station and, turning left, headed for home, where his dinner awaited him.

By late summer, the Kandyan palette of cool blues and greens had been scorched off our Italian landscape, as if with a blow-torch. We were left with ochre and raw umber and burnt sienna on the canvas, all colours you might associate with an Italian old master. It was nearly time for me to go back to Oxford.

I had tried, on Luisa's advice, to get in with the girls of the village, but on the whole it had not been a success. There was Paola, a large, doe-eyed girl with a treacherous smile who asked me, 'Are you black all over?'

'Do you want to check?' I nearly replied but didn't because I lacked the courage. And if there were others, they figured out soon enough that my heart was not really in it. The week before I left, I attempted to cook a curry for them, all the young people of the village. I probably knew even less about curries than they did, never having had to cook one before. In fact I had never cooked anything before at all. It was not a success, and I was left to pick at the copious remains in the kitchen after everyone had left.

Luisa and I had made our peace somewhere along the way: it was not something that had happened overnight, more a slow and weary realization that this thing in our past would never go away. It was an old-fashioned milestone along the road, a weathered marble slab receding into the Tuscan landscape as we drove on. There was no sex, once again; but we were happy in each other's company. In some incomprehensible way, her position in the village was strengthened by my being there. People assumed we were lovers though we were not.

Another relation of Luisa's, a retired general who lived in Rome, had offered her the use of his holiday villa in the hills. Luisa preferred to stay with the Signora in town, paying rent. 'That way I'm not under obligation to anyone,' she said. But we went up to the villa occasionally of a free afternoon, using it as a sort of picnic site. There was an old, deaf caretaker, though he was never very much in evidence.

That afternoon, without any warning, it happened.

Luisa had her own keys and we let ourselves in through the back door. We wandered through those beautiful, high-proportioned, eighteenth-century rooms; there was something ineffably sad about its shuttered interiors, like a sleeping old woman who might never wake up.

I opened the front door to step out into the garden, and we were suddenly flooded with the horizontal golden light of late afternoon. I looked at Luisa: it was as if she were bathed in honey, a golden goddess just stepped off the plinth of an ancient Greek temple and come to life. I held my breath. We had nothing for food, only a jar of plum jam and a knife to eat it with. Sitting on a garden bench facing the view, eating pieces of plum with a knife, I was suffused with this feeling of intense happiness such as you only ever get once or twice in your lifetime. As if I was here and not here at the same time, as if my arms and legs—indeed my entire body—was being drawn with intense longing into the arms of some greater existence. I thought to myself: It is never going to get better than this. It was a solitary experience lasting only a few seconds, yet it left me absolutely clear about what I must do next. I turn to Luisa. 'Marry me,' I said.

There was no ring to put on her finger, not even the ring of a Coke can I might have produced had I been the hero of a romantic comedy on the big screen. Luisa looked at me with that bemused look of hers.

'You know,' she said, 'I just might?'

And so ended my brilliant Oxford career, barely had it even begun, in the summer of that year, 2003. There was nobody among the ancient stones of that university, if truth be told, who was sorry to see me go. I explained myself in great detail to my tutor: how I felt that the degree I had chosen was not the correct one; that Oxford was somehow unsuited to my temperament; how I had discovered this urgent and unexplained desire to become a writer; how did I know this was the correct choice until I tried? Dr Handel Davies sat silently, listening to my floundering about with over-lengthy explanations; a murder suspect with too many alibis. When I finally stuttered to a stop, he stood up and shook my hand. 'Good luck,' he said briefly.

Tom, of course, had the last word. He sat me down on that fine Georgian sofa and poured me a glass of vintage port. In the background was the recording of Strauss's *Four Last*

Songs, cold as the touch of a dead man on the back of my neck. As far as he was concerned, and most of Oxford would have agreed with him, I was no better than that idiot Adam who chose a woman over Paradise.

'And an American?' he asked, shaking his head sorrowfully. 'An American?'

PART 2

10

'I'm getting married, Ma!'

'*What?* What did you say?'

'Luisa's a lovely girl, Ma. I'm sure you'll really take to her—'

'Married? You bloody bastard! Are you trying to kill me?'

'Ma, aren't you even happy for me?'

'I know what you're trying to do here. Don't you dare—you hear me?—don't you dare even *think* of bringing that white bitch here.'

'I thought maybe you'd come to London for the wedding? And afterwards we can all come back to Sri Lanka together!'

'And make me lose face in front of the relations? What would Beta say, hah, and Bella?'

'Please, Ma.'

'You keep that prostitute there, you hear me? I will have nothing to do with her . . .'

I put the phone down, shaking. Luisa had done nothing to deserve this stream of invective and I felt murderous on her behalf. My mother had an unfailing way of getting to me every time. But I should have known better than to imagine she would put her prejudices behind her and rise to the occasion. She was always the first to point out racism and bigotry in other people when she came across it. Here she was, outplaying them at their game, making a virtue of her own racism, taking an unholy pleasure in it.

Luisa hugged me. She had not heard the full conversation, but must have had a fair idea of what was said. 'She'll come round,' she said thoughtfully, after a little while. 'It's only natural. Which mother wants to lose her only son to another woman?'

I looked at her pityingly. How could I even begin to explain the truth of it?

Luisa's parents were more sanguine about the wedding when we phoned them, though they did not attend either. Not that a wedding was such a big deal for Westerners, the way it was for us Sri Lankans. They did, however extend that offer of their Putney flat for us to live in and, in a purely practical way, this was far more valuable to us than their approval. When you are young, you really do own the world; you really do not care what others think.

It was a strange thing (at least for a Sri Lankan) to wake up in bed with your wife the morning of the wedding. We got dressed, hurriedly, and rushed to the registry office before we missed our slot. There was no one else, no one we knew. The witness was a complete stranger, plucked from another wedding in the queue. It was a grey autumn day, moist and cool, the sort of day London does so well.

Afterwards, I didn't dare call my mother. Instead we called Luisa's parents, and she put me on the phone to them:

a formal, stilted conversation devoid of much warmth or enthusiasm. Perhaps there was love in there, buried deep, hard to tell. At the end, when I handed the phone back to Luisa, her father gave her one piece of advice culled from the wisdom of centuries of Italian marriage.

'Always sleep with a knife under your pillow,' he told his daughter. 'If he comes home late, don't be afraid to use it.'

∽

I won't lie to you about this marriage thing. It is bloody difficult. Each of us expects something different from it, so it is a war of attrition: a question of grinding down your partner, of wearying her into submission, so you can exist smoothly, side by side, while all the time she is doing the same to you. No, it isn't quite as bad as this, but you get the general idea.

Marriage is like murder. (Some people say it *is* murder.) By committing this heinous act of union you become desensitized to your partner, throwing out of the window all the tact and delicacy and solicitousness that went before. There are no secrets between murderers: you have seen each other at your worst, there is nothing more to hide. And like murder, it gets easier the more you do it. It was a rare enough act when we committed it, but a once-and-just-once-in-a-lifetime marriage was a very rare fish indeed. The few friends we had were either unmarried or much married.

In a way, it was easier for Luisa, who went out to work every day. She had another life she could escape to, an unmarried one at work. The marriage stayed at home with me, with last night's unwashed dishes in the sink, the radio endlessly on, and other minute and incremental additions to the status quo within the four walls of this Putney jail that I had constrained myself to. It was of my own choosing, so I could not complain. Writers are solitary people, they say, prone to brooding. I had plenty of time to brood upon my own marriage; in fact, we became quite close, this marriage and I, as we waited at home together every day for the wife to come back from work.

By the way, a word about my writing. I have not mentioned it much because there is actually not much to say. Somebody had told me at one of those crazy Oxford parties that the only writers who made money were children's writers. I had begun a book about Rathu Catherine and the Amberalla Tree. Around page twenty I came to realize that, perhaps, I was not cut out to be a children's writer. I didn't really like Rathu Catherine. She was an awfully presumptuous plump girl who ate too many milk toffees. I was seriously considering having her murdered halfway through. A child's murder mystery— would that work? It was earth-shattering questions such as these that kept me going through those long empty mornings in the Putney flat.

Of course, it was not all gloom and doom with Luisa and me. On the contrary, we had the best time of our lives, all alone with no one else to interfere. And, as time went on, the daily abrasions we caused each other—the cap of the toothpaste left open, the long hairs in the bath, the snoring (her, not me, ha!)—began to hurt less and less. So, if it was a difficult time, it was not a desperate one. And, as time went by, we became garrulous and over-familiar with each other, like two old whores sharing a cup of tea in between clients. It was only that between the two of us, we had successfully managed to murder romance.

I began to think more and more—anything to avoid writing—about the medieval life I had left behind in the process. I had been in an awful hurry to get away from it then. I was only just beginning to become aware of the gravitational pull Sri Lanka exerts on all its children, silent and inexorable like the moon's pull on the tides, making us sway this way and that throughout our lives, powerless though we might be to respond to it fully. I had not called my mother since that day, nor she me. I should have liked to have taken Luisa to Kandy just the once, if only to show her my curious and quaint pre-Luisa life, now a thing of the ancient past, if only to show her who I had been: a murderer proudly showing police the scene of his first-ever crime. It was just not to be, I realized, and that was that.

The Devil was having a hard time of it. He had been sent upstairs to drum up business as a one-man trade delegation, and Sri Lanka had been the obvious choice. (If that fine and upstanding cleric Bishop Heber had noted in the nineteenth century that in Ceylon's fair isle only man was vile, and if Ceylonese themselves were fond of singing this hymn ad nauseam in their churches and chapels, who was he, a mere Devil, to contradict it?) But he had found soon enough that things on the ground were different. The Civil War had been going on for twenty years, and all manner of evil had been practised on both sides, which the Devil's bosses down under had noted with approval; but evil itself ceases to have validity if the intention is missing, and it was very difficult to keep people's evil intentions up to the mark, so to speak, over a long period of time. They became desensitized, so that after one or two bombs, one or two judicious assassinations, they ceased to care at all: they just turned the page and carried on reading. It seemed to him that Sri Lankans had no stamina for wickedness—all too soon they would subside into that morally parched no-man's-land of the don't-know-don't-care variety.

'Remember, it's the souls we're after,' his trainer had thundered at that last three-day intensive workshop. 'Not the number of deeds themselves.' Ten people each committing a single murder were far more valuable to his firm than one committing ten.

So far, the Devil had identified two people at the walauwa worthy of attention. The Kumarihamy, though an absolute given, had been something of a disappointment.

'Stop twirling that cape!' she had snarled at him only the other day. 'People will think you're a nancy boy. Remember you're Australian. Try to be a man.'

The Devil did not exactly know what a nancy boy was, but it did not sound good. Clarice seemed to be a thoroughly nasty woman. She managed to put the very devil into him each time they met. His nerves were all in shreds.

Then there was Pandu, the garden boy, who exhibited great potential for wickedness. He spent most of his afternoons weeding the flower beds that dotted the terraces around the big house. Since there are only so many weeds you can pull out, and Pandu was bored much of the time, he turned his attention to the flowers themselves.

'When in doubt, pull it out,' he sang to himself, as he hurled perfectly good flowers over the terrace edge.

'Ahem,' said the Devil, who had been watching this wanton destruction for a little while. 'I see you have green fingers.'

Pandu looked at his fingers. They looked perfectly normal to him. 'Are you a goat?' he asked.

'Don't be an ass!' hissed the Devil. 'Now listen to me closely. You like to earn a bit of pocket money?'

Pandu nodded. This was more like it. The Devil began whispering in Pandu's ear, outlining his fiendish plan.

There was a sudden click of the walker and the Kumarihamy stood above them, swaying gloriously and blocking out the sun, majestic and forbidding like some hairy old prophetess from the Old Testament.

'Ha!' she cackled. 'Caught you!'

Pandu and the Devil sprang apart guiltily.

'Watch out for him,' said the Kumarihamy to Pandu. 'He has wandering hands. He's Australian.'

Sita looked down at the hole. Was it her imagination or had it got bigger? No digging had been done these last few days, as Girigoris had pulled a muscle in his back and was laid up in bed. Tucking up her dress—there was no one around to see—she climbed down into the hole and started digging herself. She used the pick to loosen the great clods of earth, then switched to the shovel to fill the bucket. The earth was heavy and damp, a great, clammy prehistoric beast, breathing and beginning to stir beneath her feet.

Nobody had asked her to dig. Her job had been to remove the dug-up soil to a heap out in the garden. Now that she was digging herself, she found it easier than she had imagined. And as she dug she realized she had never been more aware of the sheer physicality of her own being: the taut sinews of her arms, the soft brown skin that never seemed to lose its translucent lustre however much she managed to abuse it in the harsh efforts of her daily routine. She held her mud-streaked fingers up to the thin yellow light. They seemed to glow, softly, like jewels recently excavated from the deep. Her thick hair had come loose. She coiled and pinned it back up. It struck her then that at this moment she too was a creature of the earth, her whole life circumscribed by the walls of this hole.

Sita knew that with her looks and pleasant manner she could have found herself a better paying job in town. But the Kumarihamy had been kind enough to offer her the shack which went with the job. There were more lucrative jobs in factories that offered dormitory accommodation. But where would she put her father? In addition there was the free food, for what it was worth, at the walauwa. All in all, even if the salary were higher, she knew she would not be saving that much more. Most of all, there was the loyalty factor. Clarice had taken her in as a child of six: she knew that if she left, Clarice would never find anyone else to replace her, nobody these days was willing to endure the shouts and curses, insults and irregular payment she had to put up with. Those feudal days were long gone, though the Kumarihamy had yet to realize it.

She missed Sonny. With his wicked wit and gentle ways, he had been the only one able to stand up to Clarice. He had always been good for a small loan when funds were running low at the end of the month. And when she went to pay him back, he would wave her away with a smile.

'You can repay me in kind,' he would say, and she would swat him playfully. But in the look that passed between them there was an unmistakable spark. Out of the question, of course, as unthinkable as romancing the Pope.

The Kumarihamy was forever trying to 'fix her up' with any itinerant jobbing worker who came to repair the house: any random, randy roofer, plug-ugly plumber or cataleptic carpenter. Sita shuddered. For the most part they were pot-bellied drunkards smelling of medicinal hair oil, whose idea of a good time was to thrash their wives of an evening. The Kumarihamy seemed to think this a perfectly acceptable form of Kandyan behaviour. A servant girl marrying a carpenter looked fine on paper.

Sita understood that for many girls of her position it was the only way out: you lost your looks, you lost your health, in return you gained your children and a monster to father them by. Oh, and if a few teeth were knocked out along the way, what did it matter in the general scheme of things? Sita shuddered. It was not for her and she knew it. Marriage for her was a cop-out. Secretly (and she had told no one, not even her father), she longed one day to train as a nurse and get a job in some Western country, where it was said they were desperate for them. This would be her escape: one day, when she had collected enough money.

It was time to make the tea. She climbed gingerly out of the pit, and going to the kitchen, put the kettle on. Pandu was hovering outside the kitchen door.

'You look like a wild woman from a hill tribe,' he said, tenderly removing a clod of earth from her eyebrow.

'Thanks,' she replied. 'You don't look too bad yourself.' She watched him from the kitchen door, hands on hips, while he slurped down his tea.

He gave the empty mug back to her. 'There are lots of rare and precious things inside the house, aren't there?'

She looked at him puzzled. 'So?'

'The Kumarihamy must trust you an awful lot, especially now with her eyesight so bad.'

'What do you mean?' she asked fiercely. 'What are you trying to get at?'

He smiled, a candid and innocent smile. 'Nothing. Just saying.'

'Clever boy,' murmured the Devil admiringly, from his rather scratchy place of concealment inside the gardenia bush. 'Clever boy.'

11

It is a curious thing, this living in the big city. London seems to have so much to offer, its galleries and museums, plays, films and concerts—the list is endless. So much is written about all this, so much written about current affairs, about who did what to whom and when. It is all in the public domain, and the glossy pictures are to die for. The debate rages so strong in the secondary sources of the media that we the public fondly imagine we have a say in all this moving and shaking. We are forced to have opinions about people we are never likely to meet, talk intelligently about events we have never witnessed, and have great confidence that our opinions are somehow managing to shape the future as it unfolds.

London offers you this vast virtual world, when the reality—if you were fool enough to stop even a moment to consider it—consists of the four walls of your bare flat, the lonely piece of cheese in the fridge, the designer bag you so coveted, for which you maxed out your credit card.

Yes, yes, of course I exaggerate. But there is also a small-town cynic lurking within, peering out through my eyes in a mad way, one that I will sadly never be rid of. I thought of Kandy, which had so little to offer—and yet you were so much an integral part of that little, where you were not far wrong when you imagined you were an agent of its unfolding future. The only quasi-virtual world we knew in Kandy was that of demons flying about the hillside. If they were virtual, the actions we took to propitiate or expel or control them were real enough. Oh yes, we had Father Rosario and Kodivina Peiris, but they were primary, not secondary. They were very much protagonists in this daily play of good and evil, and we were all, in our own way, agents of this change.

Did this difference between then and now—the reality of the small town and the virtuality of the big—make any change to the quality of my life? I do not seriously think so. Luisa, of course, was different, she had always been a big-city girl, who might indeed have suffocated for lack of intellectual oxygen in a small town like Kandy. She was curious, nevertheless, about what I had left behind when I came to the West.

'Tell me about your friends,' she said, in that imperious, rich-girl way of hers.

I had had one or two so-called friends from school; then there were my Kandyan aunts Beta and Bella, and of course, Sita and Girigoris and the other servants of the household. None of them would I have consciously chosen as friends, for reason of our shared likes and dislikes. I had simply grown up with them. They were above and beyond friendship; they were my de facto family.

Luisa, too, was an only child. 'I have loads of friends back in NY,' she said. 'I might only see them once a year, but when I do, we pick up from where we left off; as if I'd never gone away.'

I laughed. 'At least yours are proper friends, unlike mine.'

'And your mother?'

I looked at her curiously. 'My father died when I was young. My mother's been so much a part of my life that I can't really see her to comment. Like sitting in the front row of the cinema.'

I did not tell her then about the part my mother had cast me for—from birth—as the villain of the piece, the horns she was always convinced she could see growing out of my head. It was too early in the marriage for home truths. Yet she must have sensed some meaning beneath the gentle wave of my words, half-glimpsed the shifting sands beneath the saltwater. She took my hand silently, and held it.

This essential loneliness of London, the enforced poverty, meant that one free thing, sex, was plentiful. Before work. After work. Many a time I thought seriously about going to her office and giving her one *during* work. We were newly married and very, very poor; and little else in London was free.

Perhaps because of what had gone before, perhaps in spite of it, we both wanted children. I do not remember ever talking about this. There was just never any question of taking precautions and, as that very first shot in the dark had found its mark, it was only going to be a matter of time.

௪

The Kumarihamy made her slow progress through the dim gloom of the walauwa interior. The high, wide opening in the wall between the front and rear reception rooms was flanked by two rather idiosyncratic columns with corn-sheaf capitals; she noticed the speckled green of damp stucco on the brickwork above the opening. The two enormous sections of the roof drained into a galvanized iron valley gutter that ran precisely along this wall. This valley had leaked for as long as she could remember, despite the galvanized iron having been replaced at great expense every seven years. How she longed for the lead of a London roof, tasty and soft, malleable and waterproof, which would have given no trouble for a lifetime; lead was, alas, unavailable in Sri Lanka.

Nobody had told Clarice that when she inherited the walauwa she would end up a master builder, developing over the years an instinctive nose for all things that could—and did—go wrong with a big house in the tropics. At times it seemed to her that her life was one long litany of failed carpenters and roofers and plumbers. Some days she longed for her pre-Kumarihamy existence in the little shack down the hill. (Though not for that long, obviously.) In moments like these, its memory came back to her—its cosy, compact warmth on a grey rainy day, its soft mangowood planks still exuding after all these years the faintest fragrance of ripe tropical fruit just fallen from the tree.

Where was that bastard son when she needed him? He should have been here to supervise and oversee: Wasn't it a man's job, after all? Ha! Just as it had been hers, she supposed, to stand behind her husband's chair at mealtimes serving his food. What a joke that had been, before she quickly put a stop to it. As for her son—she suddenly remembered that it was she who had banished him. For his own good. Here he would have been ensnared in the work of the devil, with his natural-born propensity for badness. What does it profit a man to gain the whole world, yet lose his soul? If he was going to lose his soul—and by all accounts he already had, to that white prostitute—it was better he do it where nobody could see him, abroad, rather than parade his licentiousness publicly up and down the mountain, making her the laughing stock of all and sundry. How Beta and Bella would laugh!

No, she would manage the running of this house alone even if it killed her—and it would, she knew that. Those damned sisters-in-law were only waiting for her to die, seething with jealousy that the big house had come her way. Let them wait, she would outlive them all. It was a constant source of pride to her when she reflected on how well she had done: Bella and Beta, for all their splendid Kandyan marriages, had amounted to very little in the general scheme of things. God was good, she knew; God would reward her for a lifetime of goodness and sacrifice, a lifetime of prayer and purification.

She moved, slowly, to the back of the house. It was not often that the Kumarihamy ventured beyond the kitchens to the storerooms and servants' quarters at the rear. Indeed it was a daring thing to attempt, entailing as it did a severe loss of face if an outsider happened to see her.

In the corner of the pretty, sunlit, ochre courtyard there was an eighteenth-century meat safe leaning drunkenly on three turquoise tapered legs—the fourth providing some much-needed nourishment for termites. She leant against it for a moment to get her breath back. She noticed that some tiles had slipped off a section of the verandah eave. They would need to be put back. Pausing to pluck two overripe fruits from the sun-dappled, lemon-hued lime tree—how wasteful these servants were, did they really think money grew on trees?—she made her laborious way across the courtyard, click-clacking on the polished cement floors.

When she reached Girigoris's room, she called out, 'Are you there?'

This was not a clever metaphysical question—of course he was there!—more a way of announcing her serendipitous arrival in these foreign parts.

Girigoris groaned inwardly, saying nothing. The demoness was at the door.

'Are you well?' Clarice asked loudly, as if speaking to a deaf child of somewhat impaired intellect. She did not ask *Are you ill?* because it would have been only too easy for him to answer, *Yes, I am dying.*

Girigoris groaned, this time out loud.

'Good,' said the Kumarihamy. 'Good. You're already sounding better. You'll be right as rain in no time. Our Sita has been managing marvellously in your absence. *Marv-e-llously.*' She cackled. 'Who said digging was a man's job? A few more days of this and we can promote her to your job and retire you. Then you can have all the time you want to spend with your delightful wife in the village.' Clarice smiled sweetly. It was well known that Girigoris was married to an old harridan whose famously bad temper was the talk of all the villages around Kandy, so this was intended to strike terror into his heart. On Poya days and other holidays, he had to be begged to take leave and go home to his wife.

Making her painful progress back across the courtyard, Clarice seethed in fury. The bastard! Sleeping for the last two days, eating her out of house and home, taking advantage of her sweet nature. She would give him another twenty-four hours because she knew in her heart she was a generous woman. On the third day, he had better rise again. If it was good enough for Jesus, it was good enough for him.

Sita, meanwhile, back in the house, was toiling in the bedroom under the light of the kerosene lantern. (The Kumarihamy absolutely forbade the use of electricity during the ongoing excavation.)

What a treasure Sita had proved to be! She had got into the hole, replacing Girigoris unasked.

Clarice watched her silently for a few moments. 'You know, I've been thinking . . .' she said. 'About that salary advance?'

Sita looked up hopefully from within the pit. 'Yes, my lady?'

'No, nothing,' Clarice said quickly. There was, after all, no need to spoil such a good girl. None whatsoever.

12

'She wants to speak to you,' whispered Luisa.

I shook my head, making frantic hand signals. Luisa ignored them. 'Here he is,' she said, calmly handing me the phone.

'Son Nee. How are you.' It was a statement not a question, the voice low and urgent and controlled. There was a strong echo of Signora Sirra in that voice, dressed up in a business suit, perhaps.

'I'm very well, Mrs Palazzi.'

Luisa's mother cleared her throat, like a chairman of the board about to sack the CEO. 'My husband and I would like you both to come visit with us. You will stay overnight at our house in Miami and the next day Luisa will drive the car over to Sanibel.'

It was not an invitation, more a set of instructions for the precise execution of a minutely planned tour.

'Thank you, Mrs Palazzi—'

'Our pleasure entirely.' She hung up the phone.

I looked at Luisa. 'What was that all about?'

Her eyes were shining. 'Don't you see? They want us there for Easter.'

I could hear the enthusiasm in Luisa's voice. It made me disappointed in a way I could not fathom. Almost as if this present excitement discounted all our own previous pleasures, which seemed to count for very little in the light of this new turn of events. Luisa was responding unconsciously to the call of a higher power. Where did that leave me?

'They've booked our tickets.'

'That is *so* good of them. Of course you'll be able to get leave at short notice and we'll cancel any other plans we might have. Naturally.'

She looked up suspiciously. 'Plans? Since when have we had other plans?'

'You know what I mean,' I said huffily.

She smiled tenderly. 'Oh, Sonny. We should be grateful they're paying for our holiday. You think we could have afforded this otherwise?'

She was right in what she said. It did not make me any happier.

'You know we've been dying to have a holiday. You know where we would have ended up otherwise.'

A week before, we had been joking about the pleasures of Margate—about the only place we could afford. Even the Victorian name seemed to have a common music-hall ring to it.

'You never know what might happen on holiday.' She looked at me meaningfully. 'Things tend to happen when you're more relaxed.'

It was the first time she had alluded to it, the first time either of us had put a voice to what had been in both our minds.

We had been married half a year, and still no sign of a baby. Given our previous track record, this was highly unexpected. A baby was probably the last thing we could afford; and for me, if I was being truly honest, it probably did not matter one jot either way. But for Luisa it was different: there seemed to be an unspoken need for a fracture to be healed, a memory erased, a box ticked. Though I did not see what America had to do with all of this.

'Miami?' I asked. 'Sanibel? How many houses do these people have?'

'"These people," as you so quaintly put it, are my parents. They can have as many houses as they want. It's their hard-earned money. Not some crackpot inheritance that happened to fall into their lap.'

I was stung by this. Was that what she really thought about the old house on the mountain that would one day be mine? This was not the time and place to answer back, so I shut up. It was churlish of me to be ungrateful, to dampen her enthusiasm.

'We'll go to America,' I said hugging her. 'We'll enjoy ourselves hugely. And we'll get pregnant. Both of us.'

It was impossible not to subscribe to Luisa's high spirits in the days that followed. She was one of those people who packed a month before she went anywhere. Making feeble attempts at the book I was supposed to be writing, I followed her saga as she packed, unpacked, shopped for more clothes, repacked.

I could see why this was important to her. She was returning for the first time as a married woman, a fully validated adult on equal footing with her parents. Never mind that they were paying for everything, I could see in Luisa's face and sense again that feeling of quiet enjoyment very rich people have, the warm glow of a banquet well consumed, that complacent look of entitlement as they put their hand over the wine glass. It made me jealous because it was something I would never be part of. It was odd, come to think of it, how her parents had ignored us (or more specifically me) for so long. Had they felt that if they waited long enough the marriage would just go away? Wasn't America famous for its four-week marriages?

Perhaps I had, by some esoteric émigré criterion, passed the test, having exceeded the statute of limitations on a quickie divorce. They had decided I was here to stay, so it was time to get to know me. Of course they would have received enough and more gossip from their relations in Monte. Strangely, none of these had ever mentioned Luisa's parents to us, so who knew.

In contrast to Luisa, I packed at the last minute. I did not know what was expected of me, and was convinced that the less I knew, the better it would be for all of us. They would have to take me as I was. I did not even think to pack the dinner jacket. It was America, for God's sake. There was no dress code in the Land of the Free, surely?

As soon as she had her breakfast—roti and lunu miris, and a huge mug of extremely sweet, extremely milky tea—Sita began the dusting. For her part, the Kumarihamy had phased out breakfast some months back, in a ceaseless (and, of course, selfless) drive for greater economy. Nowadays she had taken to appearing in the kitchen during the servants' breakfast hour, lecturing them on the dangers of diabetes while they sipped their tea. Unaccountably, the more she cut back on household items, the more the sugar bill seemed to go up.

'See what happened to Sita's father,' she thundered, wielding her walker like a conductor's baton. 'Has to inject himself twice a day. *Twice!*' She was particularly gratified that here was a living, breathing, *injecting* example of what she was preaching.

Sadly, the sugar level in the kitchen jar seemed to have a will of its own: in spite of her best efforts, it dipped at an ever more alarming rate. How she longed to put a daily mark on it with a fat, indelible felt-tipped pen!

Picking up broom and dustpan Sita escaped, leaving her employer alone with Girigoris—who had risen miraculously from his bed for breakfast—and Clarice switched seamlessly from diabetes to the dangers of over-resting any muscles you might happen to have pulled while going about your daily business.

This was the part of the day Sita loved best, alone in these blued *chunam* drawing rooms with their Arts-and-Crafts furniture in blackened hardwood, the stucco walls exuding a comforting damp smell that took her right back to her arrival at the walauwa as a child. For all the strictness of its regime, it had been a happy childhood in the little house of mangowood planks. She remembered how the Kumarihamy would turn up at their home every birthday in her ancient green car. There was always some squeaky toy in shiny cellophane wrapping that she would shake in the little girl's face, eliciting a smile from her.

'Ten rupees in the Kandy Market,' her father would mutter sarcastically, loud enough for the Kumarihamy to hear.

'In that case, why didn't *you* get me one?' she had always wanted to ask. More often than not he would have forgotten it was her birthday in the first place. Only years later would it occur to Sita how odd and unexpected the affection of this strange woman had been. As a child she had never questioned it. Love was thin on the ground; you had to take what you could get.

Every Sinhala New Year she had been taken up to the big house, dark and fearsome, and full of strange smells, for the obligatory annual visit that all estate staff made. All these years later, as an adult, these high, wide rooms still held a special meaning for her.

She looked up now at the wooden fretwork panels that were set here and there in the high ceilings to allow the roof timbers to breathe, through which she occasionally glimpsed the curious black eyes of a polecat. There was actually a pair of them—the roof was polecat country—and they were generally up all night, squealing and scrabbling from one end of the vast expanse of roof to the other. Sita was thankful she had only had to spend the occasional night at the walauwa. It was a close-run thing as to which was louder: the Kumarihamy by day, or the polecats by night.

A somewhat battered upright piano stood at a rakish angle in the corner. Sita opened the lid and ran a cursory duster over the yellowing ivories, which reminded her rather unkindly of the teeth of the old Kumarihamy, Clarice's mother-in-law. She had been tone deaf but fondly convinced that her daughters Beta and Bella were musical geniuses.

Many an evening the servants had been dragged out of their somnolent after-dinner quarters to listen to Bęta and Bella thump the piano, giving it the thrashing of a lifetime on the sound Kandyan principle of do-as-you-would-be-done-by. The piano had never fully recovered from this childhood trauma. It lay lonely and broken in the corner, silent and out of tune under the new regime (Clarice did not herself play, believing music to be the work of the devil).

On top of the piano were the carved animals: there was a mother rat and her baby in ivory, the mother holding a candle; a hare, also in ivory; and a third figure, a bird emerging from an egg, carved in wood. How often Clarice had impressed upon her the preciousness and rarity of these animals, minutely carved and finely detailed. Sita polished them lovingly, one by one. Later, she could not pinpoint exactly what came over her: looking quickly around to see whether she was being observed, she slipped the hare into the pocket of her dress. Heart pounding, she fled the rooms, fully convinced she had been observed, afraid that some divine alarm bell would start ringing.

She did not do any digging that day, wandering around the walauwa in a fever of apprehension, the stolen animal throbbing in her pocket like a blazing wound on her thigh.

'What's wrong?' Pandu asked when she handed him his tea. He eyed her cynically. 'Is it that time of the month?'

She flushed, saying nothing.

When it was time for her to go home that evening, he stationed himself at a convenient flower bed near the walauwa gates. 'Off for the day?' he called out cheerily as she passed him, too engrossed to notice that he too had changed out of his work clothes. Keeping a careful distance, he followed the bright yellow flowers of her dress as they dodged and darted between the great trees on the road downhill. She passed the lane to her own house and carried on to the bottom. It was easier now because they were in town and the streets were full of people going home from work. At the police station she took a left, passing the clock tower, heading in the direction of the Palace. At the pink-painted Queen's Hotel she turned suddenly and disappeared into one of the shops of the hotel arcade. Approaching cautiously, he saw it was one which sold antique jewellery and objets d'art.

'And so!' he said to himself victoriously. Through the speckled display window he saw her at the counter talking to the man behind it.

Mr Seenigama prided himself on selling only the finest pieces in his shop: Art Deco bracelets of cabochon sapphires set in platinum, pretty blue Delft plates with the VoC stamp of the Dutch East India Company on the back, and lustrous green celadon bowls.

He recognized the girl straightaway. She worked in the big house on Bhairava Kanda. She had first come in a few months ago to sell the two rather fine gold bangles belonging to her mother.

'I'll give you ten thousand for the pair,' he had said. He knew the type; they would take anything and run.

'Absolutely not,' she had said firmly. 'These belonged to the old Mahadewala Kumarihamy. They were given to my mother on her wedding day.'

'So why are you selling them?'

'It's my father. I need the money to pay his medical bills.'

It was unusual for any Sri Lankan to be so forthright about money matters. Usually, the more desperate things were, the more eager they were to show that no, they did not need the money at all; they just happened to be passing the shop, and oh, what a surprise, they just happened to have in their handbag Granny's bracelet, and would he kindly tell them how much it might be worth, purely out of curiosity, of course?

Mr Seenigama had been so impressed by the girl's honesty, he had ended up paying her fifty thousand for the bangles, slightly more, in fact, than they were worth.

She took out of her pocket and placed on the counter the hare.

Mr Seenigama picked it up. He noticed the signature on the back, and his eyes narrowed slightly. 'Where did you get this?' he asked.

'It was at home.'

'You know what it is?'

She looked up at him, saying nothing.

'It's an early-nineteenth-century netsuke. They were used in Japan as toggles, to secure the pouches men wore on their kimonos to store tobacco and money.'

'How much?' she asked.

He was pained a little by her directness, her mercenary attitude. 'I can give you seventy-five thousand.'

She put the netsuke back in her pocket with a slight shake of the head. 'I would need a lot more than that.'

'It could be a fake,' he pointed out. 'I would need to know its provenance. With an old piece, the provenance is almost more important than the quality.'

'It's from the walauwa,' she said quickly. 'I can assure you it's genuine.'

That was what he had already guessed. But it made no difference to him, the rights or wrongs of the transaction. He was a purveyor of fine objects: there were plenty of customers in this game willing to buy stolen pieces and, as a supplier, it was not his business to question their morals, or indeed his own in selling them.

In the end he paid her a lakh, in soiled hundred-rupee bills from the iron safe in the back office. She folded the money up in the brown paper bag he gave her, and left without a word.

Through the glass, Pandu watched the money being counted out. 'Got her!' he thought jubilantly. He did not follow her as she returned home, making his own way later by a different route.

Sita took the smart navy blue box out of its wrapping and looked at it once again. It appeared to be a very expensive case for pens. Inside nestled what in fact did look remarkably like a pen, together with a set of needles in their clear plastic covering. I now have six months' worth of insulin for the old man, Sita thought as she trudged wearily back up the hill. Was it really so bad then, what I did? How could I have bought all this otherwise? She shook a fist at the darkening sky in a gesture of defiance. It's so easy when you're rich, isn't it? This poverty only serves to make criminals of us all, she thought sadly.

Halfway up the hill was a small corner shop where Sita bought her daily needs. All of last week she had sneaked past it on her way to work, praying she would not be seen. Now she walked boldly in.

The shopkeeper gave her a rueful smile. 'I'm afraid I can't give you any more credit, Miss.'

'I'd like to settle in full, please.'

If the shopkeeper was surprised, he did not show it. While he totted up her tab, she went around picking out a few more provisions. At the last minute, she put into her basket a packeted slice of seer, the most expensive Sri Lankan fish.

She had not eaten seer for at least a year, not since the Kumarihamy had given up fish at the walauwa. She cooked it straightaway because she did not possess a fridge: salt, a tablespoon of chilli, three cloves of garlic and two of goraka, a stick of cinnamon, and she swirled the fish in this mixture before poaching it for seven minutes, its fragrance gently floating around the hut like a good spell.

The old man wrinkled his nose. 'Fish? We're Kandyans. You know we don't eat fish.'

'In that case, I'll eat it all myself.'

'Where did you get the money for fish, anyway? Up to your old tricks, are you?'

Sita flushed. Three years ago, Clarice had caught Sonny kissing her in the kitchen. It had only been a playful hug and peck but Clarice had been apoplectic with rage, threatening to drive her out of the house, accusing her of being a prostitute and shamelessly selling her favours.

The house was used to Clarice's rages. In her pantheon you were usually a murderer, drug addict or prostitute (or you were Clarice). If Sita had lost her job, she and her father would have been out on the streets. After a week of abject grovelling by the old man, Sita had been reinstated. Even now, so many years later, it was a source of severe embarrassment to her.

'You know,' he said at the end of the meal, 'you might just be able to get yourself a job as a cook somewhere?'

It was the most she was ever going to get out of him. She said nothing, though she was secretly rather pleased.

Up at the walauwa there was just the one phone, a solid Bakelite construction which hardly ever rang. In the silence of the empty house the Kumarihamy prowled around it like a cat around a mouse. It sat there looking at her, bold and black, glossy and unrepentant, its silence an affront to her good nature. At times she felt like taking it off the hook. That would teach them! Who was she to be trifled with in this cavalier manner? The 'they' in Clarice's mind were vague and undefined: people, *others*, the great unwashed that seethed in their numbers at the foot of her mountain. But her ire was concentrated on the one member of this group guaranteed to get her goat (and good God what a goat!): that son of hers, that Sonny.

Wasn't it the bounden duty of a son to ring his mother? Particularly after such a cheeky marriage? By now Clarice had completely forgotten the undiluted stream of trans-Asian telephonic invective she had aimed at him during that last call, and how she had hung up on him. Indeed she prided herself on her forgive-and-forget approach. It was really quite simple: if she could forget, why couldn't others forgive? She was often puzzled when others held grudges that in her mind had been wiped clean long ago. Besides, a clean slate was so satisfying, it left you space for so many more fresh quarrels. So why wasn't he calling? Surely he must recognize the obligation he was under, to humour a lonely old woman of such severely limited means? He had always been a selfish child, thinking only of himself. Did he not, even for a moment, consider the sacrifices she had made to educate him? Did he think she actually got pleasure from her fish-free life?

After much deliberation Clarice put out a reluctant paw to the phone. It remained silent and unresponsive; uncaring, really. How much more satisfying if it had given a sudden squeak of alarm and scurried off towards the nearest mouse hole. She could then have chased it round and round the room, ruthlessly whacking it with the walker.

Sonny had carefully printed out the telephone number, together with the country code, in that first letter he had written when he moved to Putney. Clarice peered at it now, deciphering the numbers with difficulty. An international call was a momentous occasion, Clarice could truthfully not remember ever having made one before. Praying to God to forgive her, she dialled with trembling fingers.

The phone rang for a long time in the silence of the empty London flat, whose occupants had long since embarked upon an adventure of their own to Miami. But Clarice was not to know, and she took this ceaseless ringing as a personal insult. 'Bastard!' she said, her ill humour returning like a welcome gust of rain after the drought. 'He can bloody well go to the devil! I'm off to bed.'

The Devil was not in the best of moods. He was disappointed with Sri Lanka. People were simply not as evil as he had been led to believe, their propensity for wickedness woefully blunt. He blamed it on the hot weather and the small-island culture that allowed people to be happy with what little they had. This was plainly wrong. Where was that killer streak of cut-and-thrust competitiveness he was so used to in the West? The go-getting dog-eat-dog culture that set his blood pounding and his chin hairs quivering? What you got here instead was a bland, milk-fed sort of passive-aggressiveness. Nobody could be bothered to do anything well themselves, yet they deeply resented you if you tried: damning you with the faintest of praise when you succeeded.

So far he had managed to recruit the excellent Pandu and the fractious Kumarihamy. He noted with approval the missing netsuke from the top of the piano, which would set off a train of events rich with consequences.

But in the main, he was bored, head-bangingly, wrist-slittingly bored. He sat at the piano twirling round and round on the rosewood piano stool, his cape flying behind him. Bored with this too after a while, he opened the piano lid and began picking out a tune. The Devil had perfect pitch, and it pained him to hear an instrument so desperately out of tune.

'The hills are alive . . .' he sang in his fine countertenor voice, 'with the sound of museeeec . . .'

Cosily tucked up in her high ebony four-poster bed at the other end of the house, the Kumarihamy thought she could hear singing. Was it a choir of heavenly angels? Was it the neighbourhood cat?

'I must get my ears checked tomorrow,' she decided.

13

Outside Miami Airport in the long-term car park was a small silver-grey BMW. Luisa fished about in her handbag, took out a key and opened the door.

'Whose car is this?' I asked, perplexed.

'Mine,' she said, trying hard not to smile. 'Rodrigo parked it here for me to pick up.'

'Yours? How come you never told me?'

'There's lots about me you don't know.'

In London we went about in buses we could barely afford. To possess a BMW was something beyond my ken. 'And who's Rodrigo?'

'My parents' chauffeur.'

BMWs, houses, chauffeurs. I was in deep water here.

'Get in,' she said. 'Stop moping.'

On the way into Miami she drove us through Hialeah, the Latin quarter, where house frontages were prettily decorated with bougainvillea and bullet holes. She told me about Bimini, the westernmost part of the Bahamas, only 53 miles away, from where all the drugs came in at night on boats, making Miami the drug capital of the States.

'So all this bad stuff is supposed to make me feel at home, is it?'

She chuckled. 'I just wanted to show you—before you get too enamoured of this place—that behind every glamorous façade there is a skin of evil, just below the top layer.' Like I needed to be reminded.

What it did show me yet again was that other side of Luisa, the mature one, quietly aware and philosophically acquiescent of the big bad world outside. There was no room here for the raucous and principled occupation of moral high ground that is every young student's terrain, and which was certainly mine. Her conception of evil was so much more nuanced and subtle and worldly-wise; a stark contrast to the essentially immature, black-and-white demons-and-angels tableau of my Kandyan childhood.

It was getting dark when she finally drove me to a little house on Mary Street in Coconut Grove, dense with green foliage and the shrill sounds of birds settling for the night. Drinking mojitos with her in the backyard jacuzzi, I felt I was once more in a tropical paradise. I marvelled at how willingly she had given all this up for a council flat in Putney.

'I'm surprised at the house,' I said, next morning.

It was small, with two bedrooms up a spiral black iron staircase; downstairs was that rarest of amenities in the eyes of a Sri Lankan: the open-plan kitchen. The sliding glass doors of the dining room gave out on to the deck at the back where the jacuzzi was, surrounded by trees. We were sitting on handmade cream Cuban floor tiles, drinking coffee.

'It's not at all what I expected . . . It's not . . .' I struggled for the proper word.

'It's not flash?'

I nodded.

'All my parents' friends are extremely flash. Palatial houses, fancy cars. My parents were never like that. They believed in keeping their heads down. Even as an only child I was never given everything I wanted just because I wanted it, the way my friends were.'

I was silent, beginning to discover a new-found respect for Luisa's parents.

'Long ago I was told that what they made in life was theirs to spend. I had to make my own way.'

I thought: How different from our traditional Asian way, where every ounce of one's belongings was hoarded with care, to be passed on to the next generation. Then I thought of my mother, who had somehow bucked this trend, willing to sacrifice my birthright on the altar of her firmly idiosyncratic principles. In some strange way I missed her, missed all that daily sparring, all those glorious absurdities. I wondered what Sita was up to, that childhood playmate of mine.

'Hurry up and finish your coffee,' Luisa said. 'We have a long journey ahead.'

If the chronicle of this relationship begins to sound like a travelogue, it is because that is how it is when a rich girl hooks up with a poor boy. He has to be ready to go, at a moment's notice, where the call of duty takes him. In those early days it seems to me we went everywhere, Luisa and I, and everywhere we went it was with a different Luisa. I can honestly say I went to bed with a different woman in each country; and each woman left me a little less sure of a judgement I had once thought so sound. The woman whose beauty had first struck me dumb—the girl-child-turned-teacher at Oxford—became in Italy the screen siren of 1930s Hollywood. The impoverished worker in the London office had become in America the world-weary sophisticate whose vision encompassed an evil far beyond my provincial scope.

Who are you now? I wanted to ask. I felt like the man who turns up in jeans with a bottle of plonk to someone's supper only to find a full-scale black-tie dinner going on, with many courses—and we were not done yet, by any means.

We crossed the Everglades that day, an endless primeval swamp infested with crocodiles, half-lit by flickering trees. Yet ancient as it was, at no time did I feel the oppressive presence of evil that permeated those jungles close to my childhood home: the silent, open-mouthed screams of long-ago human sacrifice, the ceaseless chatter of demons, the cruelty so alive it walked, heavy-lidded and gloating, up that Sri Lankan mountainside.

You will say I am being fanciful: that just as each of us creates the God we desire in the form most fitting to us, we find evil too, when and where we need to find it. But I will tell you this. I have always been alive to all forms of beauty and goodness in their finger-quivering splendour; yet I am susceptible too to their opposite. An opposite that lives and breathes and walks; and not only because I find a need for it to do so.

America was different. There was a sort of pre-lapsarian innocence about America that seemed to invalidate old world concepts of good and evil. I am ashamed to say it turned Luisa and me into the worst sort of cynic. If Italy had brought out the American in Luisa, America brought out the Italian.

We hit the Gulf of Mexico around lunchtime and drove across the causeway to the island. I was struck by how the light changed: from the full-throated parrot-green of Miami to the scaly grey of the Everglades. Now we were in a land of winking white skies and crystalline sand, the seas churned to milk with crushed seashells.

'Welcome to our humble home,' said Luisa's mother, Giovanna, and no, she wasn't being ironic, though I rather wished she had been.

The place was huge, a giant's playhouse on stilts, with an acreage of seafront that would have satisfied the navy of a small Third World country. Luisa's father, Carlo, explained how he and a few friends had got together at dinner when a chunk of the island first came up for sale. By the end of the meal they had carved it up like a roasted chicken.

'The trick to owning land is to be able to control who your neighbours are,' he said. 'One devil in the pack can ruin your entire life; in the end you're forced to sell.' He looked hard at me, and for one mad moment I thought my mother had morphed into a bald Italian in a candy-coloured seersucker suit.

Luisa's mother had short hair bleached platinum, with very black eyebrows. She was everything her voice had proclaimed her to be. Here in the eighty-plus heat she wore a cream suit, carefully neutral, her heavy gold chains and rings more suggestive of the boardroom than the beach.

'Do they always go around looking like this?' I whispered to Luisa, when we were alone for a moment.

'Looking like what?'

She understood what I meant, of course, but was pretending to be thick. They were her parents, after all.

In spite of their very Italian looks and obvious immigrant credentials, they were far more Americanized than their daughter, with that buttoned-down, dinner-jacketed attitude of the East Coast. At lunch—a spare goat's cheese salad, Giovanna pushing the leaves here and there on the plate in between brave sips of iced water—the talk was of the Met Ball and season tickets to the Opera.

'Stop!' I wanted to shout. 'You don't need to impress me. You're wasting your time. It's all way over my ugly little Third World head.'

But I realized they were not doing it for me. The money had hardened in their arteries, rich and salty, calcifying their attitudes, turning this rigid live performance into a sort of kabuki theatre for the very rich enacted by the very rich. That 'the right sort of people' were absent from the audience went largely unnoticed by the performers.

'I want to know all about your mother,' Giovanna said, cosying up to me all of a sudden. 'Has she met my daughter yet?'

I did not know quite what to say, so I shrugged and smiled.

'Would you like to call her from here? Tell her you're with us?'

'Oh God, no!' I burst out. I could just imagine my mother using the B-word on them. 'She doesn't use the phone much,' I added lamely. 'Only for life and death matters. A call would only make her nervous.'

You will never be the same again after a call from her, I nearly added. I can guarantee it.

That night we slept on Frette sheets—the only reason I know is because it was explained to me at great length, the thread count, the length and quality of the yarn, the number of years it took sixty-two little old Italian grannies on half rations to weave each square inch. I would have been just as good with Gehantex, though I was too polite to mention that.

Next morning I could not raise my head from the pillow.

'I'm dying,' I told Luisa. 'My body aches all over.'

The plan was to take the boat out into the Gulf of Mexico. The minute details of this operation had been outlined the previous night (along with the Frette sheet discourse).

Luisa was furious. 'You can't let everyone down like this!'

'I'm not letting everyone down. I'm letting myself down. I'm the only one here who's not sailed in the Gulf before.'

'At least get up for breakfast and explain yourself,' she said. '*Bastard!*'

Fine. Now everyone in Florida was beginning to sound like my mother.

The old couple was at the breakfast bar in matching sailor suits, broad horizontal blue-and-white stripes, navy boat shoes, he in peaked cap, she in beret. I did all I could not to burst out laughing. (It would not have done; I was ill.) I imagined them running around the Blue Plate Diner in similar fashion, playing Immigrants the way other children might play Doctors and Nurses, flipping burgers in matching striped aprons.

'Sonny has something to tell you,' Luisa announced.

'I'm so sorry,' I said coughing, a little theatrically. 'I'm too ill to go out in the boat. I have flu.'

You could see the different emotions flash through their eyes, like buildings past a train window. Disbelief, first of all; then hurt; then resentment. I have no doubt that later, somewhere out in the white heat of the Gulf of Mexico, there would be rage, lots of it.

'It's all right,' I said. 'I can look after myself. I have plenty of writing to catch up on.'

They were not really interested. Nobody said, you poor thing, would you like some Valium, there's the kitchen, help yourself to tea, coffee, fillet steak, Dom Pérignon. Luisa ignored me. Plainly, she felt I was shirking. This boating trip was for my enjoyment. How could I be so insensitive as not to enjoy it?

Once the boating party had departed—great meaningful sighs all round—I found I actually had more energy than I had bargained for. Perhaps I should have made the effort, after all: lain motionless in the bottom of a boat staring up at a cloudless Mexican sky. I wandered around the house a bit, marvelling at its bareness, the ease and comfort of its clean and spacious all-white nothingness: what a contrast to the permanent purple dusk swirling inside my beloved walauwa, busy with its rush-hour traffic of random treasure and deadly demon.

There was a TV in the corner the size of the piano back home. All I could receive on its one hundred and one channels were various preachers, sleek and crew-cut, shaking their fist at the camera, singing songs of hellfire and brimstone. Oh, if I could put them all on a boat to Sri Lanka, to get a taste—just one sip!—of the real thing. I turned the TV off and went to sleep.

At dinner that night—white fish poached in white wine and sorrel—I saw Giovanna do that thing again, spearing a piece, bringing it up to her mouth, putting it down again to start another sentence. It was what actors did in films to avoid eating the same food over repeated takes. I watched, fascinated.

'I'm taking Sonny on a road trip,' Luisa announced suddenly.

'Are you?' I asked. This was the first I had heard of it.

'What a *good* idea,' said Carlo.

'Florida has so *much*,' said Giovanna, putting her fork down yet again.

It was like a bad script with amateur actors.

'I've upset them, haven't I?' I said to Luisa later, in bed.

She did her usual trick, opening her eyes a little wider. 'Why would you think that?'

I said nothing. I was only just beginning to learn, you see, that when the rich invite you to their houses it is for their pleasure, not yours. There is a clearly defined contract. You are expected to sing for your supper, not sit there like a sack of potatoes, eating and drinking. If you are found wanting in the entertainment department, a non-performing liability, they will have no hesitation in tearing up your contract.

As they say in hospitals back home, my ticket had just been cut. I was discharged. As we left next morning—oh, how sorry they were to see us go—Carlo put his capable doctor's hands around my neck.

'Look after my daughter,' he said and squeezed, gently but firmly, the way you might squeeze pus out of a boil.

So here we are, taking the road back over the causeway, and I know I am in the doghouse. What she does not say—and the polite, eminently reasonable answers she provides when she does—is what gives the game away. I recline in the passenger seat of the BMW in an influenzal haze, barely able to take in the changing social landscape as we go further north into the Florida hinterland, the deep south of the USA: the tin-roofed shacks off dirt-track roads, with little boxes of star-fruit left outside on the porch for sale, the heat, the midges, the barefoot children playing in black water. We could almost have been in the deep south of Sri Lanka.

Then, a funny thing happened. We stopped at one of those towns somewhere up near Tallahassee with a raging thirst.

'I think, a bottle of Schramsberg,' said Luisa, rather preciously. I had no idea what Schramsberg was but in this heat it sounded good. We parked the car and began walking up the high street of this one-horse town. The air was as still and shimmering as in a spaghetti western. I could almost hear the harmonica play that familiar theme tune. 'Now see what happens,' she said with ill-concealed glee.

It was as if a natural disaster had struck. The locals stopped and stared, open-mouthed; we were a very unnatural disaster, an unblemished white woman in the hands of a horrendously black man.

We walked into a liquor shop. There were two other customers so we waited till they made their purchases and walked out, though not before each had given us The Look.

'Do you have Schramsberg?' asked Luisa. The man at the till looked up, looked through us at the door as if we were not there (I had had no idea till then that black was such a transparent colour). Finally we walked out. Perhaps the man had taken an Easter vow of silence. Perhaps there was a natural suspicion of strangers, as it was less than two years since 9/11. Perhaps self-service meant just that—go find your own Schramsberg. So we did, in another shop, and we were lucky, because they were actually willing to take our filthy dirty money in exchange.

'I think,' said Luisa when we were back in the car, 'it is time for us to leave this God-forsaken country.' She took my face in her hands and planted a kiss on my lips. She seemed to have forgotten she was ever meant to be angry with me.

I looked at the carved Roman profile of her face, and it struck me yet again: my unbelievable good luck that a creature of such lapidary beauty could be in love with an ugly devil like me.

14

The digging had stopped entirely. Girigoris, having made a brief reappearance, had promptly suffered a relapse and taken to his bed again. In a fit of unaccustomed benevolence, the Kumarihamy had called in Dr Dep, the now ancient family GP who had fallen down the stairs during Sonny's exorcism all those years ago and broken his leg. He was still alive and kicking, though not kicking so much since that broken leg.

'The man has sciatica,' said Dr Dep.

'He what?' exclaimed the Kumarihamy in a shocking display of bad grammar.

Dr Dep emphasized that Girigoris must under no circumstances be digging; he had a trapped nerve in the small of his back.

Imagine the nerve of it! Clarice packed him off unceremoniously to the village. 'Your wife will do a *much* better job of getting you back on your feet,' Clarice said, with a grim smile. 'This is not a hotel. Please, please don't feel you need to hurry back.'

In spite of her better judgement, Clarice was quite philosophical about this new turn of events. With Girigoris gone, she was saving a sizeable amount on the food bill. Meanwhile, an opencast mine, a huge mouth in the shape of an O—like the O in reproach—greeted her every time she went into Sonny's room. That hussy Sita did not seem so keen to descend into the pit these days. Clarice could not force her—it was not a woman's job—but having dug so enthusiastically before, it was most inconsiderate of the girl not to continue. In fact, Sita looked quite different these days—it bothered Clarice that she could not quite put a finger on it—and there seemed to be a sort of uppity air about her. She had better watch out—Clarice had her eye on her.

On the whole Clarice was somewhat disappointed with the walauwa staff these days, absconding or incompetent as they all seemed to be. Karuppayah the cook was continually and continuously drunk—though alcoholism was the province of cooks, and the country had one of the highest rates of alcohol consumption in the world. (Men had their needs, she knew, and alcohol was one of them. As long as he bought his own hooch and did not raid the liquor cabinet, everyone was happy. 'Show me a cook who isn't a drunk,' Clarice was fond of saying, 'and I'll show you a culinary calamity.')

The one bright star in this servitorial firmament was Pandu, who had been brought to the walauwa at the age of seventeen. He was turning into a fine-looking young man, with a streak of bold and resourceful cunning that had earned him the Kumarihamy's grudging admiration. She could see that he would go far. In all honesty she did not much approve of him hobnobbing with that transgender Australian.

(Who knew where that might lead? Who knew better than she about men's needs?) But there was not much she could do to stop it. The walauwa had no boundary walls, just low stone terraces that led all the way down to the bottom of the hill. She often saw the caped crusader leaping over them with dizzying ease, in a flurry of crimson. Perhaps she could speak to Bella and Beta politely about this unwanted intrusion. The Australian was bound to be a friend or lodger of theirs—she had always had her suspicions about Beta's LGBT sympathies.

Pandu knew that timing was everything. He pounced when he was good and ready, the day after Girigoris had been packed off home. He had watched his quarry carefully for a couple of days, seen the little telltale signs of extravagance— the shiny hairclips, the crimson silk shoes, the touch of eyeliner on those smoky eyes. He liked a woman who looked after herself.

'I followed you,' he said. 'I saw you, at that jeweller's outside Queen's.'

'What are you, some kind of stalker?'

'I saw him give you money.'

'Yes? How *dare* you spy on me!' Though she spoke boldly, she felt a sudden lurch in the pit of her stomach.

'Shall I tell the Kumarihamy? That you stole something?'

She laughed. 'What nonsense! You have no proof.'

Pandu shrugged. There was a thoughtful look on his young features. 'I could take her to the shop, I suppose. When they see who she is, they'll be forced to own up.'

Sita knew when she was beaten. 'What do you want, you bastard?' she muttered softly.

He said nothing for a moment, finishing off his tea and handing back the mug. 'I want you,' he said simply.

'Well, you can fuck off!' she shouted, slamming the kitchen door in his face.

She put the mugs into the sink. When she turned round, she saw he had come in silently. He was standing behind her, his handsome, insolent face inches from her neck. She opened her mouth to scream but he clapped his hand over it. He gripped her shoulders roughly. 'Shut the fuck up, bitch,' he said softly, grinning to himself as he bent her over the kitchen table.

Barely able to move from the pain, she sank into a chair. It had only been five minutes by the kitchen clock, that was all—but if you measured it in pain and humiliation and the sheer grinding down of a life, it was more like five years. Even worse than the pain was that betrayal of trust. I've seen you and worked with you these last five years of my life, she thought miserably. How could you do this to me? He was like that faithful dog you feed and care for every day that suddenly turns round and savages you. What strange force had taken possession of his mind?

Then there was that other thing. Why didn't I struggle? she thought miserably, deeply ashamed of herself. Why didn't I pull his hair, scratch his eyes out? But she knew the answer. Any struggle would have meant violence and noise she could ill afford because it would have brought the whole household running into the kitchen and into the mess of what she had done. She would have landed in the lock-up, and her father out on the streets.

There are those, her father had once remarked, upon whom the world waits. They skip through life blithely unaware of its dangers or responsibilities, never having to pick up the tab. Then there are those others whose job it is to wait upon the world, shouldering its responsibilities, its pain, its blame and, ultimately, its cost. She had always belonged to the latter category.

Who would get the blame here? Who would end up homeless with an elderly diabetic patient on her hands? I stole and am being punished for it, she thought. But I did it for a good cause, not for myself. Does that not excuse me? The laws of karma seemed harsh and relentless, swift and to the point. Was there no higher power that could see and judge beyond the initial crime and punishment? The powerlessness of her position came back to her and she broke down again. Oh Lord, help me out here, she whispered, please.

When he had finished, he wiped himself on the edge of her dress and exited through the kitchen door cockily, whistling, as if it were the most natural thing in the world. All she could hear now in the empty kitchen was the ticking clock. She smelled again the acrid whiff of his excitement as he raped her, his breathy disgust on the hairs of the back of her neck; she heard him chuckle as he laboured away.

She raised her head. 'I will kill you,' she said aloud, to the empty dark. 'I don't care how long it takes me, how long I have to wait, so help me God, I will kill you. And when you are dying, when your breath is draining out of you, the last thing you will hear is *my* chuckle.'

ॐ

The Kumarihamy rang the bell to have the tea things removed. There was no response from inside the house. Why were they not answering? Her eyes might be feeble but her ears were acute. She thought she could hear squeaks and scuffles from inside the house. Really, she must get the municipal rat-catcher in. The last time she had called him, he had turned up with a wire cage.

'What do you intend on doing with that?' she had asked him. 'Make a pet of it?'

The rat-catcher sat on the verandah steps and gave her a long speech on ahimsa—oh, the cheek of it, a rat-catcher lecturing a princess!—and how it was municipal policy not to destroy life, in whatever form it came.

'Is that how you eradicate malaria?' the Kumarihamy asked. 'By not killing mosquitoes?'

'Mosquitoes are different,' said the rat-catcher, slapping his thigh to prove the point. 'As for these rats, we take them down to the Mahaweli River and let them loose on the banks. Their quality of life is much better there,' he confided.

'And they're free to spread more disease,' added Clarice.

The rat-catcher did not reply. He did not do irony or sarcasm. He was a rat-catcher not a writer.

'Well, don't just stand there,' bellowed Clarice. 'Get on with it! That rat will have kittens by the time you get to it.'

But it was no good. As soon as you got rid of your rat another appeared, courtesy of your non-violent neighbours releasing their own rat over the garden wall. At times, Clarice was convinced Beta and Bella were breeding them specially to annoy her. She could hear rats in the kitchen now. Rising slowly to her feet, she click-clacked her way down the kitchen passage.

The kitchen was empty. She saw Sita in the corner, sobbing.

'Stop that at once!' ordered Clarice. 'If your father has diabetes, that's his problem. You don't need to cry over it. Who asked him to eat all those bananas when he was young?'

She made her way to the kitchen door. 'Where's Pandu? I need him to bring the car round at six. I'm off to see those big lumps, Bella and Beta.'

She opened the kitchen door and looked out into the garden. 'Pandu?' she called out. 'Pandu?' She could see no one outside, just a wisp of crimson disappearing behind the gardenias, though she could not be sure, her eyes were so weak.

15

The trip to America highlighted an essential difference between Luisa and me. She knew that I found her parents' great wealth amusing and somewhat absurd. She could see that far through my eyes; but deep down within her was a tremendous respect for this wealth, unstated but assumed. It was, after all, what kept us afloat in London. She saw, too, that there was an element of sour grapes to my cynicism. They had become an easy target for me, particularly after the visit: I made fun of their accents, their rather parvenu taste in clothes and what I felt was their sadly misplaced reverence for all things American. They may have had the money, but I had the words. I could sense Luisa's disapproval of my behaviour, of its unkindness. I was making fun of innocent children who hadn't the weapons to fight back.

And I could sense the conflict in Luisa: the resentment at her parents for not being ordinary, middling people undeserving of my acid cynicism, and the resentment at me for not being more understanding of the essentially childish ways of their grown-up millionaire world.

In a similar way—a sobering thought—I wondered how I would react had she found my Sri Lankan life hilarious—in all its surreal, grotesque, filthy, medieval splendour. There was plenty to laugh about in a rather tragic way, I recognized that. At the same time I might have resented her at some deeper level for finding it funny. I did so want her to be aware of it—this rather highly coloured, melodramatic backdrop to my life—however risky its exposition to our relationship. The fact that I was not being given this opportunity might have contributed to a general sense of dissatisfaction that sharpened my sarcasm and vinegared my words.

Perhaps there was another reason for the appearance of this new fissure in our relationship. There was still no baby. The official position was this: we had neither the time to devote nor money to spend on a baby. We were both young, so what was the hurry? Luisa was teaching English to European businessmen at a college in Regent Street. She was happy in her work even if it was not as rewarding as teaching her Oxford students. But secretly, the more she failed to conceive, the more obsessed we were becoming. There were times of the month when we went at it frenziedly, like rutting rats, with no success, while, somewhere else, karma was having the last laugh. Frankly, it took the joy out of the sex.

In the meantime, my literary creation Rathu Catherine was getting fatter by the page. I had tried killing her off on page thirty-two with agrochemicals in the milk toffee. She had spent a week in intensive care on a drip, returning refreshed and thin and raring to go, triumphantly ready to re-embrace her former obesity. On paper, one child was refusing to die. In real life, another was refusing to be born.

Putting the gear into neutral, Pandu freewheeled the ancient Toyota Crown downhill.

'Stop!' shrieked the Kumarihamy, like a hysterical driving instructor. Pandu made an emergency stop outside the corner shop. Nothing could spoil his good mood after that invigorating episode in the kitchen.

'Go inside and get me a kurakkan loaf.'

Pandu looked puzzled. 'Kurakkan?'

'You heard me.'

He returned a minute later, with a small brown loaf of millet bread. 'That'll be fifty rupees, my lady.'

The Kumarihamy opened an antique plastic handbag and proffered a fifty-rupee note. 'Now drive down to the *lali gedera*.'

Moments later they came to a stop outside the familiar wooden shack. 'Go inside and tell the old man to come out.'

Pandu came back to the car. 'He says he's ill.'

'Remind him,' said the Kumarihamy with barely suppressed rage, 'remind him just who it is who has come to see him.'

The old man came out grumbling.

'Do you know what this is?' asked Clarice handing him the loaf through the window.

'A football? No, tell me.'

'It's kurakkan,' said Clarice loudly and clearly. 'Ku-rak-kan.'

'I'm not deaf,' said the old man. 'Just diabetic.'

'Ku-rak-kan is good for you. There, your daughter is in my kitchen blubbing away even as I speak because you have done this to yourself. I told her, Your father has only himself to blame. So remember: no white bread, white sugar, white rice. Anything white is bad for diabetes. Even white people.' She thought for a moment. 'That must mean I'm diabetic too.' She cackled uproariously. The old man just looked at her, as if she were suffering from some rare medical condition he was unable to cope with.

'Tell me about my humble home,' she said, recovering from her mirth.

This was the part of the weekly visit the Kumarihamy loved best. One of the rewards of her almost biblical generosity was that it gave her the lifelong right to harvest the gratitude of her recipients, like plucking mangoes from a tree you had once planted, whenever you happened to go past. The fact that the mangoes were often sour had somehow escaped the Kumarihamy's notice.

'Have you fixed the leaks yet?' she asked.

The old man remained silent, his mouth twisted in a rictus. This might even have indicated gratitude.

The Kumarihamy leant forward and tapped Pandu. 'Drive on,' she said confidentially, 'I can't seem to get anything out of him today.'

The old man looked at the retreating car. He briefly considered hurling the loaf at it. Changing his mind, he went inside.

Upon their respective marriages, Bella and Beta had each been given, as dowry, parcels of land at the back of the walauwa.

Though physically abutting the rear of the big house, in practice they could only be accessed by going back up the private drive to the gates, and along the main road further up the hill. On these, the two sisters had built themselves houses that had been at the time of their construction the very last word in sixties chic, but were now coming to be recognized more and more for what they actually were, sixties horrors. They had granite crazy paving, and windows with louvered, frosted panes, and many random fixed-glass portholes, handy for collecting any passing tropical dust. But the houses had one supreme advantage: being above the level of the walauwa meant that the sisters could look down on the Kumarihamy at all times, a pleasing prospect in every way.

The sisters met every evening at six, at one or the other's houses, for a glass of very sweet sherry. From the window, they saw the aged Toyota Crown clanking and wheezing up the hill, a journey it made every fortnight or so.

'Quick, hide the Bristol Cream; she's on her way!'

By the time Clarice and her walker had been extruded from the car, the Bristol Cream was safely stashed away, the cooking sherry taking its place on the sideboard.

'Your usual, Clarice?'

Clarice looked suspiciously at the oily brown bottle. Before she could say anything, a glass was thrust into her hand. She looked at her two sisters-in-law. They seemed to have grown even larger in the fortnight since her last visit. For conscientious reasons neither ate meat, making quite a virtue of their regimen of native Kandyan vegetables. What this meant in practice was jackfruit, breadfruit, manioc, sweet potatoes, ash plantain and milk potatoes. Starch with a capital S. Clarice discreetly shuddered. She would rather starve than give up her meat. Then she remembered that she had, and she did. Oh well, at least she had not run to fat like these two, with their very traditional Kandyan backsides.

'Bottoms up,' said Beta just then, and the Kumarihamy nearly choked on her cooking sherry.

'I have come about your Australian friend,' she said.

'Australian? Friend?' The two sisters looked at each other mystified.

'The transgender person,' Clarice explained. 'LGBT?' She flicked her wrist a couple of times in a provocative manner and pursed her lips at them.

'You really must get that wrist looked at,' said Bella.

Clarice had a better idea. Getting up, she scrutinized through the window the gardens of the old house below. 'There he is!' she said triumphantly. 'Look, in that cape. He's twirling on the edge of that terrace there.'

'Where?' asked the sisters in unison. 'Where?'

The Devil, meanwhile, had spotted the three creatures, each glassed in at her own porthole, as in some esoteric and recondite museum of unnatural history. 'Cooee!' he said, waving. 'Cooee!' He knew that only one of them could see him, the other two being morally mediocre—neither too good, nor too bad.

Interesting, thought the Kumarihamy. He obviously knows them. But it was plain to see that they were disclaiming all knowledge of this cross-dressing Australian convict. That could only mean one thing: they were definitely harbouring him, and it was illegal. Goodness, he might even be LTTE! What would that make him? LGBTTTE?

'I can see why he would want to practise his twirls,' said Clarice. 'But why can't he go to dance class like everyone else?'

Bella sprang up. The penny had finally dropped. 'LGBT?' she said, her eyes shining. '*Of course*. FACE! EGBDF! He's a *musician*, just like me!'

'How's Sonny?' asked Beta, in a bid to shine the light away from her sister's extreme dimness. 'A little bird told me that he's now m—'

'Little bird? *Little bird?* How ornithological you're getting in your old age, Beta!'

Ever since news of the marriage had reached Kandy— glowing red hot on the wires of the bush telegraph—the sisters had been trying, unsuccessfully, to get official confirmation out of Clarice. 'Will he be back from Oxford for the summer?'

'If I can possibly afford it,' said Clarice. 'It's so difficult . . .'

This was the wrong line to take with the sisters, since they had got next to nothing from the inheritance, and she had scored virtually everything.

'Tell him he must come and spend a week with me when he does,' said Beta.

'Me too!' said Bella, eager but sadly unable to follow the undercurrents of the conversation.

Over my dead body, fumed Clarice on the drive back. How dare they try to get round my son. They'll have to kill me first. There was no danger, anyway, of him coming back, she would see to that.

She could hear Pandu quietly whistling in the front seat. 'What are *you* so thrilled about, you horrible boy?'

Pandu grinned at her in the rear-view mirror.

'If you're not careful, I'll have you married off,' threatened the Kumarihamy. 'That'll wipe the grin off your face.'

'Why? You have anyone in mind?' he asked curiously.

'Well, there's Sita,' said Clarice thinking aloud. 'She'll certainly put a stop to your wicked ways.'

'Oh really?' said Pandu boldly. 'Sita? Now there's an interesting thought.'

'Just think,' said Clarice, aiming below the belt with vicious accuracy. 'Just think what a charming father-in-law you'd then have.'

16

One day at a time, she said to herself. Take just one day at a time, in this infinite line of days all the way to the end of your life. She wanted to short-circuit this infinity, revenge herself on this self-satisfied illusion of longevity, this fool's paradise of an existence: by ending it now. But she had responsibilities to shoulder, a patient to look after, bills to pay. She was one of those waiting on the world, remember?

She hated going home because it was the worst there. At home, in the wooden shack, she could not afford the luxuries of terror or anger or pain; most of all she could not afford the self-indulgence of tears. She had to be 'normal' for the sake of her father. He was the patient, not she. He had long ago cornered the market in whatever self-indulgence there was going. From her he demanded steadiness, discipline, an iron will.

Work was different. Nobody knew, nobody cared. Sonny, she thought, where are you? He was the only one who might have held her hand, comforted her, perhaps even slain the dragon, though this was doubtful. He was not here. Briefly she had considered laying herself at the mercy of Father Rosario. He might have helped without judging. But there was a risk he would go straight to the Kumarihamy with this tale. Even if he didn't, she was rather afraid she knew what he would say. 'Give the money back. Replace the carving from where you took it. God will forgive you.' But the money wasn't all still there to be returned: the medicines had been bought. The carving itself might already have been sold on at a higher price to someone not too bothered about its provenance. There was no going back.

By staying inside the house, she avoided having to meet her tormentor. She descended into the pit and dug with an effort both blind and frenzied. The physical exertion, the ache of muscle, felt good; at the end of the day she was able to fall easily into a stupefied slumber. Sometimes, if she was lucky, she slept through till morning. Other nights the demons came.

Four o'clock in the afternoon was the worst time, because it was her duty to make the tea. She looked carefully along the edge of the window sill till she found some mouse droppings. She stirred them vigorously into his mug. Then, for good measure, she spat in it.

He was at the kitchen door when she opened it. Wordlessly, she handed the tea to him.

He put his foot in the door to prevent her closing it. 'We're not done here are we, little sister?' He insinuated the bulk of his body into the doorway. Finishing the tea, he handed her the empty mug. 'Put this away and come outside.' He grinned again. 'You'll love the gardenias, I promise.'

She resisted the temptation to get the short, sharp knife she used for garlic from the kitchen drawer. She would have to be more careful and subtle than that. Wordlessly, she followed him into the gardenia bushes.

I will not resist. By doing so I will only damage myself more. Instead, my mind will rise above us both and watch these two bodies and laugh; because one of them is due for the dustbin, and it isn't mine.

It was easier the second time. She allowed her mind to wander far and free, to observe dispassionately this absurd coupling of flesh and blood, gristle and bone, thirsty with its desire for those few drops of gratification. It was a matter of regret that no one would ever know the sacrifices she was having to make; equally, it was a matter of utmost importance no one ever should. Please God, she prayed, let me not get pregnant by this devil.

∽

I separated the bulb of garlic into cloves, slicing each one into pointed slivers, which I inserted, with the help of a sharp knife, into the chicken. I drizzled olive oil over it and slid it into the oven, ready for the evening. But I knew something had happened to take us off course when I heard the key in the lock two hours too early.

Luisa walked in, a bottle of champagne in her hand, her eyes shining. She just stood there, smiling, as if she had asked me a riddle and was waiting for the answer.

And then it hit me. 'No,' I said, 'it can't be. Can it?'

She nodded.

I swept her up in my arms and whirled her round and round the tiny sitting room as if some devil had possessed me. I put her down, weak with shock.

'Are you sure?'

She nodded again. 'I just tested.'

We sat there on the leather sofa in the fading light of this jailhouse flat, getting quietly drunk (mostly me, that was), listening to Roberta Flack singing *The First Time*. It was one of those moments again—a tipping point in my life.

'There's just one thing I want,' she said, 'and you can't say no. We have to do it before it's too late for me.' She looked down at her stomach. 'I want you to take me home. Your home, I mean. I want to fit in the last bits of the puzzle, complete the picture. My picture of you.'

I sat there in silence for a moment, listening to the evening traffic on the Upper Richmond Road. 'I'll call her,' I said. I prayed then for something I had always both wanted and feared at the same time. I prayed she would not hear the fear in my voice, those base notes of worry way below the piano keyboard, the ones you feel more than you hear, deep within your ribcage.

PART 3

17

Every day the sun sank at the back of the walauwa, behind the steep hillside into which the house was embedded. Already the verandah was in deep blue shade though down below, garden and terrace, lake and palace, were still aflame. Every evening at six thirty the town died its daily death to the expiring rattle of ice-cream vans and lottery-ticket sellers, temple bells and trains. After that only the roar of silence, beneath a flying carpet of embroidered lights.

The Kumarihamy sat on the verandah with Sita on the floor at her feet.

'Towards the end of his reign,' she was saying, 'the last king of Kandy had become increasingly erratic in his behaviour, paranoic and unpredictable. Perhaps it was mental illness, no one knew. He had already beautified Kandy to an exceptional degree—the Octagon, the lake, the bathing pavilion—because he truly had an unerring eye for such things. The court was riddled with plots and counter-plots. Everyone had their own agenda, their particular axe to grind, their secret and often absurd plan to supplant the king with their son, their niece, their mother-in-law, their pet dog. In spite of their best efforts the British still had not cracked Kandy; so naturally they did their best to encourage all this, demonizing the king's character, driving a wedge between him and his nobles, fomenting rebellion. The king played right into their hands with every cruel act, with his many madnesses. In all honesty, many of those supposedly barbaric and draconian punishments that he meted out were absolutely in accordance with the current laws of the land: the foreigners too had had such laws in their own countries only a hundred years before, something they chose to ignore in their drive to vilify the king. The fact was, quite simply, that the laws of our society had not developed as quickly as those in the West: these simple-minded foreigners could not understand why this was so, why everyone could not be on the same page at the same time.'

The Kumarihamy rapped Sita sharply on the head with her knuckles. 'Pay attention,' she barked. Sita, who had heard this diatribe many times before, dutifully composed her face into one of rapt attention.

'There was virtually no one in court the king could trust. To his face, his courtiers were fawning and oily and unctuous. Behind his back, they were sharpening their knives. It was absolutely no different from Parliament today, come to think of it.' The Kumarihamy sighed. 'You know what we Sri Lankans are like.

'There had been many efforts to buy the treasurer over, because rebellions needed money—to buy guns, train men—and he had the keys to the treasury; but he remained steadfastly loyal to the king. On one of the king's walkabouts one day, a palm leaf from the *gok kola* decorations poked him in the eye. The king flew into a murderous rage. "Who was responsible for this?" he roared.

'All eyes turned towards the treasurer. Now this was plainly absurd. His department had paid for and was responsible for the decorations. But to blame him for the poke in the eye was like blaming him for a shower of rain. The treasurer knew his time was up. He packed his bags that very night and fled the kingdom.'

'So what happened next?' asked Sita breathlessly. (She had heard the story fifty times before.)

'The treasurer ended up settling in Dalugama, just beyond the jurisdiction of the king, where he built the Church of St Francis and generally lorded it over the hapless natives. The church still stands today, though they have butchered the façade with a sixties renovation. (I wonder if Beta and Bella had anything to do with that?) But inside it is still really rather lovely.'

'And then?'

'Well, the king found to his consternation that he had got rid of just about the only man in court he could trust. So he called him back, reinstating him with great pomp and ceremony. But by now the kingdom itself was well and truly on the way out, and it all went kaput quite soon thereafter. All those revolting nobles . . .'

The phone rang inside the house. Both women were lost in the past; it took them quite a while to realize that the phone was ringing in the present. Sita got up to answer it.

'Mahadewala Walauwa?'

'Can I speak to the Kumarihamy, please?' There was a fraction of a pause. 'Sita, is that you?' said the joyous voice at the other end.

'My lord?' She could hardly believe it was him.

'Fantastic to hear your voice! How's everything?'

She thought suddenly of all the things she had to tell him, all the things only he could help her with. But feudal custom dictated otherwise. 'Come home soon, my lord,' she whispered softly into the phone. 'I'll go get your mother for you.'

Back in the kitchen, she set about pouring the tea. Things had improved slightly for her with the unexpected return of Girigoris, whom she used as a buffer in her dealings with Pandu, trying never to be alone in the kitchen when he and Karuppayah were absent. She could not tell him, of course, for the same reason she could not go to the police. The end result would be the same: a life on the streets and, with a police record, no further hope of a job. As the laws of the country stood, theft from an important person, an important house, was a far greater crime than the rape of a maid.

I am not sorry I did it, she said defiantly to herself. 'Can you give Pandu this, please?' She handed the mug of tea to a somewhat puzzled Girigoris. 'I must take the Kumarihamy's tray.'

The Kumarihamy picked up the phone with trembling fingers. A call from her son could only mean bad news. She listened to the voice at the other end, saying nothing, breathing heavily.

'Pregnant?' she finally said, shocked. She had to sit down, the news was so momentous. 'How could you!' She thought of a brood of half-caste brats running barefoot around her feet in old age. What a way to end her days! The prospect depressed her immeasurably.

'So I want to bring Luisa out on a holiday.'

'Well, you can't. There's nowhere for you to sleep.'

'What have you done with my room?' Sonny asked, suspiciously.

The Kumarihamy thought quickly. 'Renovation work. It's full of building materials.'

'Ma, there are six bedrooms in the house. Don't tell me there isn't one for Luisa and me.'

'I'm not having that bally in my house.'

'You know what? It's not your house. Daddy left it to me.'

'Fine. If you want to throw an old woman out, go ahead. I'll go into an old people's home. Then you'll see how people will talk. God will *curse* you for what you have done! You see what happens to you.'

'OK, so shall I stay with Auntie Bella? Or Beta?'

There was a sharp intake of breath. '*What did you say?* Those bitches have been putting you up to this, haven't they? Always scheming behind my back to get the walauwa. They have charmed you, I know it! It's all right, throw me out. Bring them and the white bally into this house. Then you can all be happy together. I will walk the streets, begging, telling everyone what you have done to your mother.'

'Oh, Ma, stop being so melodramatic.'

'No, bring her. *Please*. I insist. But I'll leave the day she steps into this house, you hear me? See if I don't.'

'I'll call you once I've booked the tickets,' Sonny said, and rang off before the conversation could deteriorate any further.

The Kumarihamy looked at the vicious black instrument in her hand, now gone dead. It brought nothing but evil news.

Was there a devil inside it? How had her son learnt the art of tormenting his mother by sending demons down the line? She must get Father Rosario to exorcize it. But was Father Rosario equipped to deal with Bakelite?

She made her slow way out to the verandah, where Sita was waiting with the tea tray. 'They're coming,' she said. 'I don't think we can stop them this time.'

'You want me to fill up the hole?'

'Are you mad? Better to dig a hole in every bedroom! Though it won't help,' she continued despondently. 'He's threatening to go to Bella's. We can't have that.' She looked through the thickening light at the town, now garrulous in its daily death throes. 'What cannot be cured must be endured. Let them come. They'll get fed up and go back soon enough. Leave us in peace.'

'Do you think,' Sita asked hesitantly, 'do you think you're going to find any treasure?'

The Kumarihamy drew back, looking at her. 'Of course! What makes you think otherwise?'

'It's just that . . .' Sita hesitated. She was on dangerous ground here. 'How exactly do you know where under the house it might be, how deep? We might be digging forever.'

'If we have to dig every room, so be it!'

'The house might fall down.'

'Let the house fall,' said the Kumarihamy angrily. 'I need the money for my old age. Besides, how else do you think I can support the whole damned lot of you?'

∽

For the very first time since the rapes had begun, Sita actually felt a quickening of the senses, a solid reason to stay alive: a surge of blood running hot through her veins. Sonny was coming home!

'Someone's in a good mood, eh?' the old man called out.

'Sonny telephoned today,' she said, trying to keep her voice steady and even. 'He's coming back; bringing his *suddha* wife with him.'

The old man reached below his rattan bed and pulled out, from underneath, a flattened brown disc. 'Her Fucking Worship came here the other day, all high and mighty. Brought this fucking present for us.'

Sita looked at the kurakkan loaf, now dry and hard, a piece of modern sculpture somewhat beyond consumption. It looked suspiciously as if somebody had sat on it.

18

Every day I made special dishes: skate in black butter sauce and beef smore; moules marinière and blanquette de veau. I felt I was feeding some rare and precious animal nestling inside Luisa's stomach, one that had not yet deigned to show its face to us. I had become quite a competent cook, living cheek by jowl (oh, what a jowl!) with my literary heroine Rathu Catherine. It was this gourmet infant who had first got me interested in food: because the more cookbooks I read, the less time I need devote to writing. These were her recipes I was dishing up, starving literature to feed life. Rathu Catherine had competition now; I could see the poor girl getting progressively thinner on the pages of her book, ignored and sidelined but gamely marching on, for that was her way.

The flight was a good month away but Luisa had already packed, naturally. There would be plenty of unpacking and repacking before the month was up. I had not dared call my mother again; forewarned was forearmed and I did not want her arming the staff with muskets and pikes, fomenting rebellion up and down the mountainside in preparation for our arrival. An element of surprise was best. If I called her a week before we arrived, it would be enough.

I had not told Luisa about the blazing row I had had on the phone.

'How did your mother take our news?' she asked.

'Fine. Over the moon. She's told us to let her know once we have booked.'

'I must take her a gift. I wonder what she'd like?'

'I wouldn't bother. My mother is the most difficult person on earth to buy gifts for,' I couldn't refrain from warning her. 'She'll almost certainly recycle it. Having damned it with faint praise first, of course.'

'Never mind,' Luisa said. 'It's the thought that counts.'

∽

The Kumarihamy summoned Girigoris and Sita. 'As you may know, my son says he is arriving with his,' she coughed, 'his new wife. They have not told us exactly when they are coming—in about a month, he says. I for one do not believe him; and I certainly do not intend being caught on the hop. We must get to work straightaway. *Straightaway*, you understand? They can go into the Blue Room.'

'The Blue Room?'

'Don't look so surprised. It's the quietest room in the house. She won't be used to tropical noises and in her condition she'll need her sleep.'

The Blue Room was, in fact, the quietest room in the house. It was also the darkest and dingiest. Its particular crowning glory was its bathroom, situated in a sort of outhouse connected to the main building by an open walkway, in which resided a squatting pan. When the seated flushing water-closet had first arrived on Sri Lankan shores, it had met with severe resistance in traditional quarters. Sitting while shitting was reputed to be particularly unhealthy for you, squatting being the recommended way to go. There were three other perfectly normal bathrooms in the walauwa, but Clarice had staunchly resisted modernizing this one when the occasion arose.

'There are so many poor relations visiting at New Year,' she said. 'God only knows what I have to put up with every April. Them and their combs of bananas.' The Kumarihamy shuddered. She loathed bananas, particularly ones brought by poor relations as gifts, since they were sure to be charmed—all charmed fruit was promptly dispatched up the hill to Bella and Beta.

'The Blue Room is *perfect* for this type of person, its loo the perfect loo. I know for a fact they far prefer to squat. They would consider it an *insult* if they were made to sit.'

There was a particularly bittersweet irony to all of this. When Clarice and her husband had first been allowed back into the walauwa, this had been the room assigned to them. 'Let them squat,' the old Kumarihamy had said brutally, the way a lesser person might say 'Let them eat cake.' Clarice had endured a lifetime of squatting; there was no reason her daughter-in-law should not do the same, foreigner or not.

There were other, more subtle, delights in store for the young couple. The iron double bed in the room came with a coir mattress which housed a fair proportion of the bedbug population currently residing in Kandy. These were naturally friendly creatures—no guest, rich or poor, failed to end up on intimate terms with them—and certainly very sociable at night, so you never need feel lonely.

Sita knew and understood all this. She did not dare voice her concern.

That afternoon Karuppayah the cook was drunk again. Just as Sita was making the tea, Girigoris was summoned by the Kumarihamy. This left her alone in the kitchen. Mug in hand, she cautiously opened the kitchen door. Her tormentor was standing outside. 'Fuck the tea,' he said, pouring it away. 'You'd better come outside immediately before the old boy gets back.'

He liked to talk while he was on the job. These days a sort of tired sordid intimacy had sprung up between them, the way a kidnap victim becomes wearily familiar with her abductor.

'You'd better enjoy it,' she sneered. 'This might well be your last time.'

'And why would that be?'

'Sonny is coming back, that's why.'

'There is talk,' he said darkly, 'of you being given to me in marriage. That would be just perfect, wouldn't it? *Wouldn't it?* You'd be my bitch forever then. I would have you whenever and wherever I wanted. All perfectly legal.' He patted her rump as he finished, wiping himself on the edge of his sarong.

Oh, God, she prayed. Anything but that. Out loud she said, 'You've got a bloody hope. Sonny will kill you when he finds out what you're doing to me.'

Pandu laughed.

The forces of good and evil were gathering on the hillside, ranging themselves in rows against each other. It would be interesting to see who won.

∽

That evening, the blue Vespa puttered up the drive, coming to a stop at the foot of the verandah steps. Father Rosario, looking even more cinematic than usual, even more enigmatic, hurled himself up the steps and into the planter's chair next to the Kumarihamy.

'Good evening, Clarice. You said there was a bit of an emergency?'

'It's my son, Father. He'll be arriving any day now.'

'How happy you must be!'

'That's just the thing. I'm ashamed even to bring this up, but I need to ask you. Mothers and sons—must they always love each other?'

She poured the Father a glass of milk wine from the bottle. In the silver-grey fluorescent light of the verandah, it looked faintly radioactive. 'You know better than anyone what a good woman I am. How much I have helped the church over the years. The Legion of Mary, the Vincent de Paul Society, the Little Sisters of the Poor—I've been fleeced by all of them in my time. *Fleeced.* I have no more to give. No more money, certainly no more love.'

She took an unusually large gulp of wine, breathing noisily. It occurred to him that he had never seen her so flustered, so out of control.

'The thing is this, Father. How can someone as good as me have produced someone as bad as my son? I won't call him evil though I know that's what he is. How is it possible?' She wrung her hands helplessly. 'What have I done to deserve it? Was there some bad karma in my previous life? Did my father do anything to anyone?'

Father Rosario looked at her, saying nothing. He was probably the closest thing she had to a friend. How much of the cold truth could you tell a friend? 'It's a question of forgiveness, Clarice,' he said quietly. 'You have raged against the world for too long because you think it has always been against you. You need to find it in your heart to forgive. Particularly your son.'

'*Forgiveness*?' Clarice gave a snort. 'Don't make me laugh. Do you have any idea how much forgiveness I practise on a daily basis? Sita, for a start; then that old lecher her father; Girigoris; do you think any of them would have lasted even a second in a less forgiving home? Who else would forgive a drunken cook who's under the table every afternoon by three? But if you're foolish enough to think I'll forgive my son for marrying that white prostitute—' she clapped a hand over her mouth realizing what she had just said. 'I have nothing against white people, Father. Some of my best friends are white.'

'And some of my best friends are prostitutes,' Father Rosario nearly added. But you couldn't joke with the Kumarihamy, so instead, he smiled. 'I've lived here so long I don't consider myself white.' He changed the subject. 'How's the treasure hunt going?'

'That's another thing. Do you think I'm being crazy and fanciful imagining there's treasure underneath? Tell me I'm not mad!'

'Not mad, Clarice. A little greedy, perhaps?'

'No need to be rude, Father. If only you knew how much I deprive myself, you'd be shocked! I starve. I starve to give my son the best education the world has to offer. What does he do? He gives it up for a white p— lady. One year's money down the drain. Though, come to think of it, he hasn't asked me for any more. She must be rich. These fallen women usually are, aren't they, Father?'

Father Rosario finished his milk wine and got up. 'I must go. I've enjoyed our little chat.'

'Just one more thing, Father. Can you send demons by telephone?'

'Why? You'd like me to send you some?'

'Don't be flippant, Father. Every time Sonny calls I feel positively ill. I'm sure he's sending demons down the line. Can't you bless this phone for me?'

'There are no devils in your phone, Clarice. The only demons live at Sri Lanka Telecom. Pay your bills on time and you'll be all right. Now I really must be off.'

But as he rode down the hill, Father Rosario smelt it again, that whiff of sulphur in the night air—a wickedness, merely, but unmistakable, the scent of burning matches. It did not seem to have anything to do with Sonny.

19

The Kumarihamy had a troublesome night. Forgiveness? Who did they bloody think they were, asking her to forgive? Next thing you knew they would be asking her to forget! The Kumarihamy never did either. She never forgot how her sisters-in-law had treated her when she first came into the family, and forgiveness was not in her vocabulary. Towards the end, even her husband had gone over to the other side, blaming her for everything that went wrong in the marriage.

How hard she had tried—purely for his benefit!—to be the model Kandyan wife. It had not been easy taking over the reins from the old Kumarihamy—who had purposely not left her in possession of those state secrets vital for the running of this complicated inheritance. At times, she felt her mother-in-law was almost willing her to fail from beyond the grave. She had had to learn on the job with no help from a weak husband perfectly happy to let it all slide, as long as he had the peace and quiet to potter about; a husband who fondly assumed that everything would automatically fall into place if you left it alone.

No one but she knew at what great cost this Kandyanization of her self had been achieved, what she had had to give up to become this autocratic, iron-willed chatelaine. And how had he repaid her for this loyalty? He had, quite simply, fallen out of love: she was no longer the simple village girl he had married; she had disappointingly betrayed those principles of noble savagery he had crowned her with all those years ago in his naïve and enthusiastic young imagination. He had watched with horror through the years as his wife morphed into his mother, and then he had turned his back on her. That had been her reward.

Was it possible, then, that it was this deep-seated resentment of him she was projecting on to her son? Nonsense, she said to herself. You're talking nonsense, Clarice. Sonny's badness had been apparent from the very start; he and his demon-loving ways. Throughout his childhood he had taken every opportunity to ridicule her, as if the sarcastic jibes of her sisters-in-law weren't bad enough. And he always knew how to get to her, so that she would completely lose it with him, punishing him on these occasions far more severely than she had ever intended. Going abroad was supposed to cure him of all this wickedness; obviously it hadn't. Here he was, bringing a white demoness home. Clarice had better be careful around her. Who knew what arcane powers of stateside witchery she might be importing into the country, in the form of this new daughter-in-law?

There was, too, the question of the treasure. Are you sure you're going to find it, Sita had asked. How do you know where to dig? The fact was, she was a poor old woman with no one to help her. They were all only waiting to see her starving and destitute, begging up and down the mountainside. Perhaps Father Rosario could be coerced into pinpointing where exactly to dig. If he could find buried charms, why couldn't he find buried treasure? Wasn't it possible that the treasurer had charmed the loot before burial so no one else but he could get at it? On the subject of Father Rosario, Clarice had not liked the supercilious tone of his voice this evening. 'There are no devils in your phone, Clarice.' How the bloody hell did he know that? Who did he think he was talking to? Had he forgotten she was the Mahadewala Kumarihamy?

She turned over restlessly, her thoughts returning to the impending arrival. A fresh and rather daring notion struck her. Perhaps she might try being nice to the young couple? Something along the lines of, *Keep your angels close and your devils closer*? She began to think, with rather novel optimism, of her unborn grandchild. Perhaps it might not be pasty, after all—as so many mixed-race children were!—but, rather, possess a complexion of the palest Kandyan caramel? Nothing so brutally black as Sonny or Bella or Beta, obviously, more along the lines of her own skin colour? Upon this comforting thought, she fell into a deep and troubled sleep: peopled by the donkeys that served her at the walauwa, kicking and braying, and the demons that plagued, leaping and whirling in the firelight in a crazy chiaroscuro.

∽

'I think I'll get her a sari,' Luisa announced decisively. 'It will show her I'm not some dumb-assed Westerner unattuned to the unspoken subtleties of Eastern nuance.'

'Really?' I said. '*Really*?' She had obviously given this a lot of thought. Certainly, she had never used this many textbook words in a regular sentence before. 'I can take you to Tooting,' I offered, 'or even Southall. I hear there are very good saris there.'

She shook her head. 'I want to choose something I like. To reflect my own taste. John Lewis.'

'Oh,' I said, my heart sinking. I had spent many crushing hours in John Lewis while she shopped, pottering around the kitchenware department. It was vaguely preferable to spending quality time with Rathu Catherine—just.

We got there at nine thirty, just as the shop was opening. This is the way hardened veterans do it: in and out before the ravening hordes, an operation as precise as a surgical cut. She chose an exquisite Japanese silk in pale lilac, with a paler pattern of flowers and leaves, six yards of it for a sari. It cost her a small fortune.

'Never mind,' she said. 'It's your mother. She deserves it.'

'Really?' I thought again, though this time I did not say it. Just as were leaving the shop I asked her to hang on for a minute. I returned five minutes later with something that had caught my eye on the way in: a black silk handbag in the shape of a small flower basket, little black cloth flowers curling around its brim.

'For Sita,' I explained. I had mentioned Sita to her once or twice.

'You're getting that for a *maid*?'

'She's not just a maid. I told you, I grew up with her.'

'So what are you going to get the others?' She sounded a little combative, I thought.

'Haven't thought about it. Some shampoos perhaps?'

She shook her head in disbelief as we walked out. It was not like her to be in the slightest bit jealous; maybe it was the hormones. Throughout our relationship, I had always been taken to task for not being romantic. I won't bring you flowers, I always said. I'll tile your bathroom instead. So maybe it was the fact that I was buying presents for another woman, and with the first woman's money at that. She did not mention it again and back home I quickly stuffed the handbag into my suitcase.

Then, almost before we knew it, it was time to go. Just before we left for the airport I walked around the rooms of this tiny flat that had been our home for a year. I wanted to memorize its geography: as Columbus might have done with his Spanish city before setting sail for America.

We were off on an adventure into the deep unknown, embarking on a sea of consequences as wide as the Atlantic itself. It was the autumn of 2004 and who knew what was waiting to be discovered? Who knew what monsters lay in the depths?

20

I had been away from home for almost two years. So little had changed, at the same time so much. The paddy fields dipped in molten gold; the giant trees rearing their shaggy heads out of tiny domestic home gardens; trunks entwined by vines, their leaves the size of dinner plates; the aggressive botanical embarrassment of jungle-green riches. All this remained the same despite man's best efforts to ruin it—with half-built roadside shacks of raw cement blocks, and glassed aluminium wedding halls barely complete, already corroded.

I watched Luisa surreptitiously as we travelled up to Kandy in a hideously creaking van, our suitcases free-range and mobile, clashing amicably with the spare tyre every once in a while in the vast rear space of this vehicle. In every country so far I had encountered a different Luisa. Who would I find in Sri Lanka? She sat silently, observing the landscape through the open window, while I struggled not to say anything, knowing only too well that the more I praised the country, the less likely she would be to share my enthusiasm.

Sri Lanka affects each person differently. It catches you unawares and sometimes—no, frequently—you only realize its hold on you once you have left. I know so many people who have hated the country (or loved to hate it) while they were here: who only realize they cannot live without it once it is too late and they are gone. It is like a difficult and dangerous woman who repels you with her indifference and drives you mad with her unreasonableness: a woman whose insane logic only becomes clear to you with the separation of time and space. In fact, when I come to think of it, she is rather like my mother.

The van driver was struck dumb by Luisa. He kept looking at her, then at me, sizing up the grave discord of this mismatch. In brutal shorthand, what was this creature, flawless and nonpareil, doing with this ugly demon? Several times he actually turned around, then turned back to the wheel, shaking his head in disbelief. I felt like tapping him on the shoulder to say, Shut the fuck up and drive, that's what I'm paying you for. Of course I didn't, because I didn't want Luisa to be reminded of the unreasonable bastard I really was. It all finally worked out in my favour, however. Halfway through the journey, somewhere around Kegalle I think, the driver decided that I must have undisclosed assets—an extra million? an extra inch? who knew?—and I could see him sneak glances at me with new-found respect. Who was I to disabuse him of this notion?

I was soon to find out that all over Sri Lanka it was the same: a white wife gave you infinite cachet, she was the ultimate fashion accessory. Local men looked at you with undisguised admiration wherever you went, local women with undisguised disappointment. But as the van finally—after four bone-shaking, toe-curling hours—turned left at the Kandy police station and began its hyperventilating stagger up the mountainside, I reminded myself that the acid test was yet to come: my mother.

On the morning of the arrival, the Kumarihamy woke up feeling quite bullish. She rang the bell. 'Tell Pandu to have the car ready, I want to go for a drive after breakfast.'

'It's morning,' Sita reminded her. 'You never go for a drive in the morning.'

'So?'

'Won't people talk? Won't they realize something's up? I thought you wanted to keep Sonny's arrival quiet.'

The Kumarihamy was reluctantly forced to agree. She had wanted to be away when the couple arrived, to demonstrate that she too had a feverish and dazzling social life; that her existence did not revolve around their arrival. Ah well, never mind, she would stay put and attempt to be feverish and dazzling in a stationary sort of way, on the verandah of her house.

As it happened, she had just popped inside to inspect the dig when the van juddered and creaked to a stop at the verandah steps. Clarice returned to find a small foreign girl—really she must have been five foot nothing!—struggling to take an enormous suitcase out of the van, watched with interest by two men, her son and the van driver, neither of whom was attempting to help. The van driver looked defensive in his indolence. It was his job to drive, not to go humping other people's luggage around. They had hands, didn't they?

'Stop that at once!' Clarice called out to the girl. 'There are people to do that sort of thing.' She rang the bell. 'Girigoris!'

She turned to her son. 'So you're back?'

'Ma, I'd like you to meet Luisa.'

'Come here, let me take a good look at you.' There was silence for a long moment, while everyone held their breath. Then, against all expectation, Clarice beamed. 'You'll do very nicely,' she said, 'very nicely indeed. Come inside out of the heat.'

The girl (Clarice found it almost impossible to pronounce that brain-scrambling phrase *daughter-in-law*) was far smaller and better formed than she had been led to expect foreigners could ever be. Her experience of foreigners had consisted mostly of Italian clerics, and no women, but she had seen plenty of foreign actresses on TV. Big-boned and gauche, that's what they usually were, weren't they? But this one was different! Things were looking up.

'Have something to drink,' she commanded. 'Tea? Coffee? A soft drink?'

Luisa hesitated.

'Quite right!' said Clarice quickly. 'I don't eat or drink between meals either. That's how you get *diabetes*.' She looked meaningfully at Sita, who had materialized at her elbow.

'Sita!' said Sonny, beaming.

'My lord.' She stood there, speechless.

'Don't just stand there gawping,' Clarice burst out. 'Go help Girigoris with the suitcases. By the way, which room have you put them in?'

Sita looked at her mistress puzzled. 'The Blue Room, of course. You—'

'Are you mad? Move them at once! Move them into the Calamander Room.'

'But it's not swept. And the sheets?'

'Sweep it!' screeched the Kumarihamy jovially. 'Sweep, sweep! There's a good girl.' She turned to her daughter-in-law with a smile as warm and all-embracing as a shark's. 'Really, these servants. You tell them one thing, they go ahead and do something completely different. Of course, in this case, there *may* be a reason.'

She gave Luisa a roguish wink. 'She might be a teensy-weensy bit jealous of you, my dear. She's always had a soft spot for our Sonny here.'

'Oh, Ma, don't be ridiculous. You're exaggerating as usual.'

'Ah, but you see, I *know*. A mother always *knows*, you see. And you too will find that out soon enough!' She gave Luisa a little pat on the stomach.

It took Sita and Girigoris the greater part of the morning to get the Calamander Room ready. I wondered what had originally possessed Sita to give us the worst room in the house but it was not in my position to ask: two years away and I was already something of a stranger. The suitcases were still in the hall. Fishing about, Luisa pulled out the sari.

'I hope you like it,' she said.

'Is this for me?' my mother asked, innocent and wide-eyed, almost an injured tone to her voice. 'Oh, I couldn't possibly wear *that*. It's pink! I'm a widow, my dear. What would people say?'

'They'd say you were the prettiest widow in town,' I interjected.

'Sonny, don't be flippant. No. Take it back. Return it. It's too young for the likes of me.'

'Auntie, please. You'll hurt my feelings.'

'I feel I know you well enough already, dear, to tell you the truth; it's the truth that's important, never mind the feelings.'

Take it! I wanted to shout. Put the poor girl out of her misery. Of course I didn't say anything. I had known all along what my mother's reaction would be. Finally she took it, reluctantly, with dire warnings that it would only lie in the back of the almirah, a ready meal for silver fish, and really, weren't we better off exchanging it for ready money?

As if to make up for this shameful slip-up on our part, my mother outdid herself at lunch. There was boiled fish and boiled vegetables swimming in clear tepid water. For added refinement Karuppayah had produced a bottle of tomato ketchup, placed reverently on the table next to the dead, floating fish.

'He can really dish up the goods when he wants to, can't he!' my mother said admiringly.

'Where's my yellow rice and chicken curry?' I asked, appalled.

'Really, Sonny, have you no respect for our foreign guest? Hasn't it even occurred to you that she might not be able to take spicy food?'

'Oh, I eat anything,' Luisa said. 'Sonny cooks curries for me in London. Once you've eaten his food you can eat anything.'

I kicked her under the table.

'Is that so?' My mother looked suspiciously at me. 'Perhaps then tomorrow we can inflict our local cuisine on you?'

For dessert there was a boiled pudding accompanied by a rather starchy custard. Conversation became difficult at this point, because our tongues were getting stuck to our upper palates. 'You know,' said my mother with a supreme exercise of her jaws, 'you're really not so bad for a white person?'

'You're not so bad yourself,' said Luisa giggling, 'for a Sri Lankan.'

I kept quiet. My mother being cordial? What was she up to?

My mother reached out a scrawny hand and grabbed Luisa's olive-brown wrist. 'See, we're almost the same colour.' She cackled. 'You could almost be Kandyan! In fact . . . we could be sisters!'

'I think I rather like your mother,' Luisa said back in the room. 'I don't know what all the fuss was about.'

'Don't you? I didn't expect her to be so welcoming. She's up to something, I wouldn't trust all this lovey-dovey stuff.'

'That's your trouble. You're suspicious of everyone and everything. But for God's sake, your own mother? There must be something deeply wrong with you. I never met a son before who didn't like his mother. Actually I don't know what I'm doing with you.'

I grinned. 'Nor do I. But trust me on this. I can smell good and bad. There's a bit of a bad smell here.'

'You're weird, you know that?'

Sadly, I was forced to agree.

There was one thing of supreme importance here: it was not my mother, nor Sri Lanka, nor even our marriage. It was the baby. I had made a mistake once, and I was not going to repeat it. I felt a deep tenderness towards this woman who was going to be the mother of my child. My job was to protect it and her, even if it meant sacrificing her good opinion of me. There were depths and levels here she would never fathom, not even after a lifetime. My job was to row her across safely, and please God may she never have to look over the side of the boat.

The Kumarihamy went to bed that night with a strange sense of wonder. She could not figure out what had come over her. Having started out with an intense and pre-programmed antipathy towards her new daughter-in-law, she had unaccountably turned into a maudlin mush upon meeting her. She was now beginning to feel rather ashamed of her behaviour at lunchtime. She recognized that, like her son, she was extremely susceptible to beauty. Was it this that made it easy for her to forgive this girl the unpardonable sin of being born white? Was it not clear, after all, that she had been brought here to drive the Kumarihamy out of the house, so she would end up a pauper on the streets? Why then was she, Clarice, being so good and noble about it all?

The Kumarihamy recognized that it was tough being wicked all the time—but someone had to do it. If wickedness and evil did not exist, you would be forced to invent them, if only to highlight and burnish that much duller alternative, the concept of good. Good without evil was like day without night; in other words, no day at all. Where would we all end up if we went round drooling goodwill at each other out of the corners of our mouths?

Nevertheless, this sudden and unexpected frisson of benevolence made her tingle all over, right to the ends of her extremities. Perhaps it was not goodwill, after all, but diabetes. She had better call that ass Dr Dep in the morning.

21

Looking back upon my early life, I realize that I had the strangest of upbringings. There are plenty of people brought up by single or widowed mothers, but none so thoroughly put down and ridiculed at every turn as I was, in the medieval boot-camp of my childhood. Nothing I did was good enough for my mother—neither my academic achievements nor my sporting victories. This would have been enough to crush the spirit of any child, but with me it had the opposite effect. I was like the mouse to my mother's cartoon cat. And like that mouse, I always managed to outwit her.

'You little imp, you bloody devil!' she would scream as she chased me round the house, and I would laugh and stick my little red tongue out at her, shaking my wayward locks. I had long ago realized that I had neither the strength nor the cunning to match hers. What I had instead was a quicksilver wit, which I used to great effect against her. Like many strong opinionated people, my mother had no sense of humour, and nothing annoyed her more than being the butt of someone else's joke.

Yet that first day back I sensed that something had changed, that the balance of power had tilted in some subtle way. Was it because I had got stronger and she realized it? Or was all this lovey-dovey business towards my wife only a way of lulling me into a false sense of security, before she flattened me with a final comic-book wallop? These thoughts kept going round and round in my head as I tossed and turned that first jet-lagged and sleepless night. At last, in the early hours of the morning, I gave up. I crept out of the room and down the arched passage, high and narrow, through a kitchen courtyard touched now with the gentle opalescent colours of dawn: muted grey and shimmering pearl and the softest of mauves.

This was the route I had taken every morning of my life, growing up. I could hear Karuppayah in the back kitchen, blowing on the kindling, setting it alight in preparation for the lunchtime pot of rice. (In Sri Lanka, the rice is unfailingly cooked first thing in the morning so it can be guaranteed to arrive stone cold at the lunch table.) The front kitchen was its usual tranquil best at this hour. Though I had seen it a thousand times before, I saw it now through foreign eyes: the pale medicinal green of its walls, the striated grey cement floors, the yellowing white of its corrupt woodwork. My mother would have considered it gloriously extravagant to paint it more than once every twenty years, so I could still see the brown patch on the wall where Karuppayah had hurled his slipper at an errant cockroach. This was from at least ten years ago. He must have been suffering from an unusual and startling fit of sobriety at the time.

My mother was down to four servants at the walauwa, and as far as she was concerned this was living in an abject state of penury. There had been seventeen in my grandmother's time though I could swear the place had been no cleaner then. The seventeen were there not so much to serve as to show the world you had them, in any case: appearance was everything in this mad, medieval masque we played in Sri Lanka, the complicated and glittering procession of life.

Sita was at the kitchen table all alone, eating breakfast. She stood up when she saw me. 'My lord?'

'Please sit down. And you don't have to my lord me. "Sonny" is good enough.'

She smiled. 'Your mother would kill me.'

'Don't let her catch you, then. But when she's not around, I am Sonny, you understand? Anyway don't move, I have something for you.'

I sped back through the silent house to our bedroom. The animal smell of sleep hung over it. Luisa lay motionless under the bedcovers, gentle hand across a belly which was softly swelling, finally beginning to show.

Rooting about in my suitcase, I pulled out the handbag. When I came back to the kitchen, Sita was making my coffee. 'This is for you.'

She said nothing, but her gasp of pleasure was reward enough. 'Hide it,' I said, 'and take it back home. My mother would not only kill you but crucify you afterwards if she saw you with it. I hope you can use it when you go out.'

'Go out?' She looked at me amused. 'You have no idea about my life, do you?'

'Tell me,' I said sitting down. 'I want to know.'

She shook her head. At that moment, there came over her face an ineffable look of sadness that made me want to hug her, but I realized with regret just where I was, just who I was: no longer the child trying to hug the kitchen maid but a grown-up man with a pregnant wife in tow. In addition, I had this taint of feudalism upon me like the mark of Cain, weighting any move I made with an unwarranted significance, a false silver-mark stamped to the base of my every action. I took my coffee and returned to my room.

When he left, she thought: Why didn't I tell him? It had been the perfect opportunity—they had both been in the kitchen alone, unlikely to be disturbed. She realized that it was shyness and reticence that had kept her quiet—the silent worry that every rape victim must face, that the world, if they knew, would think them lesser beings, soiled goods. It had happened; she could not undo it, and she had come to terms with it in her own way, so why not let it be where it was, unknown to any but herself and her rapist? But the nightmare was not over, that was the problem. Would there ever be an end unless she told somebody? Was it enough to put a sticking plaster over a weeping sore and pretend it wasn't there?

It was also that everything had changed. Sonny was no longer the slightly puzzled child packed off to university by an unfeeling mother, gaining thereby the sympathy of everyone in the servants' quarters. He was a grown man about to become a father. And she? She felt old beyond her years. It was time now for the grave or the nunnery, because she was beyond help. She and he, they had each covered half a lifetime in those two years of separation: it so happened that each had covered a different half, so there was now an ocean between them in every sense.

Wearily she picked up the broom, the mop and duster, and prepared for her daily assault on the drawing room.

∽

The Devil was in a state of acute crisis. As he was the Devil, the very embodiment of evil, it was actually in his nature to be bad, much as it was in the serpent's nature to sting or the kangaroo's to hop. In other words, he had no choice in the matter, no free will. How could you then blame him for this badness? Could you blame a kangaroo for hopping if it had no choice in the matter? Could you not then take this a step further and say that by fulfilling his destiny of badness he was in fact being true to himself and therefore rather good? That the worse he could make himself, the better he was? Surely the only way he could be classified as genuinely bad would be if he committed his evil having consciously rejected the good option. Sometimes, when he was feeling devilish (as he now was), the Devil longed to commit a good deed: that would shock them into a new respect for him! That was the trouble nowadays. Nobody gave you respect if you went around causing mayhem when they fully expected you to cause mayhem. 'Ah, that'll just be the Devil,' they said, 'don't mind him, he can't help himself.' If on the other hand there was a certain malice aforethought to your actions, then you really were a star, and people sat up in admiration saying, 'Oh, that Devil, he's good; he's *really* good.' (Meaning of course, he's bad, he's *really* bad.)

The Devil shook his head despondently. He badly needed a little free will in his life. It was all very complicated theologically. One day, he resolved, I will think this thing through, I promise. Till then, I just have to muddle along in this morally wishy-washy manner.

These musings were interrupted by a strange being coming round the hill towards him with five—no, four!—heads. There seemed to be space on his neck for a fifth, which was missing. He had extremely crooked and yellowing fingernails, and was certainly no oil painting. Was he French?

'Bonjour,' said the Devil.

'Oh, shut up!' said the apparition.

'Who are you and why must you be so rude at this ungodly hour of the morning?'

'Don't you know who I am? I am the demon Bhairava, Lord of All Evil!' it roared. 'I own this mountain, the Bhairava Kanda. All who live on it must pay me obeisance. On your knees, you vile specimen of goat!'

'Sorry old boy, can't curtsy. My joints, you see,' the Devil explained apologetically. 'Arthritis. As for you being the Lord of all Blah Blah Blah,' he coughed delicately, 'I do believe in fact that it is *I* who have the monopoly. Read all about it in the Old Testament. It's in there if you doubt me.'

'Old Testament? Fiddlesticks! My bloodlines go back much, *much* further,' thundered the apparition. 'I'm in the Vedas, you cloven-hooved hobgoblin!'

Touchy, thought the Devil. These Eastern potentates can be mighty touchy, and this one seems to have lost his head completely, even if he has four more.

'Well, it's been really delightful,' he said out loud, 'but I simply can't stay here nattering all day. I have a *tremendous* amount of evil to get through before lunch. How it all piles up when you're away from the desk!' He twirled his cape prior to departure. 'Oh, and by the way, a nail spa.'

'Nail spa?'

'I would highly recommend it. It'll work wonders on those *disgusting* digits of yours.'

∽

Luisa had cajoled two months' leave of absence from work. This is what rich girls did. She was in any case one of the best trainers at the business school: those bellied grey men from Hamburg and Zurich responded more enthusiastically to her sleek and soignée presence than to the socialistic beards that constituted the norm among the rest of the staff. She could have taught them anything from tap dancing to nude yoga. (Particularly nude yoga, I think.)

It was amazing how in Sri Lanka too she swept all before her, taking command effortlessly of the mountainside: Girigoris, Pandu, even Karuppayah, all fell at her feet. My mother was a melting Motha's jelly in her presence, acquiescing to her every wish with a very un-Kumarihamyesque cringe. It was Luisa this and Luisa that, all over the walauwa. The hills were very much alive with the sound of her music. It got to the stage where my mother was even attempting to be nice to *me*, in an awkward, wooden sort of way.

It made me think again how easy it was for beauty; how much harder it is for us ugly people to cover the same distance. I was not bitter, not exactly: she was mine and I was as much a beneficiary of this beauty-fuelled mileage as she was. But still.

That afternoon I took Luisa all over the mountainside to show her my petty fiefdom. I pointed out the little shack of mangowood planks. 'That's where my other grandfather lived. Where my mother was born.'

'Your mother?' Luisa was astonished.

'I wanted to show you that there's this whole other side to me, non-feudal, very ordinary.' I grinned. 'In case you get ideas above your station.'

'So who lives here now?'

'My mother gave it to Sita and her father to live in.'

'The servant woman?'

'The maid,' I said, patiently correcting her. It was funny how the word 'servant' sounded perfectly all right when my mother said it—she was a Sri Lankan of a particular age and background—but turned ugly on Luisa's lips. As for me, after two years in the West I found myself exactly halfway between the words 'maid' and 'servant'.

'I'm *so* sorry,' Luisa said with mock gravity. 'I see I've offended your democratic sentiments.'

It was not like Luisa to be sarcastic. I let it pass without comment.

There was a shiny padlock on the door to the shack. 'I think Sita's father must be out,' I said. At that moment the old man came round the corner, jauntily swinging a bottle of local moonshine, kassipu, in either hand. He stopped short when he saw Luisa, who promptly gave him the widest, most brilliant smile in her repertoire.

We had been told at great length how sick he was with diabetes. He looked neither bedridden nor diabetic, just drunk.

'I found work,' he said, swaying. 'Building site near the police station. Daily paid.' He gave me a cunning look. 'You won't tell Sita, will you?'

Here he was, earning himself a tidy little sum on the side secretly for his drink, while Sita slogged her guts out at the walauwa to keep him in medicines and food. Again it was not in my position to comment, so I kept silent.

'Drink is good for diabetes,' he said aggressively, challenging me to contradict him. 'Didn't you know?'

He turned his attention to Luisa. 'So this is the new Kumarihamy, eh?' He let off a delicate burp and giggled. 'Fine. Very fine indeed.' Attempting to make a deep bow, he gently toppled over, a position from which he made no attempt to rise, lying on the ground and looking up at her with an inebriated leer on his face.

'You'd better get inside before Sita finds you,' I said shortly.

'What a charming man,' Luisa said as I bundled her away. 'I think I see now where the daughter gets it from.'

22

This Kandyan family lovefest nearly ended in tears that first week. Lulled into complacency by how well my mother was getting along with my wife, I had been wanting to show Luisa my old room but it was inexplicably locked every time I tried the door. The teak double doors were panelled below and glazed above, the small panes of pre-War frosted glass opaque as sugar crystals, held together by the most delicate mullions and transoms. I could see nothing through them. I shook the doors but they did not budge.

'The Kumarihamy's instructions,' was Girigoris's reply when I asked.

'Please go and get the key. I want to show my wife the room. You can close it up after that if you like.'

After a long delay he came back with the brass key. I had a heart attack when he opened the door.

The entire floor was dug up, every side, right up to the walls. It was a wonder that these had not caved in. My treasured posters, my little bedside bookcase, the bed itself—there was nothing. Where had she put them? It struck me then how so much of the reality we create, our understanding of volume and space, is defined by how we distort it: filling it with objects we love, controlling the way we light it, the subtle odours that permeate it. All were gone from this room. In their place an absence of meaning, an unreadable void, the death of memory; and the dark miasma of a more ancient presence, silent and unforgiving. I could see that it was way too late to put it all back. Even if everything were returned, I would always know now what lay beneath. Knowledge once learnt can never be unlearnt. The room was ruined.

My mother had followed Girigoris back. 'How could you!' I cried.

She gave a crooked, sugary smile and covered her mouth with her hand, like a convent girl embarrassed at a midnight feast with too many cream cakes. 'I'll put it all back if that's what you want.'

'It's too late for that. What makes you think you're going to find anything? Are you going to keep digging till the walls come down?'

'Of course not!' My mother looked horrified at this idea. 'I'll put all the earth back before I move on to the next room.'

'Just keep going. Little by little you'll destroy the entire house.'

'You're beginning to sound just like your father!' she exclaimed angrily. 'I've spent all my money on you. Can't you see how important this treasure is to us? Just who do you think it's for? Am I going to take it with me when I die?'

At this point Luisa intervened before it could get any more acrimonious. 'As long as your mother lives in this house she has every right to dig where she wants. Don't you think that's fair?'

'That's right,' I said bitterly, 'gang up on me, all of you!'

My mother's eyes shone with emotion. 'Thank you,' she said to Luisa. 'I knew I could count on you.'

∽

'That's right,' I repeated when we were back in our room. 'Take her side, she's your new best friend, now, isn't she?'

Luisa gripped my arms and looked imploringly into my eyes. 'Sonny, when will you learn? She is not the enemy here. Can't you get that into that thick skull of yours?'

'Don't kid yourself,' I said fiercely. 'She doesn't want us here. She certainly doesn't want you. She can't wait to see the back of us so she can take control again.'

'And so she should. It's her house, after all.'

'Actually, no, it's not. My father left it to me.'

Luisa's eyes narrowed in amusement. 'Yeah, right. I can just picture you here, walking round the property every day in your sarong, inspecting the roof, screaming at the servants when things aren't done right. And while we're at it, maybe I can wear a sari, just like your mother.'

'You don't have to be so cynical.'

'Why can't you admit the truth to yourself? We will never come back here. Yes, for a holiday, maybe, but not to live.'

'Won't we?' I was stung by her answer, mortally offended. How could she even begin to think I would not want to return?

Luisa laughed. 'What? To this damp old house? You're joking, right?'

I remained silent. It struck me then how like every other Sri Lankan I was turning out to be. There is this unspoken assumption in the heart of every one of us that we will return to the home country one day. Even second- and third-generation expatriates who are not born here and have never even seen the place carry the gene, corroded and defective and deadly: a sleeper cell that activates unbidden at some point of our life when we least expect it.

The fact that Luisa was unaware of this new me was my fault entirely: till now I had disparaged so thoroughly everything in my past that I could hardly blame her for this deeply cynical attitude she was displaying, however hurtful it might be.

∽

Sita placed the early morning tray on the little bedside table and drew back the curtains. It had rained last night, and through the windows of the Calamander Room she could see a smoky, damp haze, curling like fine strips of paper here and there on the hillside. The figure in the bed stirred a little and opened her eyes. Sita's English was halting at the best of times but she could manage a few words. 'You want anything else?'

Luisa slowly sat up in bed. 'No,' she said. 'That'll be all.' There was no smile, no thank you.

She sees me as the maid, Sita thought matter-of-factly—without blame or recrimination. I am just the hand that feeds them, invisible the rest of the time. She was momentarily suffused by an unexpected glow of fondness for the Kumarihamy, who bit that hand frequently—and bit it hard—

but who at least took the trouble to bite it. Sita lingered by the side of the bed, smiling uncertainly. No, I won't blame her, she thought again. Probably I would do the same if I were in her shoes and she in mine. Yet she so wanted to sit on the bed and seize the other girl's hand. I'm a woman too, she wanted to say. Look at me! My lustrous hair, my long eyes. The sort of eyes they used to write poems about in the old days. I am in trouble. Tell me what to do. I badly need your advice.

'That'll be all,' Luisa repeated. There was a brief smile that vanished as quick as it came, like the click of a camera.

Sita left the room hesitantly.

She had imagined her misery-drenched life would improve dramatically with the arrival of Sonny, but she had been proved wrong. She could see how beautiful his wife was, how well she managed her difficult mother-in-law. She had a genuine admiration for this foreign girl and wanted to tell her so, but there was never any opportunity. The young couple was always out and about—encouraged by the Kumarihamy who, having got accustomed to having the house to herself these past two years, was more than happy to send them off on pointless excursions.

'Only one thing I would ask of you,' she said rather dramatically, breathing hard, hand on chest. '*Please*. No going up to Bella or Beta, you hear me? It's a matter of life and death. I'm not joking. They will put a *curse* on you and your baby. No, it's not funny, don't laugh. It's very common out here. We specialize in charms, we Sri Lankans.'

'Peace at last,' she would say to Sita once they were gone on yet another useless errand. 'Relax, my girl, we have the whole day to ourselves.'

And Sita would pray grimly: *Please come back, I'm not safe in this house alone.* Because the horror continued, the most dangerous time being those dead hours between lunch and tea when the whole house slept.

'It's really changed your life, hasn't it, now that the stupid little fucker's back? He's really brilliant at protecting you, isn't he?' Pandu whispered as he dragged her by the wrist.

'Where are you taking me?' she asked in a low voice.

'Shut up and enjoy the ride, bitch.'

The kitchens were not safe any more; there was a series of disused storerooms at one end of the kitchen quarters. Opening the door to one, he pushed her on to a heap of gunny sacks.

'Give us this day our daily rape,' she prayed and was immediately shocked at the blasphemy of her thought, and its coarseness. She seemed to have demoted herself to his level, degraded herself to no better than a piece of meat. To understand is to forgive, they said. Hatred ceases not with hatred, but with love. She had got to that dangerous point where she almost did not hate him any more. I must not let that happen, she thought. I must take a hold of myself and keep my disgust and despair alive. Hate must be the juice that flows in my veins, the fuel that fires my engine. Rat poison. But I must be careful to make sure I'm far away when it happens.

The Kumarihamy rang Father Rosario for her weekly chat.

'I called to give you the fantastic news, Father. There are no demons in this phone!'

'Really? I think I hear one now.'

'What did you say, Father?'

'I said, "I live in the here and now."'

'Is that so? I'll take your word for it.'

'Did your children arrive, Clarice?'

'Oh, yes! She's fabulous, Father. Guess what? She's Italian!'

'No, really? What a coincidence! So, was there anything in particular you wanted to ask me about?'

'Now that you mention it, yes. Will you exorcize the house, Father? You see, it occurs to me that any buried treasure must have a curse on it. Doesn't that stand to reason? So if you can just run your hand over these rooms with a little bit of light prayer, you might get a feel for where the charm is buried and *bingo!* we have our treasure! Brilliant, no?'

'Clever. But I told you. I don't do these things for fun or monetary gain.'

'Ten per cent of all findings to the Church? Gold vestments for everyone at the seminary, including gardeners and cooks?'

'This is no laughing matter, Clarice. It's for the protection of your soul.'

'Exorcizing is good for you, Father.'

'Very funny, Clarice.'

'So you won't have any objection to my digging up all of the Blue Room, then?'

'Dig away, Clarice. It's your own grave you're digging.'

'That's mean of you, Father. Very mean. By the way, you know how you always say faith can move mountains? Well, it's not faith moving this mountain. It's Girigoris.' Cackling, the Kumarihamy put the phone down.

23

I woke next morning to a commotion on the verandah.

'Tell him to come out, I know he's in there. Tell him I just want to have a look at the Baby Lord.'

I recognized Jane Nona's bass voice. Sighing, I put on some clothes and went out on the verandah to show myself. I knew she would not leave till there was a sighting. She probably had strict instructions from Beta not to return without first-hand information.

Jane Nona, with her iron-grey hair cut short, kitted out in sarong and T-shirt, was part of Auntie Beta's household. Long ago my Kandyan grandmother had adopted six girls from the convent that lay just below the walauwa premises, whose lands had been donated to them by my great-grandfather at some point past. The status of these six girls was curious: they were not exactly servants, nor were they family. They did not eat at table, for instance, but they were given precedence in the servants' quarters. When they got to a certain age, they were given in marriage to suitable boys and sent out into the big bad world. Were these adoptions an act of charity on my grandmother's part or just slave labour? I could never decide.

Jane was the last of the six, and had steadfastly refused to get married. In another life—another world, I thought sadly—she would have had a female partner. As it was, she had to content herself with lording it over the weak specimen of hapless male usually to be found in Beta's household, pinching them with her stubby nicotine-stained fingers when they refused to cooperate.

'Ah, Baby Lord! Stand right there in the sun so I can take a good look at you.'

This crazy nomenclature irked me. Growing up as a junior member of a walauwa household meant you usually ended up with a diminutive, like Little Lord or Baby Lady, a name which stuck with you for the rest of your life. All over Sri Lanka there were octogenarians who were still called Teeny-Tiny Lady or Miniscule Lord at home—and my father, when he was young, had been called the Good Lord, which I think wins the prize.

'Are you happy now, Jane Nona?' I called out. 'Seen enough to satisfy you?'

'You have fulfilled my heart's desire,' she growled. 'Oh, I have brought you a present from the mistress.' She brandished aloft two pineapples like grenades. 'And I have been instructed to invite you and your, erm, friend, for lunch.'

'Oh dear, we're off on a trip today.'

'Tomorrow then?'

'I'll check with my mother and give you a date.'

'Ha, that'll be the day!' she said with a snort. Turning on her heel, she strode away in disgust.

My mother, who had been lurking in the shadows of the drawing room, charged out on her walker into the sunlight. 'Put them down!' she screeched.

'Put what down?'

'The pineapples, you fool! Can't you see they're charmed?'

'They look perfectly all right to me.'

'Of course they would. That's the whole point. Put them on the ground at once.'

My mother prowled around them like a lioness around a zebra. The pineapples just lay there, looking prickly but not very fierce.

Sita came out to see what the fuss was about. 'You take them,' my mother ordered her. 'Give them to your father. I'm sure they're good for diabetes.'

'Didn't you say they were charmed?'

'Idiot girl! Don't you know anything about spells? They only work on the person they're intended for. They're perfectly safe for anyone else.'

'Then why don't *you* eat them?'

This was going too far. My mother flung her a look and wheeled herself back inside. 'I don't care what you do. Just get them off my land. Burn them if you have to.'

My mother was dispatching Luisa and me on a day trip that morning to see three historic temples close to Kandy—Embekke, Gadaladeniya and Lankatilleke. The cook had packed us a picnic, boiled eggs and sandwiches—tinned fish mashed in ketchup (extremely good in a ghastly sort of way)—and bottled ginger beer. Pandu had brought the car round to the front. There remained just one thing: for Luisa to wake up.

Things had not been so rosy between us lately, mainly because neither of us was getting much sleep. The house was full of night-time noises—the creak and groan of the great roof timbers settling for the night, the sibilant hiss and rustle of winged creatures—none of which I remembered from the past. Once I even thought I heard the piano being played. In the early hours, just as we were dropping off, the birds began. Whoever called it the dawn chorus has plainly never come across Sri Lankan birds. At times I longed for a shotgun.

On top of this was the fact that the sex had tapered off dramatically. This is a problem endemic to marriage, I am given to understand, as the years go by. We ourselves had just begun to downsize, so to speak. Perhaps it was all to do with the hormonal changes during pregnancy everyone banged on about, though this was only partly the reason, it seemed. Under my very eyes Luisa was changing into yet another woman, even if I had anticipated it, this time one who was opinionated and waspish, less tolerant, less understanding. If America had brought out the old-world cynic, in Asia she was realizing hitherto undisclosed deposits of savagery. Could one woman hold with equanimity so many contrary qualities? I marvelled at the complexity of this being who had become my wife.

It was mid-morning before we set off.

'First I show you Queen's Hotel,' Pandu said. For reasons of his own he had decided to speak only in English. Since his English was fractured and idiosyncratic, it made life rather difficult for all of us. 'British hotel,' he added for Luisa's benefit. Of all the household staff, I knew Pandu least well. He was only a little older than me, having arrived at the walauwa in his late teens, a year or two before I had made my escape. I could see he was wary of me, though at the same time determined not to be cowed. He was the only one who did not my-lord me, using instead an obsequious 'sir' which bordered on sarcasm, though in front of my mother he took great care to behave himself.

'I think we'll go straight to the temples before it gets too hot,' I countered.

'Queen's Hotel cool. Lemonade. Ginger beer. Swimming fool.'

Employing a driver is always a mixed blessing in Sri Lanka. All too often you end up doing what they want out of a misplaced sense of guilt and charitability. I was determined to put my foot down this time. 'The temples,' I ordered.

'Oh, let's go to Queen's,' Luisa said, in her new-found spirit of contrariness. 'I'm already a little bored at the thought of temples.'

Pandu brought the car to a stop outside the pink arcade of shops at Queen's. 'Shop,' he said. (Whether this was a verb or noun I could not gather.) 'Antique. Jewellery.'

At that last word Luisa gave a little squeal of delight and rushed inside. I groaned silently. Then I thought: this trip was for her benefit; if she was happy shopping for the next two hours, who was I to complain?

In the dim interior was a small oleaginous individual in a shiny shirt. 'I am Mr Seenigama,' he said. 'Welcome to the Paradise Isle, the Emerald Teardrop. Also, the Pearl Beyond Price,' he added in case we had not got the message.

'Also, the Snot at the Tip of the Indian Nose,' Luisa contributed sotto voce with a giggle.

At this point Mr Seenigama must have pressed some hidden buttons because two things happened. The air conditioning came on with a lovelorn sigh and, simultaneously, a spirited rendition of Abba's 'Gimme! Gimme! Gimme!' I wondered whether Mr Seenigama had been practising his disco moves in the back room before we arrived.

Luisa tried on a pair of amethyst earrings. 'Oh, look,' I said, 'a netsuke. We used to have a whole collection, little carved animals. I remember we had a rabbit just like this one.'

'So what happened to them?'

'My mother locked them up when she saw me playing with them. She said I'd lose them. I was very young at the time.'

Mr Seenigama saw me admiring the carving and shimmied over on dainty feet. 'Very antique,' he said. 'Very previous. Genuine old family. Very decrepit.'

I smiled. 'Very sorry. Can't afford.'

We emerged from the shop two hours later, not having bought a thing. It occurred to me that this was the way our life was now, with this aggressively random quality to it. For a minute I longed for my sterile but structured life in Putney where not much happened, perhaps, but it happened to order and to time. I thought guiltily of Rathu Catherine; in the country of her birth I was ignoring her entirely, finding her fiction far less gripping than the dramatic unreality of our current existence.

We ended up at the Botanical Gardens—with its glorious avenues of flowering trees, its curiously erotic coco-de-mer palms brought over from the Seychelles in the nineteenth century—picnicking on tinned-fish sandwiches. Afterwards

Luisa handed round a Tupperware box of pineapple pieces. 'There were a couple of pineapples in the kitchen,' she explained. 'I got Karuppayah to cut them up.'

She only said this after we had finished eating them. In fact the last piece was still in my mouth, and I nearly choked.

No sooner had the car disappeared down the drive than the Kumarihamy rang her bell. 'Sita!' she called out. 'Girigoris! Karuppayah!' It took a while for Clarice's ragged army to assemble. Indeed it was entirely unusual for Karuppayah even to be seen on the front verandah, his natural habitat being the kitchen courtyard, where he staggered from front kitchen to back, with frequent stops at his bedroom for a refreshing drop or two from a bottle kept permanently stashed under the mattress. Karuppayah was the only member of staff who spoke perfect English, having worked in an English household as a young man in the first years after Independence. As a result he was fully conversant with all those colonial dishes so beloved of memsahibs—boiled mutton in caper sauce (usually made in the tropics with old goat and salted capers out of a jar), toad in the hole, jam roly-poly pudding—all of which Clarice too had learnt to love at second-hand. The fact that Karuppayah was present at the reveille only demonstrated the gravity of this council of war.

'No doubt you all know why you are assembled here,' the Kumarihamy said, knowing full well that none of them did. 'The Baby Lord's room.' She looked at their blank faces with some satisfaction. 'I am restoring it to its original state with the help of you three. With this in mind I have decided to *invest in a second bucket!*' If she had expected oohs and aahs of amazement at this evidence of entrepreneurial wizardry, she did not get any.

Somewhat disappointed, she continued. 'We will form a chain. Girigoris, you will be filling the buckets. Sita, you will hand the filled buckets to Karuppayah, who will fill the hole. Once it is full,' continued Clarice, 'we will see about the floor.'

'I have never laid a floor,' said a somewhat nervous Girigoris, who knew that this onerous duty would ultimately fall to him.

'Brick on edge,' shot back the Kumarihamy. 'Three inches of concrete on top. But first you have to tamp down the soil really hard.' Never let them forget, she thought, who amongst us is the master builder.

Still, her raggedy army of three remained motionless, open-mouthed and goggle-eyed.

'Any questions?'

'Who will make the lunch?' asked Girigoris hesitantly. Lunch was a hugely important part of his day.

'Lunch?' screeched Clarice. 'Lunch? You will all get packets for lunch. Vegetarian rice packets. I am not foolish enough to imagine you will finish this in a day; when my son comes back, he will naturally want his dinner, so all filling must stop and the door securely locked. We will conduct this operation in secrecy, when they are away from the walauwa, understand?'

There was silence.

'Now chop chop! We haven't got all day.'

And so the filling began, Clarice exhorting her team to ever greater heights (or depths), brandishing her walker, cracking jokes, singing occasional snatches of song out of tune.

She had not enjoyed herself so much since that glorious day when Bella's daughter had run away with the conductor at the Kandy Bus Stand, and that had been quite some years ago. At lunchtime she called a brief armistice and they all sat around the kitchen table eating their buth packets. The Kumarihamy briefly considered cracking a bawdy joke or two the way they did on building sites, but desisted. For a Kandyan princess to dine in the kitchen with her staff was unprecedented—a supreme and sublime breach of etiquette—and the servants looked at each other in wonder, knowing how unlikely it was ever to happen again.

24

'Look,' I said, 'the netsukes I was telling you about the other day. My mother must have put away the rabbit.'

I was showing Luisa around the cavernous drawing room: the ebony sofa or *kavichaya* that had belonged to the last treasurer, reeded and scrolled, with gilded anthemion leaves, and the caned blackwood bergères, their backs woven in the sunburst pattern.

Luisa yawned. 'I'm all antiqued out,' she said in a bored voice. She began to play chopsticks on the piano. A rustle and click at the far end of the room and my mother shot in, as if propelled forward by a clockwork mechanism someone had overwound by mistake.

'Ha! Thought it was you! What on earth are you doing indoors on a fine day like this? You need to get out of town. Galle, Yala—you really must see the wild life in Yala!— Trincomalee.'

'Give us a break, Ma, this is a holiday not a package tour.'

'Disgraceful. You bring her all the way here, then keep her locked up.'

Luisa sprang up. 'We're going for a walk.'

'Are you?' 'Are we?' my mother and I said in unison.

'Why not? There's so much for us to see in Kandy on foot.'

At the end of the drive outside the main gate we turned left to go uphill. She gave me a sly smile.

'You're not!' I said shocked.

'Oh yes, and you're coming with me.'

'Luisa, you can't!'

'Just watch me,' she said aggressively.

'My mother will murder you.'

'Not at all. I'm in very good odour with the old bird as it is. In fact I'm her only ally here. These are your aunts. It would be shameful of us to go back without visiting them. We might never see them again.'

There was a profusion of flowers along the road up the hill—sharp blue ones hanging on vines—I did not know what they were called. A lot of rain the previous month had cut a channel along one side, exposing laterite soil rich and red, like mango jam. I thought again how much like Tuscany it all was, the same clear light, the same slightly unrealistic colours suspended quivering in the perfect air, though washed here in darker tones of tropic gold.

Beta's and Bella's houses, built on adjacent narrow vertiginous blocks of land, must have taken all the ingenuity of the architect that built them. They had more spectacular views than the old house, being higher up, and were built on many levels, so that you entered at the top and descended to the bedrooms.

'Ah, the foreign party,' Jane observed, ushering us into a cavernous open-plan living room built of rough granite, random rubble, inset with a row of portholes. 'I'll tell the mistress you're here.' She paused at the door. 'It might have been nice, mightn't it, if you had called to give us a little prior warning?'

My aunt came in and enveloped us both in a hug. There was quite a lot of her and relatively little of us, so it was a comprehensive, all-embracing sort of hug.

'Does your mother know you're here?'

We looked at each other. 'Of course,' Luisa said defiantly.

At that moment, as if on cue, the phone rang. I could hear my mother's voice full of false cheer. 'Beta, Beta! You have my children with you?'

Beta looked at us speculatively. 'Thank you so much for sending them up.'

'Well, it's the *least* I could do. From the day they arrived I've been telling them, Go and see your aunts, go and see your aunts. By the way, thank you for those pineapples. So sweet.'

'What, me or the pineapples?' Beta asked suspiciously.

'I so wanted to come myself but you know how it is, running a large old house.'

'I'll send them back straight after lunch,' Beta said, pressing her advantage to the full.

'Lunch?' screeched my mother.

'Why? Is there a problem?'

There was a pause. 'No. At least I don't think so. Do you think I could have a word with Sonny?'

Beta handed me the phone. 'Don't eat a thing!' my mother hissed into the phone. 'Make an excuse. Say you have a bad stomach!'

'Huh?' I said, but she had already hung up.

At this point, Beta called Bella. 'They're here,' she whispered urgently into the phone. She might have been talking about an enemy invasion. 'Come quickly.'

Within five minutes Bella was with us, as if she had been mobilized and ready for action since dawn. There were the usual exclamations of delight at how pretty Luisa was, how sophisticated and beautifully turned out, how far too good she was for their nephew.

There were about a hundred-and-one curries at this impromptu lunch: two years away and I had forgotten how in Sri Lanka they will not let you go without feeding you even if you happen to drop in unexpectedly at the humblest household, managing to produce so much from so little. There was baby jackfruit curried, manioc game chips and breadfruit cooked with spinach and dry chillies; whole eggs boiled, then deep-fried, and served in a bubbling brown gravy; a host of mallungs—various types of steamed green leaf in grated coconut and lime juice; and a pickle of local olives in coarsely ground mustard.

'You should have given us fair warning,' Beta said mournfully. 'You might have got a proper meal, then.'

'Now that you're here,' she continued, 'there's something I need to tell you. I see that you're a grown man now, so the time is right. Your mother has had her differences with us over the years. Perhaps we were not as kind to her as we might have been when she first came into the family. But all that is water under the bridge now. She must understand that!'

I sat silently, my ears burning.

'She must understand that we mean well. You are now the head of the family whether you like it or not. And we only want what's best for the family.'

I nodded. 'I'm sure she understands that.'

'Be sure to repeat what I said,' my aunt told me as we left.

Walking back downhill, I thought sadly: not in a thousand years would she understand; even if she did, she would not forgive. All would be lovely on the surface, as it was whenever they met for their sherry. Underneath, her soul was fissured, cracked apart and boiling over with the molten lava of hate.

There was a rush of air behind the Kumarihamy as she put the phone down, sucking the breath out of her body. Was she having a heart attack? A stroke? Perhaps it was diabetes. It was, in fact, the Devil fanning her with his crimson cape, as concerned for her health as she was.

I trusted them, she thought. I let them into my house. This is what they go and do in repayment. Bitches and bastards. I should have gone with my first instincts when I felt the demons down the phone, and not let them past the front door. They hoodwinked me with their pink saris and honeyed words, their *Clarice this* and *Clarice that*. It was all planned, I see now. They were hanging around just waiting for an opportunity to consort with the enemy. All I wanted was for them to be out of the house so I could restore his room, in order to please him. Ha! This is the thanks I get.

My days are numbered. It won't be long before Bella and Beta (and that frisky animal Jane) are in here with the new American Kumarihamy and my son the devil. And I'll be on the streets, so God help me!

And just like that the honeymoon period came to an end, with a crash and a bang. It quite made the Devil's day.

I will spare you details of the earth-scorching, oxygen-sucking conflagration that awaited us upon our return. A writer has the duty to tell the truth: but when the balance of that truth is so impaired, the violence of its actions so extreme, it ceases then to be plausible. And plausibility is what the reader is after, whatever the reality. Truth without plausibility is as unsatisfactory as meat without salt.

The illogic of my mother's reasoning left me breathless. There was no reason why Luisa and I should have been banned from seeing my aunts. It was as if the mere knowledge of us were a prize possession enclosed in my mother's fist, to be shown fleetingly and occasionally to those of her selected choice; the way a child might hold a seashell picked up on the beach, like a great secret, giving you the occasional flash if she really liked you.

I noticed though that the violence of my mother's words was directed only at me, that she switched to Sinhala so Luisa would not understand. So there was some method to this verbal madness, after all. I was used, since childhood, to her explosions of rage. I had never thought to question them till now. It showed yet again how alien I had become— so Westernized—that I sought reasonable explanations for events that were essentially beyond reason. And where was that famous antidote, my childhood wit, when I so needed it?

The force of the fire having finally spent itself, we returned to our room exhausted.

'I can't take this,' Luisa said. She got into bed and pulled the sheet over her. 'It's bad for me in my condition.'

'I'm going for a walk,' I replied. 'I need some air.'

'By the way, what does bally mean?'

I looked at that exquisite face peeping out from under the sheet. 'It's a term of endearment,' I replied wearily. 'Like darling or something.'

25

Sita saw him standing outside the closed door of his former bedroom. He looked lost and forlorn, like a stray dog that had wandered into the house off the hillside, looking aimlessly for shelter, not really understanding where to find it. Where was the man she had welcomed back to the house with such relief only a few weeks ago?

'My lord,' she said softly. 'There's something I want to show you.'

He was so preoccupied he didn't even pull her up for the use of the honorific. She went to the library and picked up the brass key off the green baize board where it was hanging.

'This is why your mother wanted you away from the house,' she said, opening the door.

Half the floor had been filled back in, the earth flattened. 'Another two days and we would have had it concreted. Then your mother was going to move all your stuff back in. She wanted it to be a surprise for you.'

'So this is supposed to make me feel better, is it?' he said bitterly, wringing his hands. 'It's all a bit pointless now, isn't it?'

She had never in all her years at the walauwa seen him so despondent. There was a weakness to him that made her uneasy, a warping of the timbers after too many seasons abroad.

'Come with me for a walk,' he said suddenly.

She looked apprehensive. 'But your mother?'

'Oh, fuck my mother!' he burst out. Again she was shocked by the uncharacteristic words, the savagery of a weak man who has no other weapons in his armoury.

They walked down the steps to the lower terrace and inexplicably, quietly, she found he had taken hold of her hand. What if his aunts were watching from above? Yet she made no attempt to release herself for fear of offending him, or so she persuaded herself. At the same time she prayed breathlessly that they would meet no one they knew along the way. Then she realized with horror that his steps were leading unerringly to the lali gedera, her home.

'Sonny, no!' she cried. It was the first time in her entire life she had used his name, an action more deeply shocking than any physical intimacy. 'My father's in there.'

'No, he's not,' he whispered. 'He's away at work. Open the door.'

Trembling, she took the key out of her pocket. Inside there was a faint smell of the morning's cooking lingering in the air, the single bed with its sheet stained and rumpled. However much she tried, it was impossible to keep the space clean and tidy with a drunken old man in occupation.

Once inside, she found herself being backed gently towards the bed. With a sudden sickening lurch of her stomach she thought of that other man, her daily tormentor.

Then that flood of pent-up emotion and loneliness and frustration washed over her, two long years of it, and she sank gratefully down on the mattress, pulling Sonny on top of her.

〜

When my parents first married, they had lived in this one-roomed house with my astrologer grandfather. It was only after I was born—perhaps even as a direct consequence of it—that they were invited back to the big house. As a child, I had been banned from ever associating with this grandfather and all he stood for, my Kandyan grandmother exerting her iron will in this matter much as my mother does now. But Jossie Amma my nanny (one of the seventeen) would sneak me in on clandestine visits.

I remembered him in his spotless white sarong and tunic, the faint bittersweet odour of the little parcels of betel and tobacco and areca nut that he folded up so precisely and chewed so thoroughly. I was terrified of his red mouth and discoloured teeth, the result of all that betel, and when he hoisted me on to his lap I did everything possible not to look into that open gaping hole in his face, one that freely gushed blood more copiously than any demon's.

After his death, the house was padlocked and abandoned for a few years till Sita and her father came upon the scene, but as a boy, I had managed to dislodge one of the timber planks of the house low down at the back, and I was skinny enough to be able to wriggle through. It was my secret place of refuge in times of stress, with its comforting warmth, the organic softness of the materials used in its building. It was no surprise therefore that I found my feet directing me to it now.

I suppose I should tell you that this fast and furious coupling in a secluded shack on a tropical hillside took place on account of a temporary leave of my senses, or some such similar justification. After all, I am the protagonist of this novel, and so must demand satisfaction at all times from you, my reader.

But when your own mother chews you up and spits you out in indigestible chunks, is it not bound to leave you distraught and cut up, seeking solace where you may, in the arms of whoever happens to be at hand, particularly someone you had always been fond of, who was so pretty and sad and sweet?

Or was this some desperate act of reaffirmation, of a Sri Lankan identity that was faded and found seriously wanting after a two-year hiatus? By bedding Sita, was I groping blindly, trying to find my way back home?

Or was it simply an urgent animal need of the moment, one that was not currently being met in the marriage bed? An 'It's the sex, stupid!' sort of thing, as Bill Clinton might have said had he been living in Kandy?(And who knew better than old Bill about sex?)

The sad truth is that during every moment of that carnal act, I was aware of the woman and baby asleep in the bedroom of the big house up the hill. I was aware of the betrayal involved. You cannot block these things out. You cannot help what your mind thinks, just as you cannot really control what your body does. I realize that this awareness of wrongdoing, while doing it, makes me worse rather than just bad. Badness needs the stamp of goodness on the reverse to be really wicked. So be it. I was the devil, after all, that is what everyone had been telling me all my life. It feels good sometimes to live down to other people's expectations of you.

I left her that afternoon no sooner had I finished—in a selfish, seigneurial sort of way—having taken what I wanted as was my right. After all, her father might arrive any minute, so I could hardly wait around, could I, I told myself.

Oh, and one last thing: remorse. A small vial of clear distilled liquid deep inside my body leaking out in spite of my best efforts to keep it stoppered. Though I do not expect you will like me any better because of that small detail.

∽

Afterwards she thought: What have I done? *What have I done?* The American, Sonny's wife, had done nothing to her to deserve this terrible revenge. She had few of the airs and graces about her that so many Sri Lankans loved to affect in their dealings with the 'servant class'. Yet here she was, stabbing this woman in the back, taking her man away from her.

Ah, but I had the prior claim, she thought defensively. I knew him long before you ever did. He was mine always, even if he did not know it at the time. I was possessed, am *in possession* of him, she thought exultantly: of the master of the house, the Lord of the Manor.

But that other thing—that constant worry, the piece of grit in the shoe—came back into her mind. Why had she not come clean about the theft of the ivory carving and its consequences? The mind can do strange things to the body, she knew. He might physically desire me now; after that other knowledge, I will be only a common thief to him, and who has ever desired a thief? It was even more difficult to tell him about the rape. What man ever desired another man's leftovers? No, she thought, it will be enough for me to have him as he is, for him to have me as he finds me now. Further knowledge would be disastrous, because knowledge once learnt, can never be unlearnt. The simple fact of being desired was enough for her: it gave her the confidence and strength to meet that other evil head on.

Desire. No one said anything about love.

That night when she got back home from work, her father greeted her with his usual malicious eyes.

'I know your secret, old man!' she wanted to shout. 'You can bloody well buy your own medicines from now on.' But the irony was that she couldn't. More than ever, she needed him out of the house; she needed the space in case there was a repeat performance.

Repeat? You must be joking, she said to herself. You happened to have caught him at a weak moment after his mother yelled at him. He just wanted a taste of what he had been fancying all these years. He will go back to his wife a happy man, more loving than ever before. And you will go back to being abused on a daily basis, because that is what life has chosen for you as your particular treat.

26

The Kumarihamy possessed one supremely positive quality: though she never ever forgot other people's transgressions, she never ever remembered her own. So it was always something of a surprise to her to discover afterwards that people disliked her as much as they did. What did I ever do to them? she would ask in injured tones, shaking her head sadly. It was the price she had to pay, she knew, for being so very good. Never mind, she would reap her rewards in heaven.

She imagined heaven as a sort of über-walauwa with hot and cold running servants, and not a postman in sight to interrupt your snooze on the celestial verandah. And there would be a view, of course, of the earth spread out below you, with X-ray binoculars conveniently to hand, so you could peer into the intimate lives of anyone down there you chose.

In the days following the fracas, she awoke every morning with a spring in her step. She half considered hurling her walker over the edge of the terrace in the general direction of Kandy, but rejected this as somewhat premature. She did not regret one bit having said what she had that other day. Sonny and Luisa were young. They had neither the benefit of age nor her knowledge of the inside workings of Sri Lankan society, where you could only survive if you avoided the many human snakes residing therein. Only man is vile, she said joyfully to herself. Only man is vile.

It was odd that the young couple seemed to be avoiding her, turning up irregularly for meals, sticking to their room most of the time, speaking in hushed whispers. But the Kumarihamy was secretly quite pleased at this: it re-established her suzerainty over the domain. Indeed, their mouse-like behaviour exactly echoed her own when, all those years ago, she herself had first arrived at the walauwa, then in the iron grip of the old Kumarihamy. Clarice had been a renegade bride too, in the care of a son completely cowed by his mother. It was truly a wondrous thing to watch history gently unfold in repetition of itself.

As a reward to the household for this triumphant return to the status quo she upped the stakes on the gastronomic front, exhorting the cook to ever greater heights of culinary mountaineering. For lunch there was beef smore, the classic Portuguese pot roast—thick slices of Portuguese shoe leather arranged prettily on a china platter, smothered in fried onions. Then there was Karuppayah's glorious duck padre, essentially a curry-and-chips combination, doused liberally with arrack and flamed, a recipe beloved of the whisky priests of colonial times. For duck, the Kumarihamy had substituted a somewhat ecclesiastical chicken, lean and rangy, that you fully expected to arrive at the table dressed in purple gaiters, rising up from the pot briefly to say grace, before offering itself up for consumption.

'Eat!' said the Kumarihamy jovially to Luisa. 'Eat. Remember you have to eat for two now.'

Luisa gave a weak smile, pushing the pieces hither and thither on her plate—no prizes for guessing whom she had picked up that manoeuvre from. In the meantime I sat there marvelling at my mother's mercurial changes of mood; she was completely happy now that she had caused panic and dissension in the ranks with her outburst. It occurred to me that her happiness had always been contingent on other people's unhappiness. Perhaps we all had this quality, but it was more apparent in her.

The fight, instead of uniting the two of us, had unexpectedly driven a wedge between Luisa and me. It was as if I was being blamed for my mother's behaviour, as if I represented Sri Lanka in this matter, and she the rest of the world. It was tempting for me to say, 'I told you so, I warned you about my mother' but I held my tongue. I took to going for long walks instead, especially in the dead hours of the afternoon when the whole household snoozed. Those walks led me all too often to the shack where I met Sita by prior arrangement. We had devised a signal: I scratched my left ear, and if she responded similarly, we would meet. If she scratched her right ear in reply, it meant she couldn't.

For some reason we both seemed to need the sex, for nourishment as much as physical pleasure. Though we hardly said a word during those brief trysts. We were strangers to each other, an ocean lying between us, so the physical fulfilment was enough. Any more would have only served to highlight how alien we had become to each other in those two years away. We had too much ground to cover to become friends again, and neither of us had the time; that easy childhood bond was gone and any adult connection would take a lifetime to put in place. It would involve a total annihilation of feudal bonds, unseen but still very much in place.

In this love triangle I was between the devil and the deep blue sea. Though I was the devil himself, so that couldn't be right, could it?

'I want to go on a trip,' Luisa said to me. 'You're keeping me locked inside this miserable house—it's driving me crazy.'

'What's the hurry? We have a month more. We don't have to rush.'

'Didn't your mother mention Galle? Yala? I could do with the beach, a bit of swimming. I really could.'

'Wrong time. The currents are too strong. November's off-season. Next month is better.'

'It's all right for you. You vanish every day on your walks, leaving me here alone to face the music.'

'You could come with me.'

'You know I can't. Not now.'

In the last few weeks Luisa had thickened noticeably. It was curious how even her features had got more muzzy, less defined. The pregnancy, having started almost invisibly, like a sort of well-behaved house guest, was really coming into its own now, throwing its not inconsiderable weight around, ruling our lives. So when I suggested that she accompany me on my perambulations, I knew I was safe. There was no likelihood of it happening, thank God.

I did not want to go anywhere else in Sri Lanka. Not Yala, not Trinco. I wanted to stay right here where my daily pleasures lay, inside a little house of mangowood planks, while the rain pattered comfortingly on the tin roof above. You will wonder how I could keep both lives running parallel, mutually self-contained, mutually pleasurable. All I can say is that this is the way it was. Every now and then I had read in the papers of some man—usually some insignificant creature in a lowly paid job—who was found to have been running two parallel households, each as complete as the other. I had till now thought this highly improbable (surely the lipstick on the collar? the note in the pocket?). I was beginning to find this not so. Not only was it perfectly possible: it had become perfectly acceptable, completely natural.

In those days, Sri Lankans of our milieu were brought up eating Eastern food for lunch, Western for dinner: this was how it was. It was the perfect, if banal, comparison to my current love life.

∽

The Devil felt distinctly uncomfortable. They were all ranged around him in a semicircle, looking uncannily like those very ancient, superbly vicious nuns you sometimes find remaindered in convents, sophisticates in the art of savagery, at the very top of their game.

'There have been complaints about you,' gobbled the Devil Superior through his turkey-wattled throat.

'What?' said the Devil disbelievingly. '*Moi?*'

'Our Hindu colleagues have issued a strong diplomatic note. They say you've been caught poaching in their territorial waters. What do you have to say to that?'

'Outrageous!' squeaked the Devil. 'Just because I set up shop on a mountain claimed—*claimed!*—by some Hindu chappie called Beaver, I mean Bhairava. As for poaching, ha! So far I've only managed to land two fish—one irresponsibly spotty youth and one very old trout. Beaver can definitely have her back—I find I can do very little with her.'

'Then there's the question of your dancing,' continued the Superior.

'Dancing?'

'You've been spotted doing pas de Basques. No, don't deny it. Last Tuesday you attempted a grand jeté off a random rubble terrace and landed in someone's pumpkin patch. *Disgraceful!*'

'Do you have any idea what that pumpkin did to my tomatoes?'

'This behaviour is not at all in the Spirit of Darkness, frankly. Not at all. You're giving evil a bad name.'

'Pray what exactly do you mean by the Spirit of Darkness? Milk wine?'

'Anyway, we in Hell have far more important things to worry about in the coming months for Sri Lanka.'

'Oh?' said the Devil. 'And what might those be?'

'Never you mind. In the meantime, try not to step on Beaver's—I mean Bhairava's—toes.'

'Toes? *Toes?*' said the Devil in a disgusted tone. 'Have you seen the state of his toenails? I recommended a nail spa. I begged him. Would he listen?'

‿

'Time for your daily exercise,' said Pandu, draining his mug and hitching up his sarong.

'You can fuck off!' she hissed.

'What do you mean, slut?' He seized her wrist.

'I am never going with you again, so help me God!'

He became dangerously calm then. 'In that case I suppose I should go see the Kumarihamy. Is she free now, do you think?'

'Go and see her!' Sita shouted. 'Tell her everything. See where it gets you.' She sat down on a chair, heart pounding. She was taking the risk of a lifetime. This could mean the end of everything, the end of the life she currently took for granted.

He drew back, saying nothing, examining her expression minutely for clues. Then the realization spread over his face, slowly, like a dirty stain on a dishcloth thrown over spilt tea. 'You fucking bitch!' he said admiringly. 'You're screwing him, aren't you? *That's* what's going on here. The master of the house is fucking the bitch servant!' He shook his head in amazement, looking at her with new-found respect. 'Quick fucking worker, aren't you?'

'Oh, go to hell!' she said, pushing him out of the kitchen and slamming the door in his face. She sat back down again, breathing heavily. I have to be doubly careful, she thought. He's on to me. He's always outside in the garden. If he sees us going into the shack together it will spell the end of everything. Should I go easy, let things cool off for a while?

27

The Kumarihamy was supremely confident she would strike gold any day now. The young couple had been with her for over a month now—how splendid if it could happen before they departed these shores in the New Year! Sonny's former bedroom was back-filled and concreted over, the skeleton crew moving on to the Blue Room accompanied by its cutting-edge excavation equipment (one pick, one shovel, two buckets). This room had been the site of the original guard hut during the time of the king: what better place to hide the treasure?

There would have to be a second wedding, of course, a proper one, that went without saying. A mere registration in a foreign country simply did not count. So what if the pregnant bride was forced to float down the aisle like a galleon in full sail? People would forgive, knowing she was carrying that precious cargo of a son and heir. (It had to be a boy—the Kumarihamy would not countenance a female firstborn, the very idea was plainly absurd.) Weddings in Sri Lanka were more for showing people who and what you were than for mere marriage. They were for putting the uninvited firmly in their place. The entire mountain would be festooned with lights, so that all over Kandy parents would say enviously and bitterly to their children: 'Look, the Mahadewala wedding! They don't do things by halves, do they? Look closely, because you won't be seeing the likes of it again, not in our lifetime. Oh, and please don't think you're going to get the same when *your* turn comes. It's the Jayamangala Caterers for you, my girl!'

In the spirit of joyful anticipation, and as a palate-whetting hors d'oeuvre, the Kumarihamy decided to throw a party. Fearlessly she picked up her demon-free Bakelite instrument.

'Good morning, Clarice! To what do I owe this early call?'

'Tuesday's off, Father, that's what I'm calling to tell you. I'm throwing a party that night for all my friends, my nearest and dearest. I want to introduce them to my lovely children.'

'Wonderful. Who'll be there?'

'Well, you, Father. You are my nearest, and absolutely my dearest.' The Kumarihamy paused. She could not really think of anyone else.

'Bella and Beta?'

'*What did you say?*' There was a hostile half-second before the Kumarihamy recovered swiftly and smoothly, like a professional tennis player returning a wayward serve. '*Of course.* Yes, Bella and Beta. No, sadly they can't make it, I'm afraid. Something about pickling pumpkins that night before the crop gets entirely ruined.' She paused for breath. 'I may invite their friendly lodger though. You know he's . . . he's . . .' She could not quite bring herself to say the word. 'He's Australian,' she said finally.

'Australian? Poor man. How difficult for him.'

'Oh, and Father? It's smart casual that night.'

'When am I ever not, Clarice? When am I ever not?'

∽

I was floating around the house watching my mother mastermind this cleaning operation, the likes of which I had not seen since my father's five-year almsgiving all those years ago. Even that creep Pandu had been pressed into service, scrubbing up the servants' quarters. He kept giving me odd looks now and then, his lip curled in a contemptuous smile. Luisa was staying firmly inside the bedroom because she was allergic to dust. And what a storm of dust!

My mother was talking of a wedding. I had explained to her in no uncertain terms that Luisa and I were very much married, the evidence of it prominently on show. She dismissed this with a flick of her elegant hand. 'Marriages have to be seen to be believed,' she said. 'A foreign registration is not worth the paper it is written on, not in Sri Lankan eyes. What is required here is a proper baila-bashing, family-feuding, drink-yourself-into-a-stupor-on-cutprice-arrack sort of wedding. That is the only sort of wedding the poor relations understand. And where would we be if we couldn't rub our poor relations' noses in the dirt?'

In the meantime, something strange had happened to me. I was beginning to yearn for just that little bit more: I wanted to know what went on inside that pretty, coconut-oiled head I lay beside on some afternoons; I wanted to be able to translate those inscrutable expressions that flickered now and then across those heavy-lashed eyes, ephemeral as mosquitoes across a pond at dusk. What did she think about all this? Who was I to her? Did she see any future in us? For that matter, did I see any future in us? When the time came, was it a divorce my mother would be celebrating with fairy lights instead of a marriage?

But the more I wanted, the less she seemed able to give. These last few days, she had not even bothered to meet me. Was this some trick of hers to keep me wriggling in exquisite anticipation? If so, the strategy seemed to be working. I was frustrated and lonely. What I wanted to know was this: Did this happen to every bigamist? Did they always begin by priding themselves on the belief that their split was a controlled and deliciously doable fifty-fifty, only to find months later that the pendulum had swung where it would and come to rest at a natural equilibrium of eighty-twenty? And if so, what was the remedy for this inequality?

∽

The night of the party, as he rode his Vespa up the hill, Father Rosario could feel the presence of evil even more clearly than usual, the bass notes, the growl of a voice deeper than human that spoke in a language he did not know but understood only too clearly. It spoke of destruction and misery, a chronicle of many deaths foretold.

'Go home,' he wanted to tell the young couple. 'You are too innocent for all this. Leave it to old hands like your mother and myself. It doesn't matter too much what happens to us. We have had our day, you see.'

He was introduced to Sonny's wife and they conversed in halting Italian—she because it was very much her second language, he because he had been away from home so long, his Sinhala and Tamil were now more proficient than his mother tongue.

'Isn't she wonderful, Father?' said Clarice.

Pandu, all got up in his Sunday best, was circulating with a tray of milk wine. The Kumarihamy, looking at it, vanished into the bowels of the house as if she had just remembered something. She reappeared moments later brandishing an aged bottle of Red Label. It dated from the time her husband was alive; if you looked closely, you could see where rats had nibbled on the label, though thankfully nobody did.

'Ta da!' said the Kumarihamy, like a magician with a white rabbit. In the event everyone passed on the whisky because they knew what was good for them, all except for Father Rosario who was feeling brave that night. Simultaneously there emerged from the kitchens a tray of mutton patties just fried in hot oil, into which Karuppayah had cunningly inserted bits of gristle and bone; these were guaranteed to crack your teeth if you bit into them too enthusiastically.

A sudden commotion below the verandah revealed the ample forms of Beta and Bella mounting the steps, magnificently upholstered in full Kandyan regalia, pleated silk fanning out from extravagantly ample hips, like plumage on two large jungle fowl. Perhaps it was the third glass of milk wine inside her, but the Kumarihamy rose to the occasion with superbly aristocratic insouciance. 'How excellent of you to come!' she said in her best superior manner. 'But I thought the pumpkins?'

'Jane's been telling us from last week that something was afoot. She said she'd never seen the walauwa being cleaned so thoroughly.'

'How good of her to notice,' said Clarice.

'So we just couldn't resist, could we, Bella?'

'Try the mutton patties,' said Clarice, 'they're full of surprises.'

Beta looked pointedly at Luisa's stomach. 'Are you going to have it here?'

Luisa shook her head. 'We're going back on the first of January. It's due in about five months.'

'And will you be joining her, Clarice, for the, for the *accouchement*?'

'What a long word, dear! Did you swallow a dictionary on the way up?'

'No, dear. Quite possibly something in this patty though.'

The Devil had the best time of all, finishing off milk wine in people's glasses when they weren't looking. 'The Spirit of Darkness,' he whispered, smacking his lips, 'oh give me more Spirit of Darkness.' He kept judiciously out of the Kumarihamy's line of vision, for fear she would insult his manhood in public. Who knew, she might even accuse him of being Australian? Occasionally he would wink at Pandu, sadly getting no response in return.

For my part, I tried unsuccessfully to corner Sita in the melee. She shook her head, warning me off. She studiously avoided me the rest of the evening.

When we got back to the room, Luisa said, 'I want to go home. To Putney, I mean.'

'Why?'

She shook her head, looking unhappy.

'Was it something Father Rosario said?'

'Maybe. I just feel, you know, there's something wrong here.'

'Is it me?'

She looked at me speculatively. 'You're different. Something's happened. I no longer feel I have all of you at my disposal.'

'It's my mother. Makes too many demands on me.' I silently prayed the lie was convincing enough.

'There's something more than that. I feel it's bad here for the baby. I want to park it somewhere safe till it arrives.'

'Look, I'm here to protect you, right? You don't have to fear anything because I'm here.' I held her tightly for the longest time, and I think I meant every word. 'At least let's wait till after Christmas. You know my mother's looking forward to that. Maybe we can go down south. Take her with us.'

'Two more weeks,' she said unhappily. 'How on earth am I going to manage?'

She let me make love to her that night, though I could see it was uncomfortable for her, that she was suffering through it. It was the closest we had been to each other in quite a while. I thought back with a sort of grim nostalgia to that time, only a month ago, when she had been my whole world; I had loved her then, and that world. It had been more than enough for me.

'It's my father's diabetic clinic today, my lady. I may have to leave a little early this evening.' The Kumarihamy snorted but did not say anything. She was still on such a high from last night's party that nothing could ruin her mood.

For days, Sita had been denying to herself the truth. By the time she made her excuses and left the walauwa that evening, the conclusion was long lodged in her brain, like a piece of food gone stale in the fridge. As always in Sri Lanka the hospital was jam-packed, so much so it was impossible to believe that the country was not in the throes of some epidemic.

'Is your husband here?' the doctor asked.

'No!' she wanted to retort. 'Why should it matter to you if I have a husband or not? Bad news is bad news whether there's a man to hold your hand or not.'

Having given her urine sample, she sat outside in the waiting hall with sixty other people. They can't all be here for the same thing, can they, she thought in sudden alarm. There were toothless grannies and men in wheelchairs and shaven-headed children, so perhaps not.

She had always been regular, never missing the day. So when she was late she knew, without necessarily having to come to hospital for the test. It was only one more nail in the coffin, after all. The fates had ensured that her punishment was thorough and comprehensive, almost as if they were saying: so you thought you could be good, did you, and get away with it? (Because she still believed in the intrinsic goodness of that original theft, whatever the laws of morality might decree.)

Almost an hour later she was called back in. 'You're pregnant,' the doctor said.

PART 4

28

How well she remembered the day only two months back, when she had made this same journey up the hill, Mr Seenigama's dirty money safely in her pocket, her father's diabetic medicines already bought! She had raised a victorious fist at the sky then, armed with the unshakeable conviction of her moral superiority.

She thought now: so this is what it is like. A brief sunlit high noon, followed by this plunge; and just when you think you've hit bottom you notice the hole in the seabed that sucks you deeper down into that land of hideous neon creatures, squeaking and gibbering, sightless and ugly, where you now find yourself. This is where you will stay. Because remember that thing called redemption they told you about at school? It was a fiction.

She was an expert on misery now, this last coup de foudre yet another failed attempt by fate to finish her off. The trick was not to stack all your miseries together, one on top of the other: that way led to death by landslide. Instead you split them into friable pieces, crunching up each one separately, balancing the crushed material on the tip of your spade, flicking it over your shoulder to join the pile of other miseries you had already excavated. Unconsciously, she squared her shoulders. I have nowhere further to fall, she said to herself. I may have hit rock bottom. But I am not dead, or even mad. I will survive.

ᔕ

Sita went past me at lunchtime scratching her left ear. She had not scratched that itch in quite a while, so I raced to the shack after lunch, my expectations (and everything else) rising. Her hands trembled as she opened the padlock.

Once inside, she made me sit on the bed. This was actually her father's bed—Sita slept on a mat on the floor—though this had never stopped us from making maximum use of it. What sort of indescribable perversion had she got planned for me today? I reached out for her but she pinned both my hands under one of hers. This was beginning to look better and better.

'I brought you here,' she said (please note the verb 'brought': how quickly the balance of power shifts when a man is besotted), 'I brought you here not for that. But because there is something I have to tell you. I'm pregnant.'

And here we were, yet again. It seemed to me then that my life was one long list of unwanted pregnancies, one-shot wonders. It seemed that I only had to look at a girl to get her pregnant. How could I have been so cavalier and irresponsible? Had nobody explained to me the meaning of the word condom? Did I think that I was under the protection of some guardian angel of birth control?

'I'll stick by whatever you decide,' I said. 'I'll pay for whatever needs to be paid for. It's your decision, I'll respect that.' I felt very good saying this, a saint almost.

She hit the ball straight back into my court. 'What do *you* want me to do?'

'I don't know,' I replied.

There was a maddening familiarity to this script. I began to feel the slow build-up of rage and frustration inside: this country had gotten to me yet again. I remembered now— only too well, only too late—why I had left it in the first place. It had a way of trapping you with its easy charm, its skin-deep smile; before you knew it, you were pinned beneath, breathless and suffocating, in the embrace of its tentacles. A sort of death by love.

This island granted you the greatest freedom to do exactly as you wanted. Only after the bill was presented did you understand at what great cost this freedom came; but by then it was too late and you realized there was no one to blame but yourself—for fondly imagining it was a free offer. Did this make Sri Lanka a fool's paradise? Perhaps it did. But I knew now that it was also a paradise inhabited by fools: because I had just been proved to be one of them. Only a fool would think of blaming paradise for those problems of his own making.

༄

The Kumarihamy sat on the verandah with Sita at her feet. Below her lay Kandy in all its glory, her favourite topic of conversation. As was ever the case, not being of the blood, she held a far more proprietorial attitude towards the city than her sisters-in-law; and was far more knowledgeable about its history than they.

'A fact little known,' she told Sita, 'is that from the time of King Karaliyadde in 1551, for virtually the next one hundred years, the Kandyan rulers were Catholic. In fact the whole court converted during his reign. Though you can imagine that many of those conversions were not genuine, and made more for political and social advancement than anything else. You did what your boss did, that was the feudal way. At the same time, the kings firmly upheld the Buddhist faith, the official religion of the country. They considered themselves caretakers, responsible for the structure and upkeep of this precious and ancient building they had inherited, even if they privately subscribed to a different architecture. This is nothing new in history. Even today, the Thai kings are upholders of Buddhism in their country though privately the royal family is Hindu. And in England—ha, don't talk to me about England!—the royals were in fact German, and spoke the language of the enemy in the privacy of their palace till about fifty years ago. It was at the time of the Second World War that they changed their good German name of Battenberg to the lovely but totally fake English-sounding one of Windsor.

'The Sri Lankan royal bloodlines ran through King Karaliyadde's daughter, Kusumasana Devi, better known as Queen Catherine of Kandy, whose two husbands (they were first cousins of each other) ruled the kingdom one after the other for the next half century. The queen's children from these two marriages were taught by Portuguese tutors, and

Portuguese was the court language, never mind that Portugal was the official enemy. Long after the Portuguese had left the island, their influence continued: much as the upper classes of Sri Lanka continue to speak English at home today, half a century after the British exit—the language of the colonial oppressors they so affect to despise.'

'And the Dutch?' asked Sita. (Sita didn't give a tinker's cuss about the Dutch. She had been well trained, over the years, to add the right interjection at the right time.)

'The Dutch?' snorted the Kumarihamy. 'The Dutch? Ha! Those mealy-mouthed merchants with their gilded gifts? All they ever wanted was the cinnamon concessions to the king's vast landholdings. Vulgar commerce. The British now, they were a different bunch of crooks altogether. They played the long game: they were in it for the power and glory as much as the money.'

The Kumarihamy saw that Sita's attention was wandering. She half considered giving her a sharp rap to the head, but decided to be kind this morning because she could see the poor girl was a little under the weather.

'The British were masters as always of dissemination and disinformation. Had the last king been alive today I have no doubt they would have planted weapons of mass destruction on him.'

The phone rang inside the house and Sita leapt to it with an alacrity Clarice found somewhat annoying. She was never so prompt when there wasn't a lecture going on.

'It's for Luisa Hamu,' she said, returning a few moments later. 'Something about having to pay for that Christmas booking. Otherwise they can't keep the reservation.'

'I'm not going to some damn fool hotel for Christmas,' snapped the Kumarihamy. 'Christmas is all about staying at home with the family.'

Luisa came back into the bedroom after the phone call. 'It's confirmed. Christmas Day and Boxing Day. I just paid.'

'What does my mother say?' I asked.

'She doesn't have to join us if she doesn't want to, does she?'

Luisa had come to a sort of understanding with my mother: what cannot be cured must be endured, preferably with a large ocean between you and it. Not long to go now, she thought. She and I had been making small trips to places near Kandy, never staying away for more than a night or two: the three temples, the elephant orphanage, the rock temple of Dambulla. Whenever I came back from a trip, I visited the Blue Room, the site of the current excavation. I knew that Sita played a major part in this and I wanted to tell my mother: please spare her, it's not good for her to be labouring in her present condition, she is carrying your grandchild. But of course I didn't.

It had been a week now and Sita still had not told me what she intended to do. Was I worried? I was in that eerily calm space in the eye of the storm. My entire life, the way it would be conducted in future, depended upon the whims of this beautiful, familiar stranger. No, I had to take that back. Her life stood to change just as radically as mine, depending upon her decision.

'Only two more weeks and we're out of here!' Luisa said, barely able to keep the victory out of her voice. 'I never thought I'd be looking forward to Putney so much. Did you?'

I summoned up as much emotion as I had left in my system, dried up as a riverbed in drought. 'Ah, Putney!' I said lamely.

In the midst of all this, I had had plenty of time to think. What did I want? What would be the perfect outcome for me? The answer when it came surprised me. I wanted Sita to have the baby. So I would have not one but two children, of the same age: two sisters. I thought of them as girls because when it came to it, two sisters would have a stronger bond to each other than two brothers, or even a brother and sister. They would have separate but parallel lives, each enriching the other with the wisdom of her particular upbringing. And me? I would have the same too, of course: two wives, two lives, distinct and complementary, like the lines of a railway track. The way the Kandyan kings had lived.

It seemed to me that I had been granted access to two rooms, each containing a treasure—winking and glittering in the half-light—each entirely unlike the other. Was it so imperative that I give up either? Was it so unreasonable to want keys to both? Or was I, quite simply, a glutton with eyes too big for his belly?

Try as she might, Sita's calculations brought her every time to the same conclusion: the pregnancy had occurred precisely at the point of overlap of the two men. Either of them, Sonny or Pandu, might be the father. She could not think of two more different men, two more different prognoses for this prospective life.

There was Sonny, blindly confident he was the father. In his mind, he was already making provision for the child.

What sort of woman am I that I continue giving him the impression that he is the sole candidate? I never told him about my treatment at the hands of the other man, she thought, hopelessly. I have now swum so far across this river of lies that it is easier to keep swimming than to turn back. Anyway, which man ever truly knows that he is the father of his child? She thought of the Kumarihamy's tale of Queen Catherine's second husband, King Senerath, who chose as his successor his youngest son, doubting the paternity of the two older princes. The story was as old as the human race itself. It was the secret weapon that every woman wielded over every man.

None of this helped her in her present predicament. There were several courses of action open to her and each one spelled betrayal: of her principles, her integrity, her morality. Whichever one she chose, she was condemned to spend the rest of her days harbouring the corrosive acid of a secret, slowly eating away at the edges of any pretensions to goodness or integrity she might still have.

29

When the storm broke, I found I had a ringside seat. Sita was dusting the drawing room. I heard a retching sound bursting out of her stomach and, as I watched, she keeled over in slow motion. She was vomiting all over the ebony and gilt kavichaya; as if on cue, my mother appeared from the opposite end of the house. She may have been virtually blind but her hearing was sharper than mine.

'You stupid girl, what do you think you're doing?' She began to slap Sita. 'Ruined, it's ruined!'

'Stop it!' I shouted. 'Leave her alone. She can't help it.'

My mother seized Sita's hair and pulled her face towards her. 'Are you ill? Food poisoning? You've been eating rubbish again at the corner shop, haven't you?'

Then, as I watched fascinated, she did that thing women often do—she homed in like a heat-seeking missile on the truth. 'You can't be,' she said outraged. 'I don't believe it!' She looked around, as if seeking some explanation from the inanimate objects crowding the room. 'Who did this to you? Tell me!' She slapped her again, hard, on both cheeks.

I had just opened my mouth to say something when Sita spoke. 'I was forced,' she said softly.

'Forced? A big strong girl like you, in this day and age? You must be mad. You're just a prostitute, that's what you are. I always knew it, flaunting yourself.' My mother looked up at the ceiling dramatically. 'Oh God, why do I allow people like this into my house? What possesses me to feed and clothe them, give them houses to live in? I'm too good, that's the whole trouble . . .'

Long before she could finish her favourite speech, Sita had run crying from the room. I retreated quietly to ours, shutting the door behind me.

$\backsim$

Long ago in ancient Sri Lanka there lived a good and wise king. Bidding his beloved queen farewell one morning, he set sail on a long journey to do what kings did best: to prosecute a war in a far-off land. He returned many moons later to discover that in his absence his Beloved had grown in width and stature. Particularly in width. Not to put too fine a point upon it, the queen was in the Family Way, without the assistance of her king.

At this point the story veers off in two different directions, as good stories always do. The first has it that a handmaiden of the queen asks for a piece of the mango that the queen is eating and, upon being refused, begins to carry tales to the king about her mistress's wayward habits.

'It's that minister for war,' she says. 'He's the one wot dunnit.' Since the minister for war is precisely the one that sent the king off on this war, it all begins to make sense.

The second version of the story takes a more direct route to get to the same point. It loses the handmaid, it loses the mango. Instead, it has the king away at war for precisely ten months. Either way, the queen is heavily pregnant, with not a father in sight. So the king does what all wise kings do: he has the queen tied to a tree and split in half with a sword. But the baby survives, living off the remains of the dead queen. When the baby grows up, he vows revenge on his dad, who may or may not be his dad. (Who's to tell, with his mom dead and the minister for war now living far away in a retirement bungalow in Orissa?) Learning the demonic arts, the baby groups together eighteen mounds of herbs and spices, and out of these the *Daha Ata Sanni Yakku* are born, the Eighteen Demons responsible for all the ills of the world, ranging from deafness to bad breath to boils on the bum.

The Kumarihamy well remembered this story from childhood, as told by her astrologer father—the expurgated version, of course, because his lack of humour was well known up and down the mountainside. The story struck her as particularly relevant to her own predicament today, involving as it did kings, queens, unwanted pregnancies and saucy handmaids. The Daha Ata Sanni Yakku were the demons to be invoked and propitiated whenever anyone fell ill and, as far as the Kumarihamy was concerned, pregnancy outside of marriage was just such an illness. Since Sita appeared not to know who the father was—oh, the idiot, idiot girl!—it was not beyond the bounds of possibility that one of the eighteen demons was responsible. Prompt action was called for.

At the bottom of the hill, quite close to the lali gedera, there lived a family of sorcerers, the Kodivina Peirises. They were in fact distantly related to Clarice on her mother's side. The two families—astrologers and sorcerers—had often worked in tandem in the past: the astrologer who foresaw your illness promptly sent you down the road to the sorcerer for remedial action. Likewise, once you were fully exorcized, you naturally required guarantee of a demon-free future, so you were dispatched up the road to the astrologer, who allayed your fears (or not, as the case may be). If the professional relationship between the families was close, the social one was cold: freezing in fact, ever since Clarice's stellar and unprecedented rise to Kumarihamy status.

The sorcerers were definitely the sort of poor relations you assigned to the Blue Room and the squatting pan. Except that their living on the same mountain meant that they were assigned nothing at all: they simply turned up uninvited to any family function, as was their right.

Thus, it was with mixed feelings that Clarice sent Sita tumbling down to fetch old Kodivina, known to one and all as Kodi. Kodi had not yet finished his breakfast when Sita appeared on the threshold. 'Who is she, to summon me at this ungodly hour?' he muttered through a mouthful of stringhoppers.

'She wants you to come now. *Immediately*,' Sita repeated. 'And you are to prepare your oils here. She cannot grant you access to her kitchens or Karuppayah will give notice. You know what he's like.' (They all knew on the hill what Karuppayah was like.)

So a potent paste of white sandalwood and turmeric root and coconut oil was ground and prepared, with suitable incantations and imprecations.

'If she's in such a hurry, Bolay will have to do the job,' Kodi said. Bolay was his eldest son, plump and unmarried and rather dim. What he did not know about exorcism (there was much) he made up for with unbridled enthusiasm.

Clarice was seated on the verandah when they arrived.

'You look very ill, Auntie, if you don't mind me saying. Quite demonized, in fact.'

'Auntie?' said Clarice in a small voice. '*Auntie?* Pray when did I become your Auntie?'

But Bolay wasn't listening. Loudly chanting, he clambered with difficulty on to the verandah and began massaging the charmed paste vigorously into Clarice's scalp.

'Stop!' shrieked Clarice. 'Are you mad? Who did you think was pregnant around here?'

By the time the misunderstanding was cleared up, much of the paste had been used and Sita had to be content with what little was left. It was no wonder then that the pregnancy refused to go away.

'Do you want me to try the charmed-thread-around-the-neck next?' asked Kodi, upon being informed. (After that last fiasco, the Kumarihamy refused to deal with anyone but the principal.)

Clarice resisted the urge to tell him to tie the thread around his own neck and go hang himself if possible. 'We need something stronger,' she said, gravely and graciously.

Kodi scratched his head. 'I'm afraid, then, it's the thovil for you. But I warn you, it'll cost.' (He knew too well the Kumarihamy's almost legendary meanness.) The thovil exorcism ceremony was a hugely expensive affair: as much an expression of a family's wealth and power, its patronage of the folkloric arts, its ability to entertain the whole neighbourhood, as a cure for its ills.

The Kumarihamy gave him a sweet smile. 'Let me think about it,' she said. 'I'll have to get back to you on that one.' Devils be damned; she had decided to take matters into her own hands.

30

We were all gathered on the verandah, my mother's idea. It was like some eighteenth-century French trial where accuser and accused are brought face-to-face to hammer out their arguments in front of innocent bystanders, so we could each judge the rights and wrongs of the case. Except that in this case I was hardly an innocent bystander—though no one was to know that. Even Luisa had been summoned from her bed, her undeniable whiteness adding a certain gravitas to the proceedings, like the presence of a foreign observer at a local election. My mother was hugely enjoying herself: no doubt this reminded her of similar incidents in the past when her mother-in-law, the old Kumarihamy, had held sway.

Sita was seated on the floor at my mother's feet. Next to her, her father, whose whereabouts at the building site had been traced. To cover up his sheepishness at being caught out, he had assumed a face of outraged piety. He looked everywhere but at his daughter, knowingly, as if he had always been in possession of certain dark secrets. *Slut*, he said under his breath, in between slurps of betel juice. *Hussy*. I could see he was entirely with the Kumarihamy on this one. *My daughter the whore.* Karuppayah was here too, lurking uneasily at the back, a lit cigarette inverted in the palm of his closed hand, from which he took the occasional surreptitious drag when the Kumarihamy was not looking.

Suspicion had naturally fallen on Pandu. 'What have you got to say for yourself?' the Kumarihamy asked forcefully.

'What do you want me to say?' His insolence was superb, an actor in full command of the stage. Was there something I had missed here?

'Have you been having relations with this prostitute?'

'What's it to you if I have?'

My mother flew into a towering rage. As it is, she was employing a shocking form of address never heard in polite society today, formerly used only when speaking to animals or slaves. 'I'll give you a thundering slap,' she said, 'if you don't mind your manners. If your answer is yes, the solution is simple. You will have to marry her.'

'No!' Sita screamed. The sound must have rung all the way across the mountainside. 'I will never marry that bastard. I'll kill myself first.' I wondered to myself if my aunts were at their portholes above, watching and listening.

My mother twisted Sita's ear. 'Shut your mouth, bitch. You will do as you are told. It is for us to decide what happens to you.'

I was shocked at the level of violence, verbal and physical, that lay comfortably submerged in our Sri Lankan system—a flash of goldfish below the skim of the water—that took so little to summon to the surface. Only two years abroad and how easy to forget what exactly it was you had left behind!

I stood up from my chair. My mother and the other actors in the drama looked at me—mildly annoyed that I should attempt to create a diversion on this most important of occasions. Who was I to be stealing their precious thunder? As I began to speak, their jaws dropped and I realized: this is what I should have done all along. It was in fact my first consciously adult act within the confines of this mad medieval world I had stumbled back into.

'Listen to me all of you,' I said. 'That baby she's carrying is mine. If any of you so much as tries to touch a hair on her head, you will have to get past me first.'

I was breathing heavily but it felt good. I felt I had just swung a heavier weight at the gym than usual, a weight I did not know till now I could lift. I was so suffused with this feeling of goodness, the blood pumping in my veins, that I barely heard the sharp intake of breath next to me, barely felt Luisa springing to her feet and running inside.

There was chaos and pandemonium. I vaguely noted that my mother was swearing at me, that Karuppayah was brazenly puffing at his cigarette, that Sita was weeping in huge, hoarse gulps like a child who had been beaten. I sprinted after Luisa into the house, but she locked the door to our room behind her. 'Luisa!' I shouted. 'Luisa!' However much I rattled the door, she did not open.

Almost by default, I went to the kitchens in search of Sita. I found her outside in the kitchen garden, on a bench by the gardenias.

'Sita, listen to me,' I said urgently. 'I want you to keep this baby. I swear I'll support it every way I can. Just promise me you'll keep it.'

She looked at me, pityingly. 'You fool,' she said. 'Since when have *your* needs had anything to do with what happens around here?'

'Sita,' I said desperately. 'Promise me.'

'Go away!' she shouted. 'Leave me alone.'

When I went back inside, Luisa's door was unlocked. Her suitcase was open and she was putting things inside it, distractedly going through the motions like a bad actor whose mind is not entirely on the script. 'They don't have a seat till Christmas morning,' she said quietly. 'The flights are full.'

'Luisa, it meant nothing. I just lost my mind temporarily.'

'How long has this been going on?'

'It ended as soon as it began. I swear. A flash in the pan.' (Please God don't strike me down!)

'And that is supposed to make me feel better, is it?'

'No, but I'll do anything to put it right. Anything you ask. I promise.' I was at her feet now, my arms around her knees, begging.

She looked at me, a long, hard, measured look. The sort of look Solomon might have given before he passed judgement. There was silence for a moment. Then she said: 'Tell her to get rid of it and we'll call it quits, shall we? Is that fair?'

I could not believe I was hearing this. How could anyone be so monstrous? How could anyone so casually wish away another person's life?

'*Luisa!*' I was so shocked I could barely reply. 'Are you serious? You're asking her to destroy the one thing that means so much to her! You have everything, she has so little. Why would you be so heartless and cruel?'

'I suppose you weren't being heartless when you asked me to do the exact same thing?' she said. 'Back at Oxford, remember? You were being cruel to be kind, were you?'

And there it was: the ace of spades she had just laid, with great neatness and precision, on the green baize. The card with which she had trumped me yet again. How could I have forgotten?

Was it, then, to be an eye for an eye, a tooth for a tooth? Where did mercy and forgiveness come into it? Or was it justice alone that the world turned on? I left her weeping on the bed and went outside, to clear this background fuzz of moral static that was scorching my mind, frying up what little brains I had ever had.

31

When the furore had subsided, the Kumarihamy phoned Father Rosario for spiritual advice. Not that she particularly felt she needed it; more a shoulder to cry on, a strong Italian one.

'You know Sita, my servant girl, Father? She's gone and got herself pregnant.'

'Pregnant? It's not the end of the world, Clarice. If you like, I can put you in touch with a convent that'll raise the child and put it up for adoption.'

'You don't get it, do you, Father? It is Sonny's child.' The Kumarihamy sighed. 'I can't have the little bastard turning up years later to claim the walauwa.'

'Really, Clarice! That's your grandchild you're talking about.'

'That's just it, Father. The obvious solution would be to marry her off to the garden boy, Pandu. It is a very good match for her, and he likes her, I can tell.' She paused. 'But I can't have a Mahadewala brought up as a servant boy. Imagine? So what do you advise?'

Resisting the strong urge to tell her to go jump in the Sea of Milk, Father Rosario said: 'In matters like this you must pray, let your conscience decide for you. Use your conscience.'

'If you have one,' he might have added, but didn't, for he was not a cruel man. She was about as likely to discover a conscience at this late stage of her life as she was to find mythical treasure buried under the Blue Room floor.

Under her breath, the Kumarihamy swore to herself that there was nothing more useless than a tropicalized Italian cleric. The devils were surely behind Sonny's misdeeds. She summoned Kodivina Peiris back urgently.

'How much?' she asked, in an unusually buttery voice.

Kodivina looked at her, noisily sucking in the air through his teeth. 'A lakh?' he asked speculatively. 'That will buy you three drummers, three dancers, masks and costumes. Bolay and myself, of course. And the cockerel.'

'Cockerel?'

'I'll be bringing my cock to the ceremony. I won't charge you.'

Clarice looked at him sharply. Was he trying to be funny?

'I need my cock to scare the patient with,' he said earnestly.

Clarice was still trying to get over the pain of the price. 'I hear they're doing thovils in Badulla for half that price,' she said.

'Please go to Badulla, then. Be my guest.'

'Anyway, what's so special about you?'

'Clarice,' he said. '*Clarice*. You don't have to take this high-handed tone with me, dear. We go back a long way, remember? You know that no one does devils like I do.'

'I suppose it takes one to know one,' she finally conceded.

'You'll have to take care of the devils' food,' he reminded her, once they had sealed the deal. 'And the bystanders' too. Though they'll be bringing their own contributions, I'm sure.'

'Contributions?' Clarice shuddered. 'That's what I'm afraid of. All they ever bring me is bananas. At times I feel my whole life is one long—unfeasibly long—banana.'

Though the Kumarihamy never mentioned it to anyone, hardly daring even to countenance the possibility herself, there was that other potential bonus to accessing this sudden surfeit of demons. Who knew, but one of them might be prevailed upon to show her the exact location of the treasure?

In the days following the Great Trial, I wandered around the house bewildered, ignored by everyone. My mother considered me beneath her contempt. It was shocking enough that I had married a white demoness; to follow this up by siring a child by a servant girl was beyond the bounds of all Kandyan decency. It did not seem to have occurred to her that hers was a similar position all those years ago: that I was the product of just such a liaison.

Sita avoided me altogether. Was she disappointed that I had not come out more strongly in her favour? Did she expect me to divorce Luisa and marry her? Up to now, I had only barely considered the possibility. I had been perfectly happy to enjoy the benefits of our unspoken arrangement without having to sign on any dotted line. I was so mixed up at the moment, I didn't actually know what I wanted: only that I wanted the child. I saw Sita as the mother of that child; not particularly as my wife. Yet—and I know this is no justification for my behaviour, much as I would like it to be—there seemed to be more to Sita's ambivalence than met the eye, something I could not quite get to the bottom of.

As for Luisa, we were back to that old Oxford habit of sharing the bed as strangers. There was an invisible line down the middle of the mattress which I dared not cross. There was a weariness to her in her dealings with me: Was this how wives of murderers reacted when they discovered deep into the marriage that their husband was not who they thought he was? Though, if I had been found to be a stranger to her, there was something even more frightening and alien to me about her response to this situation.

She had asked for Sita to get rid of her unborn child. Who was this Salome I had married, asking for the head of St John the Baptist on a silver platter? This new American Kumarihamy seemed to have a grasp of medieval ethics as brutal and merciless as those of my mother and the old Kumarihamy before her. Was this the price I had to pay to continue my life with her, watching as she developed this shiny carapace of cruelty, the way my father had watched my mother change before his very eyes? If so, was *this* what I really wanted?

I felt at times I was being pursued by three strong women armed with machetes and machine guns, through some deranged cityscape, dodging down side streets, leaping from roof to roof. I could hear the metallic ring of their jackboots on the cobbles, echoing as they closed in on me. A quick and painless chop of the neck was all I could pray for.

When my mother proposed the thovil, I seized upon the idea eagerly. Thovils had been so much a part of my young life, why not now? It could do no harm, surely, and its drama, its concentrated intensity, would serve to take people's minds off the real import of the situation. Like getting drunk at a wake, and dancing with the corpse you are meant to be mourning.

32

Kodi and his crack team of demon-busters arrived early morning.

'You'll need to clean the house from top to bottom,' he told a stupefied Girigoris. 'Understand?'

'We did it only last week . . .'

'So do it again.'

'. . . for the first time in how many years!'

It was very worrying, really. No one knew how much cleaning an old house like this could take.

In the garden, they set up an arched throne which was decorated with plaited strips of banana trunk and gok kola, the fronds of the young coconut palm. A separate eight-foot-high platform was constructed nearby with a rickety bamboo ladder up to it, for the chief sorcerer to rest when he so required, far from the madding crowd. In the kitchens, Karuppayah was having the very devil of a time preparing food for the audience. On the terrace, in a separate makeshift kitchen, the sorcerer's chef was preparing the devils' buffet—a *hathmaluwa* (a curry of seven vegetables), a fry, a steamed-greens-and-grated-coconut mallung, assorted fruits and king coconuts, and lashings of boiled white rice. Separate coconut-frond trays were woven too, to offer to the demons multicoloured flowers, raw rice, betel leaves, sprays of coconut and areca blossom, and lots of small change, because everyone knows how much devils like money.

The sisters had taken to meeting every morning. Beta's was the more logical venue as it commanded a better view of the walauwa terraces. These last few days had been intensely exciting, culminating with that mother of all rows last week. The verandah roof of the old house partially obscured their view, but acted rather as a baffle does on a speaker, amplifying and concentrating the sound with an acoustic clarity so that it rang across the valley like a knife on a wine glass.

They had heard about the pregnancy, they had heard the threats of a shotgun wedding; nobody had been more amazed than they by Sonny's eleventh-hour admission ('The little devil!' said Bella admiringly). What more was there to hear? What indeed?

'Beta, come quick,' said Bella. 'There's an erection on the front lawn.'

'Don't be vulgar, dear. You seem to have pregnancy on your mind.'

'No, I mean it. Come and see.'

They saw the minute figure of Kodivina and his helpers setting up a stand. Others were splitting banana trunks and carving decorations.

'It's a thovil!' said the sisters delightedly, in unison. It was as if the carnival had come to town.

'Shall we go?'

'Of course. Clarice would never forgive us if we didn't.'

By noon the clay lamps and cloth torches were lit and the drumming began. Blessings from all the gods were sought and the deeply sick woman led in, dressed in virginal white ('*Ha!*' said the Kumarihamy) and placed in full view of the first few stragglers who had arrived. The performance was going to be an operatic marathon, lasting almost twenty-four hours, so people knew to pace themselves. In aesthetic quality and production values, it lay somewhere in between Glyndebourne and the opera buffa. Kodi, in full sorcerer kit, a lit lamp in either hand, a smoking brand stuck rakishly in the corner of his mouth, was making feints and passes at the patient like a matador to a bull, attempting to entice the demon out of her system. Every once in a while he would charge at her with flashes of smoke.

Meanwhile the little demons that inhabited the mountainside ran here and there, squealing delightedly like teenagers at a horror film, unheard by all except the truly wicked. The Devil himself watched with bemusement this display of indigenous bravura. He was not one for Eastern mumbo jumbo, being very much a creature of the Old Testament, unbending and intransigent, from which he had sprung fully formed. (Only we are the sole possessors of the True Evil, he privately thought. All else is sham.) Next to him, in the shadow of a temple tree, Lord Bhairava dozed gently, snuffling every once in a while, dreaming as always of the head he had once lost.

The crowd was thickening now, the mood of anticipation palpable. One or two of the more susceptible members of the audience rose and began to sway, each in his own sweet trance underneath the intense blue skies of this daytime tropical discotheque. Kodi had worked himself up into a thoroughly out-of-body state.

Shaking and rolling his eyes, he climbed the rickety ladder to his abode, where he stood dangerously close to the edge, swaying double-jointedly like a drunken puppet. There was panic in the audience and people rushed to him with arms outstretched. No sooner had they reached the platform than he keeled over the edge with a great expiring sigh, sinking graciously into their waiting hands. They removed the smoking brand from his mouth and revived him with splashes of turmeric water.

It was time now for the entr'acte. Sita was led away and lunch served, courtesy of the walauwa. A separate table had been set up with plates for the lucky few. ('Plates?' snorted the Kumarihamy. 'What do they need plates for?') The rest had to make do with cut squares of banana leaf. Lunch was vegetarian, of course, disappointingly sparse. Comments were made about how much better it had been in the days of the old Kumarihamy.

At two thirty sharp the performance resumed. The devils' luncheon was dished up at the throneside—roti and raw eggs, a vegetable fry and cooked white rice, fish and chicken, even a little beef, because everyone knows the corrupt tastes of demons. For dessert, there was curd and honey and seven types of sweetmeat. A small flask of arrack was placed on the table together with an assortment of cigarettes and cigars for added enticement. Lucky devil! whispered the men enviously, though of course there were bottles of illicit kassipu circulating around the audience too, and the mood, now, was distinctly festive.

Sita was led back into the house at dusk, to be brought out again in a change of white clothes, the live cockerel placed neatly trussed at her feet. A flute began to play and the dancing resumed. A brief break for the audience dinner, again courtesy of the walauwa, and then the third act. Kodi and his assistants now appeared spectacularly dressed in pearl-encrusted costumes, crowns of gok kola on their heads, jewelled armbands and anklets on their hands and feet. A litany of the Daha Ata Sanni Yakku—the eighteen devils— was recited, their genealogies, habits, predilections and eccentricities explained in detail.

Kodi worked the crowd like the professional performer he was, leaping and somersaulting, making jokes and asking for money which the audience readily gave. It was nearly midnight now, the skies black and thick with stars. Kodi was ready for the major performance of the evening, when he would wear, in turn, each of the traditional eighteen masks, calling each devil in turn, culminating with the most frightful of all, the Bear Mask.

There was a slight scuffle in the front row. People craned their necks to see what was going on. Beta had risen. She began swaying gently to the sound of the drums. Behind her, almost as if planned, Jane Nona rose too. The two women began circling each other in a sort of gigantic and elephantine pas de deux; every once in a while they clashed gently, like two juggernauts attempting to mate on a motorway. Then, without warning, they began to mount the steps of the verandah, to the horror of the watching crowd. The verandah was a no-go area, the province of the sick person and the exorcist alone. Avoiding Sita altogether, the two behemoths vanished into the house. The crowd sighed in relief. A crisis had been averted.

Moments later, Girigoris came running out from inside. 'It's my lady Beta,' he cried in loud agitated tones. 'She's fallen into the pit.' He was wringing the chequered cloth he normally wore around his neck, his diction wooden and stagey. 'And you know what? *Her bottom's up.*'

This was more than the crowd could bear. These were people who under normal circumstances would never be allowed on the verandah of a walauwa, let alone inside one. Thovils could come and go; the sight of a Kandyan princess with her bottom up was one they were hardly likely to behold again. Almost to a man, they rose and rushed inside the house.

'I'm not sure I like these new-fangled additions to the ceremony,' said one aged village matriarch to another. 'I hear the young Kumarihamy is American. I wonder if this variation comes from there? Give me a good old-fashioned thovil straight up any day, I say.'

Beta was carried out on a makeshift stretcher by the able-bodied youth of the crowd, many of the audience choosing to follow this confusing catafalque up the hill rather than stay for the rest of the night's performance. Kodi manfully carried on till dawn—who was there now to catch him if *he* fell off his platform?—but he had been paid to do a job and do it he would. But it was no wonder that the smoke and turmeric water, the screeching cockerel, the slashing of three limes on a single stalk—none of these seemed to have any effect whatsoever on the rogue demon inhabiting the patient. Sita remained uncured.

The morning sun was now cutting through the chill, the town below just coming awake. It was time to put the demons to bed. The Kumarihamy paid Kodi his one lakh.

'In future, please employ the fat lady to conduct your thovils,' he said. 'Tell her to bring her own cock,' he added bitterly, 'if she has one.'

For her part the Kumarihamy was not entirely unhappy with the night's proceedings. The ceremony might not have had the desired effect, but it had raised her stock immensely among the people of the mountainside—they would be talking about this event for years to come. Who knew better than she that life on this magic island was far more about prestige and people's perceptions of you than the often sad and shabby reality of what you actually were? Besides, this evening of gorgeous spectacle had only served to concentrate her mind wonderfully. She knew precisely what she had to do next.

33

Sita spent the day after the thovil on her mat on the floor. They had barely gotten back, at seven in the morning, when the old man decided to go off to work, almost skipping out of the house. What sort of devil had got into *him*, for him to have such an unusual amount of energy? Sita felt wretched and exhausted, depleted and depressed. More than ever, she was aware of how little she really mattered in the greater scheme of things. 'Promise me you'll keep the baby,' Sonny had implored. He had said nothing about *her*: made no promises to *her*. Perhaps in his mind he envisaged a single mother's existence for her, eking out a living in a termite-ridden back room of the walauwa, forever at the mercy of the Kumarihamy, something in between a poor relation and a servant. Did he not realize how absurd this would look to Sri Lankan eyes— what a loss of face it would entail, how impossible it would be in practical terms?

Yet, she so wanted to keep the child. It was a part of her; it was the one thing that connected her to that slim chance of another life, the possibility of which—if she was really being honest with herself—seemed less and less likely as each day passed. But oh, how it might so easily have been, she thought, had the cards only fallen in her favour! Still, it had been a comfort to indulge in that spurious hope, to escape for one glorious moment into the gaudy plastic rose of that Bollywood film, overblown and highly coloured, where the serving maid becomes the princess overnight and lives happily ever after, to the sounds of a screeching, nasal soundtrack. The life the Kumarihamy had claimed for herself, all those years ago, having known how to do things the right way.

There was yet another, darker, possibility. What if the child were not his, but the monster's? Could she ever, even for a moment, pretend it was Sonny's? And if the monster turned up on their doorstep later and spilled the beans, what then? Would she be able to brazen it out? Would he blackmail her mercilessly till the end of her life? The outcomes to this sordid tale were endless and unreal, going up and down, round and round, like toy horses on a merry-go-round. I should have come clean that very first day, she thought bitterly. He would have understood. He would have forgiven. But then she thought: Who am I trying to kid? He would probably have walked away, never to return. And all this because I wanted to look after an old man and pay for his medicines. Though unbeknownst to me, he was making quite enough to pay for them himself, only he never chose to tell me.

One thing alone was clear, one thing she was able to take away from this nightmare. No one wants me for myself, she realized. They want me for the easy sex, they want me for the child within. I am just a mule plodding along, burdened by other people's wishes and desires, smuggling them over the border into the realms of possibility.

Climbing the rock-cut steps to the walauwa early next morning, she saw that the car had been brought round to the front. Pandu was busy polishing the windscreen.

'All ready?' he said with a smirk.

Ignoring him, she went inside. The Kumarihamy greeted her in the hallway dressed in a blouse with puffed white sleeves and a Kandyan sari the colour of tea, all hung about with pleats and brooches. Around her neck, she wore a chain of agates, the beads mounted within filigreed cups of rose gold.

'Get your things together,' she announced. 'We're leaving in ten minutes.'

'We?'

'Idiot girl! You think this is a pleasure trip? You think I like going to Colombo?'

Sita reflected that the Kumarihamy had not been to Colombo in at least a year. Why now? Then the reason reared its ugly painted head into her consciousness like a devil's mask at a thovil. She shrank back. 'No,' she whispered, afraid. 'I'm not going.'

'You what? *How dare you!* You will do exactly as I say as long as you are living under my roof. Pandu!' the Kumarihamy called out. 'Put this girl into the car at once!'

She realized at that moment she was surrounded, and her resistance left her, like a swimmer who, against every conscious instinct, gives in to the current, knowing her only chance of survival is to work through and not against it. My future is no longer in my hands, she thought, surrendering with a sort of hopeless pleasure.

Ensconced in the back seat amidst an array of brown-paper bags and her folded-up walker, the Kumarihamy talked all the way to Colombo on what seemed like an interminable trip. 'Do you know that *over a thousand* of these procedures take place every day in Sri Lanka? That this is the *preferred* method of birth control here? Amazing, isn't it?'

And I suppose that's meant to cheer me up, Sita thought. She was in the front seat next to the monster.

'They're all illegal, of course. Be grateful I'm taking you to one of the best places. Very clean. Well maintained.'

The monster whistled tunelessly under his breath, shooting covert glances at her, sly and licentious. Whenever he changed gears, his fingers seemed to brush against her thigh, however much she moved away.

'You won't find many people prepared to risk their name and reputation being seen in such places. You're lucky I'm an old fool. Far too good, that's what I am. Far too good.'

They turned into Duplication Road at Liberty Plaza and five hundred yards down, just past the electricity board offices, they drove into a cul-de-sac, coming to a stop outside a pale blue building with darker trim. Sita saw that the clinic was named after some foreign dignitary, perhaps in a bid to instil confidence in its customers. There were hundreds of people milling outside, and the Toyota Crown had to inch its way through, causing a minor sensation. She wondered how they could all be there for the same thing. Most looked blank, betraying neither concern nor compassion. She thought bitterly: We Sri Lankans have an infinite capacity for aimlessness, haven't we? Under normal circumstances she would have gotten angry. Why are you all here? Go home!

Leave us in peace to do our own dirty work! But she was beyond anger, beyond the withering, flame-thrower sarcasm she might have been tempted to train on them in happier times.

'I believe I spoke to someone yesterday,' said Clarice, cutting through the queues to the reception desk, using her walker fearlessly as a crowd-control weapon. Sita understood now the wisdom of the pleats and brooches, the agate necklace—the full Kandyan princess kit—severely restrained, fearfully formidable: designed to strike terror into the heart of your average backstreet abortionist. For the first time in a long time, Sita felt comforted; a small smile twitched involuntarily across her face.

The Kumarihamy was made to fill out a form as Sita's next of kin.

'Name and address?'

'Myrtle Perera, 72B, Old Kandy Road, Dalugama,' she said, with a smoothness that took Sita's breath away. 'I always wanted to be called *Myrtle*,' she whispered in a dramatic aside.

Nobody took any notice; false names and addresses were de rigueur. A young doctor in a white coat and stethoscope escorted them inside. He had a mouth overfull of teeth which gave him a goofy look when he smiled. Strangely, the smile was more reassuring than the stethoscope.

'We will put you under general anaesthesia,' he said. 'The procedure won't last more than thirty or forty minutes. It will take you a little longer to recover though. Then your mother can take you home, all right?'

Sita allowed herself to be led away. It is a little like dying, she thought. A little part of me will die today. As perhaps with any dying person, she was beyond all mortal struggle now, floating high up and looking down on this curiously inert lump of flesh riddled with its daily discharges, its petty corruptions. How little it all seemed to matter when you viewed it from up here!

'Into your hands, O Lord, I commend my existence,' she prayed as consciousness left her.

∽

I woke up to an empty house. I walked into the kitchen courtyard and suddenly the sun came out from behind a cloud, lighting up the ancient, mildewed, ochre walls: a moment of incandescent beauty lifting my soul out of itself, flooding me with the high-water gold of its goodness.

It took me back to that other time in the Tuscan garden, when I had proposed to Luisa. So long ago. We were old people now, looking back upon those children picking plum jam out of a jar with a knife. I felt an unreasonable anger towards Luisa, that she had never shared my awe of this house, had never wanted to: the damp beauty of these etiolated walls; the dharma chakras of its balustraded roof, like diamonds in a tiara on the brow of a dowager. Now it was too late. She would never come back. The anger was as much for this abrupt end to a life that might so easily have been, a story through whose last paragraph the editor had drawn her thin red line. As for where this left me, I did not know, could not really say.

The lime tree was laden with ripe fruit, like a tropical Christmas tree hung with baubles. It was in fact only a few days from Christmas, though so much had happened that celebration was the last thing on anyone's mind. I could hear the faint chink of the pick from the Blue Room. Girigoris was in the pit digging and Karuppayah squatted on the edge, a beedi dangling from his lips.

The hole was coming along nicely. When would my mother stop this madness?

'Her Ladyship says that she has had to rush to Colombo on urgent business. If you can find your own lunch today, she would be enormously grateful. She'll be back by evening.'

'And where is Sita?'

'She has taken Sita with her.'

I wondered what urgent business my mother could possibly have in Colombo, when she hardly even left the walauwa normally.

'Let's go into town for lunch,' Luisa said. It was the first time in days she had addressed a full sentence to me.

Upstairs at the Flower Song, she laid a tentative hand on my arm. There was a party of noisy Chinese tourists at the next table, so I did not hear what she said the first time.

'There's another seat on the Christmas Day flight,' she repeated, toying with her chopsticks. 'I mean . . . I don't know if you want to, but perhaps you could come back with me?'

It was easy to avoid giving her a direct answer, sitting as I was inside a sound cloud of many-toned, guttural Cantonese reverberating around the room. I squeezed her hand.

∽

The Kumarihamy found she was attracting too much attention, so she decided to wait it out in the car, sending

Pandu in for regular updates. Once the patient was off the operating table and back on the stretcher recovering from the anaesthesia, they drove to a roadside pastry shop. She lunched lightly on a fish bun and seeni sambal roll; Pandu, for his part, consumed three of each. After a couple of bites, she had Pandu summon the shop attendant to the open window of the car.

'What do you call this?' she asked him. She had peeled back the top of the bun to reveal half a teaspoon of filling, no more, of fish skin and bone.

'Can you see any fish in this?'

The attendant stared open-mouthed, more at her than the bun. Being a big-city dweller, he was not used to the ways of Kumarihamies.

'You can call it a skin bun or bone bun. Not a fish bun. And what is this?' she continued, excavating further. 'Starch. Pure white starch. Guaranteed to give you diabetes. Dia-Be-Tes, you got that?'

'Would you like your money back, Madam?'

'*Madam* did you say? Ha! No, I would *not* like my money back. I would like my health back!' Laughing mirthlessly, she had Pandu drive her back to the clinic.

An hour later Pandu lifted Sita into the car.

'You've been a wonderful, wonderful girl,' sighed the Kumarihamy.

Rustling about among her parcels in the back, she proffered one to Sita. Through a clouded haze, Sita noted that in the bag was a silk sari of pale lilac, with paler flowers of the same colour printed on it. She slept most of the way home. At one point she vaguely registered that Pandu must have been attempting to make small talk, because she heard the Kumarihamy say, 'Shut up and keep your eyes on the road!'

Back in Kandy they stopped at the shack and Pandu carried Sita in, laying her gently on her mat on the floor. She thought without her usual bitterness: This is the gentlest he has ever been with me.

34

I heard the car come up the drive. I saw, through the shadowed pillars of the verandah, my mother being decanted from it and helped up to her room. No sign of Sita. I waited till Pandu had taken the car round to the back, and raced downhill to the shack.

I knocked on the door but there was no answer. Then I realized it was not locked. Pushing the door gingerly open, I went inside. The late afternoon sunlight was streaming in through the wooden bars of the small window. At first, it seemed the place was empty. What have they done with her? I thought in sudden fear. Then I noticed the figure lying motionless on the ground. I knelt down gently and took her hand. She opened her eyes.

'I killed it,' she said. 'I killed it, Sonny.'

I felt cold, suddenly. As if a part of my mind had been suddenly excised and the wind was blowing through the gap, howling.

She began to cry, a small keening sound, the sound of a wild animal caught in a trap. I half lifted her, cradling her head on my lap. 'Shhh, my darling, don't cry. Don't cry. Don't cry.' I rocked her back and forth, back and forth, crooning those words as if to a baby. I tried to wipe the tears with my hand, but there were too many.

'Why do we do this to ourselves, Sonny? Why do we kill the parts we love most?'

I was crying too now, the tears flowing from every pore, my stomach awash with liquid grief. She looked so fragile and vulnerable at that moment, so beautiful, I could not believe how I had treated her so casually, let her go so easily. Had she really meant so little to me?

We stayed like this for the longest time, rocking back and forth, back and forth, the light outside turning from yellow to gold and, in its last throes, to a baby-girl pink, as the sun sank below the brow of the hill.

Finally, I broke the silence. 'I promise to look after you for the rest of my life. You will want for nothing.'

I felt her stiffen then, and knew at once I had said the wrong thing.

'What?' She pushed me away from her. '*What did you say?* Let's get this clear. I don't owe you a baby, you don't owe me money. We're done here, right? Finished. Got that?'

'But Sita—'

'Shut up!' she screamed. 'Shut the fuck up. You don't belong here. Go back to your rich girl and get the fuck out. Leave me to my life. Don't you think I've managed well enough so far?' She was crying and screaming at the same time. For a brief, perverse moment I was relieved at this flash of the old Sita, strong and invincible.

But I was ashamed too, more ashamed than I can tell, of this feudal world that had so easily seduced me into treating her in this cavalier fashion, discounting her validity, devaluing her existence.

'Can't I see you again?'

'Get out!' she screamed. 'Get out!'

It was an ignominious and shabby end. I only realized later how much it must have cost her to make it so, how painful it must have been. She was like that sculptor who takes a hammer and smashes his favourite statue into a thousand pieces, because that is the only way he knows to cure himself of his love of it.

I looked around that pitifully sparse room one last time, committing it to memory. It had always been a place of refuge, a comfort to me in times of distress. All I could see now was its skeletal bareness, the lone figure on the floor like an animal in a cave awaiting death. For me, the scene was already secure in the realms of my imagination, sepia-hued with history: but for her, it was still her reality—the reality I had condemned her to forever, by my inaction. It occurred to me then that there is only this very thin line between love and pity, almost invisible. I had crossed it some time that afternoon, and hadn't even known at the time.

As I left, I noticed it, the lilac sari thrown carelessly on the bed; Luisa's gift to my mother.

I climbed back up the hill, my anger mounting with every step. My mother had always undercut me at every turn—it was the story of my life, I was used to it—but this was finally the worst thing she had done. I could have killed her at that moment, strangled her and thrown the body over the mountainside.

She was sitting on the verandah with Luisa, looking very pleased with herself.

'Ah, the return of the king,' she said archly.

'How could you do it?' I was panting with emotion, my breath choking me. 'How *could* you!'

She gave Luisa a fleeting look. 'When the king himself wants something, who are we, mere handmaidens, to refuse?'

'Oh, cut the fucking crap. You took advantage of her in her fragile state. You bullied her into this. As your servant, she knew she had no choice.'

'Bullied? Don't be childish. It was necessary and you know it. Besides, it's what you wanted too.'

'Me?' I said in disbelief. '*Me?*'

'Only, you were too much of a coward to say it. Even to yourself. It is precisely because there are people like me in this world—prepared to do these bad things—that people like you can live, and afford to be high and mighty in your condemnation afterwards.'

'But it's murder!' I shouted.

Luisa intervened. 'What's done is done,' she said softly. 'Thanks to your mother, we can now move on with our lives.'

'Move on?' I asked. '*Move on?* I have to live with this the rest of my fucking life.'

I stormed into the house and threw myself on the bed, raging that I had not been up early enough that morning to stop it, for being such a fool as to imagine my mother would not attempt something like this. But mostly, I raged against the world, for the way it has of emptying us of any goodness we might have, so that we are squeezed hard and dry and bitter, like all the other bastards in it.

Later, when my anger had subsided, I began to think. Was my mother right? Was it necessary for one person to commit evil so others could afford the luxury of being good? If evil genuinely did not exist in the world, would we have had to invent it? Then there was that other thing—I had seen the flash of complicity between my mother and my wife. How much did Luisa know? Had she been in on this from the start? Was that why she had made those tentative overtures earlier on at the restaurant?

There are certain things in a marriage better left unsaid: this was one of those. I never asked her about it, either then or later. It was a question of survival. I was always one who believed the very best of others, a belief that was generally self-fulfilling. You found people to be good almost because you wished that goodness upon them. My mother, in direct contrast, believed the opposite. She generally thought the worst of people, finding that self-fulfilling too. She was constantly amazed and delighted at the wickedness of others which exceeded, by far, her worst expectations. But that is another story.

In the final analysis, who was responsible for this murder? My mother who committed it, my wife who condoned it, or just me, who had caused it?

I had been the cause of two deaths so far. Perhaps I really was the devil—as my mother believed. Suddenly I was weary of it all, weary of this life that was tied like a great big rock to my neck, that I had to drag around with me wherever I went. Perhaps the dead really were dead, as my mother believed, wrapped up in yesterday's newspapers and thrown into the dustbin. Perhaps it was time to concentrate on the living, the living that were as yet unborn.

35

I flew back with Luisa on Christmas Day. For lunch, I remember they served us lamb chops and a tiny bottle of champagne each; a consolation for those like us stupid enough—or unlucky enough—not to be at home celebrating with loved ones on that day. I held Luisa's hand all the way. This is what husbands do.

The language of love may be universal but I had discovered that there were many dialects all over the world, and I had been foolish enough to assume you could hold two in your head in equal proportion, with equal fluency. It was time to get back and relearn that old Putney lingo, regain my proficiency. I looked at this woman next to me, a cut jewel of many facets, flashing a different side of her each time the light changed. I remembered how my fingers had tingled at her beauty the first time I ever saw her: she could have had anyone she wanted, yet she chose me, the ugly devil. I had betrayed that trust comprehensively and effortlessly. It was time to start earning it again, learning it again.

I would always remember Sita: the way half-forgotten phrases come back to you years later for no reason at all, in the middle of your mundane life. They might once have been hot on your tongue, now they only sound alien to your ear. It is not the phrases that have changed: only you. That life had been, in principle, an equal possibility. But this country, in all its mad medievalism, would have defeated me, as it had tried to defeat my mother all those years ago when she had gone through the same thing. She had survived, I think, by becoming precisely the sort of person she so despised: because the only sure way to vanquish your enemy is to become indistinguishable from him. She was a stronger person than me. I am not sure I would have survived.

If my mother had not acted as swiftly as she did, Luisa would have flown back alone. And me? Most likely I would have been at the bottom of the sea.

On the next day, Boxing Day 2004, the tsunami hit Sri Lanka, taking the lives of forty thousand people. My mother was one of them, together with her trusted lieutenant Pandu.

Luisa had paid for our rooms at Yala Safari Lodge and my mother—parsimonious to the last—had decided to enjoy them in spite of our absence 'because it will be a terrible waste of money if I don't'. The hotel was flattened by the wave, and most of those in it. As I have said somewhere before, how can you explain a natural disaster like this? Is it the work of the Devil? Is it God polishing off so many thousand truly evil men who deserve to die? I am not sure I will ever know the answer.

Love, once you have learnt the basic language, is easy. Hate, well, now that is a different matter altogether. My mother was like that scientist who injects herself with the disease in order to fight it better, ending up embodying the disease itself.

Perhaps she identified in me all the ills of that society she had fought so hard to become part of, transferring those years of frustration and blame on to me because I would not, could not, answer back. I was glad of one thing at least: that at the end she and Luisa had parted friends, perhaps even partners in crime. As for me, I had always viewed my mother—regal and distant and impossibly grand—not so much as a mother but as a character from a fable: The Princess Living on the Mountainside, or the Wicked Witch of the East. Perhaps I had never loved her as I should, but I had never hated her either, as perhaps I also should. Indeed, you might argue that it was her wickedness that had allowed me to walk scot free, to exhibit what modicum of goodness I ever possessed. As I flew on, ahead of the sun on this never-ending day, I put my hand on Luisa's stomach and thought of the life ahead; and I tried hard to obliterate from my mind the trail of death I had left behind me so far.

I knew I would be back one day. In my absence, in the meantime, my aunts shifted into the walauwa with Jane, running the estates with an efficiency I never knew they possessed. The first thing they did was to back-fill the pit.

My mother's worst nightmare had come true. It would have killed her had she only been alive to see it. It's the charms, she would have said. They have charmed their way into my house. I told you not to eat those pineapples.

36

The night before her fateful trip, the Kumarihamy invited
Father Rosario for a Christmas Eve drink. It was to be the last
social engagement of her life, though she did not know it at
the time.

'They're gone, Father. Just left. They're catching the dawn
flight from Colombo.'

'I'm sorry to hear that, Clarice. Weren't you all supposed
to go to Yala for Christmas?'

'I'm going, Father, all on my own. Care to join me? There's
a second room all booked and paid for.'

Father Rosario shook his head. 'I've too many Christmas
visits to pay. Too many people to see to.'

'Suit yourself, Father.'

'And your other problem?'

'Oh, I sorted it out straightaway. Took her to Colombo.
Tell me I did the right thing, Father.'

'That's not for me to say, Clarice. The Church will say that
you have sinned gravely. Privately I can tell you it is a matter
between you and your God.'

So if the Kumarihamy was looking for absolution, she did not receive it.

'Imagine the complications if that child had lived? My son would have had two competing heirs. It would be just like in the days of the kings!'

The Kumarihamy sighed. 'All my life, from the time of my mother-in-law, the old Kumarihamy, I have been cast as the villain of the piece. Not that I'm complaining, of course.' She giggled, a high, schoolgirlish giggle. 'A lifetime of wickedness and I find I have *quite* grown into the part.'

Father Rosario said nothing, watching as she peered blindly into the velvety darkness, as if receiving some obscure truth signal broadcast through the chill night air. 'Whereas others seek the redeeming qualities of those around them, somehow building them up to be better people than they actually are, I see the truth: all too often and all too clearly. And I am not afraid to act on it, even though I am unfailingly penalized for my decisiveness.

'For instance, if I had not been so hasty in my actions, my children would still be here now. If I hadn't forced the secret out so quickly, they need never have known—I could have sorted Sita out quietly after they left. And we would all be having a lovely time on the coast now. All that lovely swimming in the sea!' She paused. 'I think I'm being punished for taking matters into my own hands. For playing God.'

'You never know what God has planned for you, Clarice. Often, we are up too close to the pattern. Step back and it'll appear, at least in part: that grand design no mortal is ever lucky enough to hold the entirety of.' Father Rosario stood up and walked to the edge of the verandah, taking a deep breath. 'Anyway, I can tell you one thing, the air is strangely clear.'

'Of course, Father. Why wouldn't it be, now my little devil has gone back to England?' The Kumarihamy cackled as she waved the Vespa off. 'I'll see you in the New Year, Father.'

But even as Father Rosario rode his Vespa downhill, the odour of evil returned, breathy and sulphurous, as if someone were riding pillion with him, hands around his stomach, breathing down his neck. Approaching the police station at the bottom of the hill, he braked, then braked again, but the motorcycle accelerated on. It took him a second to realize the brakes were not working.

Almost unconsciously he wrenched the wheel sharply to the right, causing the motorcycle to go flat on the road, spinning like a saucer on a kitchen table. Father Rosario had bad cuts and bruises down his leg but was able to limp away alive. Later, he wondered what alien instinct had come over him, enabling him to react so quickly. Another second and he would have shot through the busy T-junction, running bang into the police station wall, dying upon impact.

ॐ

No one was more surprised at the tsunami than the Devil. 'All that murder and mayhem, and I wasn't even told about it? They kept very quiet, didn't they, leaving me to rot in Kandy while they all went down south to the coast for the fun? I hear they're cutting off dead men's fingers for the rings, drowning survivors coming out of the sea just to rob them of their belongings.

'Disgusting!' he hissed. 'Amazing! Remarkable! These people don't need me at all, do they? They're positive *experts* at wickedness!'

And then he began to sing, in his fine countertenor voice, his favourite Bishop Heber hymn: 'Only man is vile,' he crooned happily, 'only man is vile.'

37

When it came to it, she found she had so little to call her own.

Two plastic carrier bags of clothes. Everything else she was leaving behind for the old man. Perhaps in time to come he would sell each piece—the bed, the almirah, the tabletop cooker—as and when his drinking habits required. She was beyond caring. They have taken everything from me, she thought: anything of any value I might ever have cared about. The Kumarihamy had taken away her most treasured possession. And Sonny? He had taken from her any possibility of a new life, any chance she might ever have had of making that quantum leap out of medievalism into a decent existence. But looking back, had that chance even existed?

As for the monster, he had stolen from her any last shred of dignity she might have possessed. I am as nothing to them, she reflected, no better than a piece of meat laid out on a butcher's slab. But then it struck her—with the fairness and reason that always came to the fore and were often her deepest regret—why am I surprised? I stole from them: Isn't it only fair they steal back from me? An eye for an eye, a theft for a theft.

But all this was now past. Already these events had begun to take their place among those unreliable memories that made you sometimes wonder, were they manufactured, or did they actually take place? And with this fading away came, unexpectedly, that flash of magic: a powerful sense of self unencumbered that revealed itself only after the smoke had cleared. She said to herself: I am gone; I am out of here.

She was no longer anyone's keeper. She would find herself a job far from all of this; in a garment factory, perhaps, sleeping safe in a dormitory of female workers. In time, she would be whole again.

As darkness began to fall she climbed the rock-cut steps once more, for one last look. The house was closed up, the Kumarihamy and the monster having gone south, but she knew her way in through the passage outside the Blue Room. She could hear a radio on in the servants' quarters, the faint clink of glass. Girigoris and Karuppayah would be well into their second bottle of arrack now. In the silver-blue daze of twilight seeping through the fretwork fanlights, she saw the dark shapes of the furniture; felt rather than saw because after a lifetime of dusting, she could feel their solidity beneath her fingers—their age, their comforting wax-polished patina— without having to touch. And if there were demons flying around these high, wide rooms, she was impervious to them.

She returned to the Blue Room and looked once more into the pit, moist and raw as an open wound. She saw a tiny glimmer in one corner, like a firefly, and without thinking, climbed down. It was hard to the touch. Patiently scrabbling around with her fingers for a while, she managed to dislodge it: an armband in the shape of a serpent, set with rough white and blue stones. Its two emerald eyes glinted at her poisonously.

Was this then the long hand of God? She looked up skywards. Forgive me, she said, as she pocketed it. Walking back downhill, she retraced her steps to the shop in the arcade. Through the window she could see Mr Seenigama closing up for the night. She rapped on the window. When he saw who it was, he pattered over.

'Can't it wait?' he asked, a little annoyed. 'I promised to be home on time tonight.'

She shook her head. 'No, it can't.'

When she placed the armband on the glass counter, his eyes opened wide. 'I don't have to ask where this is from, do I? How much?'

'A million rupees,' she said. 'In cash.'

Mr Seenigama almost choked. 'You think I have that sort of money lying around?'

'As a matter of fact I do,' she replied calmly. 'Besides, you know damn well this will end up in London, on sale for five times that price.'

Mr Seenigama looked contemptuously at her. 'You know an awful lot, don't you, for a servant girl?'

Sita put the armband back in her pocket. 'All right, I'll take it elsewhere.'

'Wait!' he said.

She came out of the shop twenty minutes later with the money, thick as a brick, wrapped in brown paper and secured by rubber bands. Perhaps not the garment factory then, after all. Perhaps that career as a nurse abroad? She had the money.

She shook her fist at the sky, black now as a devil's mouth. 'Thank you!' she said. 'Thank you, thank you, *thank you*!'